MAR 2 9 2016

WEATHERING

Diving Belles

WEATHERING

Lucy Wood

B L O O M S B U R Y

NEW YORK · LONDON · OXFORD · NEW DELHI · SYDNEY

Bloomsbury USA
An imprint of Bloomsbury Publishing Plc

1385 Broadway	50 Bedford Square
New York	London
NY 10018	WC1B 3DP
USA	UK

www.bloomsbury.com

BLOOMSBURY and the Diana logo are trademarks of Bloomsbury Publishing Plc

First published in Great Britain 2016
First U.S. edition published 2016

ISBN: HB: 978-1-63286-357-7
epub: 978-1-63286-358-4

Library of Congress Cataloging-in-Publication Data has been applied for.

2 4 6 8 10 9 7 5 3 1

Typeset by Hewer Text UK Ltd, Edinburgh
Printed and bound in USA by Berryville Graphics Inc., Berryville, Virginia

To find out more about our authors and books visit www.bloomsbury.com.
Here you will find extracts, author interviews, details of forthcoming
events, and the option to sign up for our newsletters.

Bloomsbury books may be purchased for business or promotional use.
For information on bulk purchases please contact Macmillan Corporate
and Premium Sales Department at specialmarkets@macmillan.com.

For Ben

1

ARSE OVER ELBOW AND a mouthful of river. Which she couldn't spit out. Which soaked in and weighed her down until she was steeped in silt and water, like old tea. But where was her arse anyway, where was her elbow? There was nothing but water as far as she could tell. A stew of water and leaves and small stones and herself all mixed up in it – a strange grey grit. Scattered, then dragged under again, everything teeming, and not sure which way was up or down. Light and dark, light and dark, like a door opening and closing.

Pearl flailed, grabbed at the water, but with what? Nothing to grab with but somehow she was back on the surface, dipping and whirling and strewn about. Bits of grey dust here, bits of grey dust there – almost impossible to recognise herself. Everything sodden and spreading out, couldn't keep herself together; she was floating in a widening circle, dispersing like seeds kicked out of a tree. A godawful sloshing, and Christ, that wind. That was almost the worst of it, blowing over the water, flinging her about. So that some of her skittered off downriver and some snagged on a raft of sticks and leaves and the rest was trapped in the current and reeling.

She floated, the water pulling and sucking at her. Hard to gather her thoughts, which drifted and wedged into the riverbank. Which had never been much use. Where was she again? It was hard to keep track of it. Washing over stones, circling around stones, lodged underneath a stone. Stones bloody everywhere and a rivery smell, like fresh air and mud and something green dying. Shadows and copper glints. Heaps of silt. And cold – the sort of cold she couldn't abide, the kind that bit right in.

There was a bend up ahead, where the water started to slow and turn in a wide circle and a nest of stuff had built up. The current took her towards it, turning sluggish, slackening, and for God's sake now she was getting caught up in it: sticks and weeds and feathers. Wet leaves. Roots. An old gatepost. Horrible yellow scum washed off the fields. Everything bumping up against everything else. Everything tangling.

Some of her sank. Some of her tangled in. She tried to speak but nothing came out except the river's drum and babble. She felt like grit, like small stones. The water turned a slow circle. Where was she again? She tried to dredge something up but her thoughts were brimful with river. A root wrapped around itself over and over. The water pushed her against the bank, unceremoniously, into a mush of leaves and foam. A fetid reek, as if something had given up. Branches weaving together, something unspeakable brushing the surface of the water. A ridiculous place. Leaves circling and tilting like sinking boats.

She struggled, tried to untangle herself but the water weighed her down, made her sodden and slow. Everything murky and swimming with silt. Leaves came down like raindrops. The wind turned the river into peaks and humps, which jostled her, which slopped her about; she couldn't keep a hold of anything: now washing against the bank, now trapped among leaves, now caught under a rotting branch. She dipped, sank, took on another huge gulp of water. Tangled deeper in. The river getting into everything. Impossible to get away from it. Her thoughts soaking, everything full of stones. And who even knew where this was, exactly?

Typical – now sideways rain, billowing in on the wind like sails, drenching everything, churning the river, turning it brown and squally, dragging her back under into the dim, where there was no sound except the river thrumming.

2

THE RIVER WAS DARK and wide and the wind was louder than Pepper had ever heard it, like a train getting closer. It pummelled her, knocking her shoulders. There were a thousand trees bending. She licked her front tooth, which was sharp and tender – she had just fallen over and banged it on the front steps and there was a tiny chip in the corner. She was riddled with old injuries: at three, had crushed her thumb in a door; at four, had caught a glimpse of a bright bird and fallen out of a window, splintering her collarbone; at five, she'd grabbed a hot light bulb and seared a semicircle onto her palm. Now, at six, she had a chipped tooth, the edge rough as a cat's tongue. But it would fall out one day and another one would grow back. And the new one wouldn't be broken, would it? She glanced at her mother, who was looking down at the water, holding the wooden box.

'The new one won't be broken,' Pepper told her.

Her mother walked up and down the side of the river, looking at the water. 'I think they've all gone,' she said. 'I can't see any.'

The wind bellowed. When her mother had opened the box, it had snatched at the bits inside and sent them flying away like a flock of birds. They had landed on the river and floated, staying clumped together for a moment before spreading out. The choppy water had pushed them around and some of them had sunk and the rest had been swept away. As they'd flown out of the box she'd smelled something musty and grey, like potatoes left in the back of a cupboard. Her mother's smell of lavender and bread. Wet breath and wet trousers from crossing the grass to get to the river. Her mother had sneezed twice – eat stew, eat stew, it sounded like she was saying. She had hardly spoken the whole day, except once to the person who was meant to be in the box. 'Back where you'd want to be,' she had said, touching the smooth lid, the carved flowers. She had told Pepper that there was a person inside, sleeping. But Pepper knew that it wasn't someone sleeping. It looked all gritty and broken up and white. And the box too small for someone sleeping.

In the distance, car lights swept across the trees and then disappeared. There were heavy clouds and it was getting darker. Late October, the sky turning deep blue. No street lamps, no other houses.

'I think they've all gone,' her mother said again. Her hair blew out to one side; it was long and tangled and always moving. 'Untameable,' her mother called it. Which made Pepper think of it as a wild horse, rearing and galloping. And she had crackly skin that got electric shocks when she touched car doors or other people's coats, and she had very red lips, and dents like thumb prints in the squashy skin on her thighs. And she was tall, like the trees. Pepper had never seen so many trees – they stretched into the distance and turned into a dark mass. Behind them, there was a big empty space with no trees that looked humped and crooked.

'Where's the moon?' she asked. The clouds were hiding it. Her mother put her dry hand on Pepper's head. Pepper used to be scared of the moon. The way it kept shrinking and growing. Its sly, shadowy face. She'd thought that, at any moment, it would fall out of the sky and crash through roofs and houses. But now she knew it was held up there somehow.

She leaned against her mother's legs. Through her head, she could feel the faint thump of her mother's heart and her belly creaking. The big buttons on her coat like hard sweets. Pepper butted her head in, then butted again harder. It was boring standing there, and her stomach all clenched up with hunger. They had been travelling for hours and hours – first a bus, then a train, then another bus, the seats smoky and scratchy and a man across the aisle who had fallen asleep with his mouth open and spit dribbling onto his neck. A bottle under the seats which had rolled and rolled. They had been running late, as usual, her mother pushing the last of their things into bags and no time to pack any food, so they'd bought sandwiches with ham in and a pot of potatoes all cut up into pieces. But the ham had yellow seeds down one side and the potatoes had green bits in them. She'd spat it all out and hidden it under the seat. Then done an impression of the man sleeping, lolling her tongue out and snoring, until her mother told her to stop, but she had almost laughed, making a strange gulping sound that had nearly woken the man up.

She butted her head and hit against her mother's hip. Dreaming of warm pancakes and thick crusts of bread. She had an appetite without end, but people always wanted to tell her how small she was for her age, as if she didn't know already.

'Not so hard,' her mother said.

'Why are we standing here?' Pepper asked. She tried to catch one of the leaves that kept spinning down, a yellow one, but missed.

'You know why,' her mother said. She looked again at the water. 'We'll go in a minute.'

'But where are we going?' Pepper said.

Her mother looked down at her and made the face she always made when Pepper asked the same question a hundred times. And knew the answer anyway. Pepper scuffed at the grass with her shoe. She knew where they were going: to the house of the person that had been in the box, but it was important to keep asking because she was never told all of the information. She was always the one that got left out of everything.

They hadn't even been inside yet. Their bags were piled up on the steps by the door. Wet steps, where she had slipped and banged her tooth, then squeezed her hands tight until her nails dug in, watching the sliver of tooth get blown away by the wind. It wasn't like any house she'd seen before. It loomed up, huge and dark. Completely by itself, not huddled in a row like all the other ones they'd lived in. Lots of dark windows, a rusty letterbox, a bristly orange doormat. A watering can with plastic flowers stuck in it. The walls were a strange grey colour that was almost blue, like an egg she'd once found that had fallen out of a nest and broken. And the river was so close. You could glimpse it over the grass and hear its deep glugging.

She looked at the water. No more bits left. She watched the river as it swept round a bend, maybe saw a clump of something pale catching in the bank further down. She glanced at her mother, licking her tooth. What she wanted to know was: what about the teeth, what had happened to them?

'I don't know,' her mother said.

'But where are they?' she asked. She crouched down and found a stick and scratched at the wet ground. 'In all that dust?'

'We should go back to the house.'

7

Pepper worked the stick in deeper, imagined she was prising open a huge lid. 'You said there was a person in the box.' The stick hit against a stone and wouldn't go any further. She thought about the white gritty stuff. She knew what it was really, but it gave her a strange, heavy feeling and if she didn't keep asking then she would be a coward. 'So the bones as well?' she said.

The wind came again, making the trees bow. 'Do your coat up,' her mother said, even though it was her that was shivering.

'So it was the bones as well?' Pepper said. She picked at the skin around her lips. Waited, then waited some more. Sometimes her mother would tell her things, but mostly she would just look away into the distance and then Pepper would have to stay very still and hold her breath, or she would have to make a loud, sudden noise, and then her mother would blink and look around as if she didn't know where she was, even though she'd been standing in the same place the whole time.

After a while, Pepper reached into her mother's pocket and tugged her hand, then tugged it harder. The nails were all bitten down. Soon the hand would move and grab her, make her shriek. But it stayed still. She tugged it again.

Eventually her mother said: 'Old snaggle-tooth.' She touched Pepper's mouth with her finger, so that it almost stopped hurting. 'Does it hurt?' she asked.

'No,' Pepper said. She pretended to bite her mother's finger and then did bite it a little bit, by accident.

The dark closed in on them. The river made noises like a person muttering. Everything was dark: the sky, the trees, the river, her mother's jacket, creased from the journey, which seemed like it had happened so long ago. But it had only been that morning when Pepper had turned back from the bus window and seen for the last time the red door of their rented flat, the spiky plant with no leaves, the bath at the front full of weeds and rust. And in the window of the flat downstairs, the two white birds. But she had tried not to look at them and concentrated instead on imagining a sharp pole sticking out of the window that sliced the top off everything they went past: trees, telegraph wires, warehouses, slice, slice.

But those two white birds, in a cage with swirls on it. Their soft faces. Sometimes she'd gone right up to the window to watch them flying around the room, or sleeping with their heads tucked into their wings. She would tap on the glass until they stared at her.

She crouched down again and dug at the ground, wet grass sticking to her legs. The wind went *hoooroo roooo* and a few drops of rain hit the water. She would never see those birds again. Her mother always said that they'd stay, but they never did. It was just like the fat brown dog in the place before, and the cat with three legs outside the place before that. Once there had been a prickly moth on a bathroom window. She'd stroked it every day until its wings dried out and crumbled off.

The rain came down harder and Pepper jabbed at the ground. She often thought about those other houses, how it would all be going on without her. Soon, that woman downstairs would be going to bed. There would be shuffling, running water, opening and closing doors. The sound of the curtains being drawn carefully. The television would click off and the woman would speak to the birds. 'Sleep tight, *mes chéries*,' she would say, which meant: goodnight, my cherries.

3

RAIN LIKE FEET STAMPING. A few fat drops slipped down Ada's back as they ran to the house. It soaked her coat, her hair. Puddles gleamed at her feet. She had forgotten this: the sudden squalls, hail to sun, gales to downpours, drizzle to fog. She turned and made sure Pepper was behind her. She was lagging – gloom had descended on her as suddenly as the weather. One minute she had been standing quietly by the river, the next, she was stomping up and down the bank muttering about birds and teeth. Somehow managed to injure herself already and obviously starving again; her stomach sounded like someone was blowing up and twisting a balloon.

She took Pepper's hand and ran over the grass. There was the house, low and stooping. It had always looked like a listing boat, propped up and lopsided with its barns and outhouses tacked on. Brick and wood and corrugated metal. A porch added haphazardly. The chimney perched at a wild angle, about to crumble off any moment. Rust bloomed like moss, moss in the gaps on the roof where tiles should be. Cracked windows, the roof buckling like an old tent. Ivy garlanding everything.

The grass turned to gravel. She slowed down so that Pepper wouldn't fall over again. Wet leaves pasted everywhere. The porch roof bowed in the middle. Their bags were piled up by the door – four holdalls, two small cases, everything they owned now that she'd sold the motley collection of cheap furniture and crockery they'd accumulated over the years. It had seemed like a lot when she was struggling with it onto the bus, but now it looked like nothing. She brushed rain out of Pepper's hair and held on to the empty box. At least that part was over with. She could hear the river: a deeper drumming than the rain. Sweeping on tirelessly, as a searchlight might. The trees sent shadows rocking over the walls.

'Those trees will be bare soon,' she said. By December the sun wouldn't come up over the valley. The leaves would gather up in drifts. Only a few left clinging on, stubborn as old bunting.

Pepper rocked on her heels. 'Are we going to go inside now?' she asked.

Ada looked down at her. A tiny thing, all eyes and elbows, dancing round like she needed to pee. Which she probably did. 'Hold this,' she said, giving Pepper the wooden box. 'I need to find the keys.' She crouched down and opened her bag. Gloves, tissues, paperwork. Pegs, for some reason, and then the whole washing line: loops of yellow plastic that she kept pulling out like a magic trick – except no keys conjured up at the end. The wind blew in cold sideways rain. How cold would the house be? She shuddered to think of it, remembering ice inside the windows, separated oil. By January there would be ice in the milk, but they wouldn't still be here in January.

Pepper ran her fingers over the box. 'What does this say?' she asked.

'I packed them in here,' Ada said. She dug her hand down to the bottom of the bag and felt for them again. There was nothing but crumbs – always crumbs, following her around like a plague. 'Christ, where are they?' She unzipped another bag. All their clothes stuffed in. Shoes on top of shampoo, a handful of cutlery.

'Are we going inside now?' Pepper said. She wound the washing line around her belly.

'We've got to find the keys first,' Ada said. 'Can you look in that bag?'

Pepper opened the other bag and looked inside. 'My snail shells,' she said. 'They're all everywhere.'

'Can you see the keys?' Ada asked.

'Hell's bells,' Pepper said. 'They've gone everywhere.' The wind kept on gusting. Ada got out Pepper's hat and pulled it down so it covered her ears. She tried the front door but it was locked. Rattled it and pushed with her shoulder. If you just open now, she thought, I will be a better person. I will never swear in front of Pepper. I will clear out this house patiently. She took a deep breath. Tried the handle again. 'Bollocks,' she said. She looked up at the window, wondered what it would take to break it. The wind shook the trees like brooms.

'We're stuck out here forever,' Pepper said. She wound the washing line tighter. 'Maybe they're in that car. That man's car.' Then she went back to winding herself up tighter and tighter, pretending that she had stopped breathing.

The bus had dropped them off in a gravelly lay-by – the closest place it stopped – and they had been picked up by Luke, who had insisted on taking them to the house. 'Am I late?' he said. He turned the car heater up to a loud whirr. 'A tree's come down across the road further back. Had to take the long way round.' He looked over his shoulder at Pepper. 'You probably thought I wasn't coming.'

Ada shifted in her seat. She was sitting on an old blanket, scratchy wool with bits of yellow grass sticking out. A green and blue check pattern – the kind everyone around here kept in their cars for emergencies.

Pepper stared at Luke and didn't say anything. Her hand came up and picked at her lips. She had never been good around people, never made friends, even as a baby had yelped whenever she was picked up. A furious little face the midwife had said. Grey wrinkly skin, pedalling the air like she was trying to escape.

'There's something of Pearl in her,' Luke said. The rain was a weak patter. He pulled the car away and the wheels spun on the wet road. The heater filled the car with singed dust.

'Who?' Pepper said. 'Who's in me?' She kicked the back seat until Ada made her stop.

'I appreciate it,' Ada said. 'The lift.' But it would only be this once; she hated having to rely on anyone, especially her mother's old friend. Her only friend. The one who'd found her and sat with her while he waited for the ambulance to come. His pale blue eyes were fixed on the road. Waxy hair pushed behind his ears. His suit jacket sleeves had been mended with small stitches and his hands were ridged with turquoise veins. A gold ring on his thumb, the inky edge of a tattoo creeping up the top of his neck. He had a dented nose from when a cow had kicked him in the face. He'd just got straight back up again, pushed his nose into place and said something about how come the grass didn't smell any more? After that, he couldn't smell or taste anything – not bread, not garlic, not anything.

'You'll be wanting to use Pearl's car,' he said.

A cold feeling gripped her. 'We won't be here long,' she said.

13

'Can't get far without one around here of course. I checked it over a while ago, when I knew you were coming.' He spoke gently, slowed round a sharp bend, where the road narrowed so only one car could get past. A branch scraped against the door.

Ada nodded slowly. But she hadn't driven a car in years. And the roads around here were the worst to drive on, what with the wet and the bends and tractors hurtling along in the middle of the road. And the ice and the hail. Dips. Potholes as big as bathtubs.

'It's still got some life in it,' Luke said. 'The brakes are stiff buggers, since no one's been using them. But I threw some brake fluid in.'

'She wasn't using it?'

Luke glanced at her. 'Pearl hadn't driven in a long time,' he said. He shook his head, started to say something else and then stopped. After a moment he said, 'You'll find some tiles off. If you need a hand I can always.'

She thanked him, but said she would be doing it herself. 'We won't be here long,' she said again. There wouldn't be much to do. Her mother had always kept up with repairs, battling the damp, the cracks, the wind-thieved tiles. An expert in anything practical, although couldn't cook to save her life. Would use a griddle pan as a hammer.

In the back, Pepper shifted and stretched. Her eyes closed and her cheeks flushed from the heater. Wispy hair all mussed up. One hand in a fist, murmuring: 'I won't do it. Three more potatoes but none for you.'

Down the hill and into the valley. It was an isolated place: trees thickening into woods, the sun barely reaching in. Gales funnelling through. The moor rose up in the distance, humped and stark as something marooned. There were farms spread out for miles: sloping fields, derelict stores, barns. Cows bunching together and shifting their weight slowly from leg to leg. Steaming out of their noses like kettles. There was no centre to speak of – most of the houses were scattered by themselves, a few huddles of newer bungalows, a shop, the church and the school two miles in the other direction. A pub down an overgrown lane, a whitewashed café by the main road that long-distance drivers stopped at, filled up with petrol from the pump outside, hunched over strong coffee, and then left without looking back. And the river. The river winding through it all.

Luke hummed the same strange tunes he'd always hummed. 'It might take more time than you think,' he said. 'Sort out the whole place.' He leaned forward over the wheel. Same squinting eyes, same chapped skin, but he looked old. She had never thought of her mother getting older in all the years since she had last seen her. She pushed the thought away, then shivered and Luke turned the heater up. 'Must have been eight years since you were last here Ada,' he said.

Ada nodded. Although it had been thirteen. Apart from coming down briefly a few weeks ago, but all that was hazy – hearing about her mother, rushing down for the funeral. She hadn't been to the house. Endless meetings with solicitors about what to do with it. Taxes. Bills. Needed sorting out, doing up. Selling. Costs of labour. Her current landlord talking about raising the rent. In between jobs again. Nobody else she could call on – how was there no one else she could call on? And now she saw herself as if from above, on her way back to the place. Her mother's place. Nowhere else to go.

'I remember you riding that scooter around the lanes,' Luke said. 'Like it was yesterday. Beeping the horn, wearing those long skirts.'

'That wasn't me,' Ada told him.

'I waved to you each time,' he said. 'When you went past.'

'That wasn't me,' she said. But her voice was suddenly childish, doubtful.

'There's the Trewins' house,' Luke said. 'Reckoned they won the lottery a month ago but lost the ticket. They haven't got over it yet.'

Ada looked at where Luke was pointing, imagined what he would say about her to people – that she was the same, different? She hardly knew herself. 'I would never wear long skirts,' she said.

They passed a house with no lights on, the gate swinging in the wind. Their headlights passed through thin curtains, showing up, for a second, the shape of a body in the room behind them. Her hands clenched and she leaned back in the seat.

'It's just down there,' Luke said, pointing as if she might have forgotten.

The wind heaved everything to one side and then the other. Could she have left the keys in Luke's car? No signal to make any phone calls out here. She thought for a second of the landline and felt relieved, then remembered the landline was in the house and they couldn't get into the house. Dappy mare – something her mother would have said. She ran her hand across her cheek and leaned against the door. It was dark. No neighbours, only a tiny light from a house in the distance.

'What's that noise?' Pepper said. She leaned out of the porch to listen. The washing line now slumped and forgotten on the steps.

'The wind,' Ada said.

'The other thing. Is it the river?'

Ada looked in the bag and found a torch. 'I need to go back and look for the keys,' she said.

'I'm coming,' Pepper said.

'Wait here. Stay by the door, OK?' She took the torch and went back down the steps. Over the gravel and then back onto the wet grass. She shone the torch on the ground in wide arcs. Everything glinted and looked like keys. She looked back at the house and thought again about breaking a window. How did people do that? Tie something round your fist and smash it? Or hurl a brick? All those hours at school struggling with algebra when these were the things she needed to know. She took a step forward, stopped, then stepped back. Scanned the grass, scanned it again, then remembered that there used to be a spare key hidden somewhere in the garden, lodged in the wall, or under a stone by the steps. She ran back and found Pepper in the driveway.

'I told you to stay by the door,' she said. When would Pepper stop wandering off? Ada had lost her in a car park once and found her, ten terrified minutes later, underneath a van cooing to a pigeon she'd been following.

'I saw something,' Pepper said.

'There's a spare key somewhere here,' Ada said. 'Look in the wall for me. Any loose stones.'

'How do you know?' Pepper asked.

'You're good at finding things,' Ada told her.

They turned over stone after stone with nothing but mud and worms underneath. Pepper picking stones up and throwing them down hard. 'I can't find it,' she said. 'I can't find it.' Her cheeks mottling. She picked up a stone and threw it at the wall of the house.

Ada closed her eyes for a moment. Wished she could throw one herself. She lifted up another stone and the key was under it. The lock was stiff and swollen and the key went in slowly and almost didn't turn. The door heaved open. Damp and mouldy smells rushed out. Cold, stale air. But they were in. Ada shoved their bags into the hallway and closed the door. The house was very dark. She pressed her back to the door, suddenly expecting to hear her mother clomping, clearing her throat, her terrible sneeze that would startle cows in the next field. There were Pearl's shoes, her long coats. The crushed waterproof hat.

The house creaked and griped, while they waited in the doorway like nervous guests.

'What does it say?' Pepper asked. She was looking at the wooden box. Running her finger over the side.

'It's just flowers,' Ada told her.

'It says something,' Pepper said. She squinted at the box and turned it upside down.

'Let me have a look.' It was probably just the date or something. Ada held the box up and tried to see in the dim hall. *A Beloved Pet.* She read it again. Her mother had been tiny – probably tinier at the end. But a pet box. She didn't know whether to laugh or cry. So did neither.

4

THE FIRST CLOUD OF dust hit Pepper and she sneezed, then her mother sneezed too, loud and sharp like she always did, so that it rang out twice in the empty hallway. Once, she had sneezed so loudly it had made a woman in a shop drop a bottle of milk. By the door, there were boots and umbrellas and a lot of knotty sticks. A long coat hanging down, like a person standing there waiting. Further up, sheets of wallpaper were peeling off and bending backwards in big arcs. A bony leaf rattled around their feet.

'Hellooooo,' Pepper said. To show she wasn't scared.

'The light switch is behind you,' her mother said. 'Can you see it?'

Pepper felt along the wall by the coats. Her fingers brushed against cobwebs. She looked for the spider but couldn't see one. She found the switch and clicked it but no lights came on. She tried it again, click, click, click, until her mother told her to stop. Then she said something about staying by the door, don't go anywhere, looked like there might be loose boards, the ceiling could be about to cave in. She opened the door, wind rushed in and billowed the wallpaper, and then the door shut and she was gone.

The house creaked in the wind. At first, all Pepper could see was the pale wall up ahead, but then it was easier to see other things: an open door further down the hall, a lampshade rocking in the draught. There were rows of photographs in frames along the wall and she stood on tiptoe to look at them. They were all birds and their small eyes were dark and bright as oil. Some of the pictures were brown, like tea had spilled on them, some were black and white, some were faded blues and greens. She followed them down the hall – there was a small bird on a branch, a blurred shape between trees, and then there was a tink tink sound, and on the floor a saucepan catching water dripping from the ceiling. Reminding her of her own full bladder.

She turned and went through the open door and found herself in the kitchen. Tried the light switch but no light came on. The floor was brown and sticky. There was a table with a chair pulled out as if someone had just got up and left. Speckled grey tiles, dirty mugs and plates in the sink. The sink was full of brown water with leaves floating in it and a greasy sheen. Pepper put her finger in the water and the plates bobbed and looked like lonely faces that had been left behind. Everything had been left behind and it was like intruding. She jabbed the plates so that they clacked together.

There was a rustling noise and she turned, expecting to see her mother, but there was no one there. The kitchen was quiet except for a clock ticking and the wind pressing against the window. There were notes stuck to the fridge. She squinted at the one closest to her. *Blue with orange, blue with orange.* What did it say? She knew it started with a 'b' at least. But words were devious; they twisted and played tricks so that you ended up writing, 'I have brown hare' and everyone laughing. What you had to do was look at them out of the corner of your eye until they turned blurry and almost disappeared, and then you didn't have to worry about them any more. It was the same with cracks in pavements and clocks with heavy, swinging pendulums.

The noise started up again, a sort of rustling somewhere in the house. She followed it past a closed door, past the stairs, making sure she stood on the carpet's big flowers rather than the gaps in between them. The hall curved and at the end of it there were stone steps going down to another room. Inside, there were thick orange curtains and shelves full of books and boxes. A row of glass birds. A toolbox with the lid open: a hammer and screwdrivers and broken watches inside. Jars and jars of silver pins on the desk. More photographs on the walls. One of the windows had swung open and rain was blowing in. She crossed the room to close it, then heard the scrabbling right behind her. She turned round. The window banged. Nothing for a long minute. Then the noise again. Her legs tingled. She needed to pee, urgently. The sound came again and she licked her tooth. The window rattled, banged shut, then creaked open. Something moved behind the chair. She stayed very still. Then a grey shape hurtled past her legs, skidded and ran out of the door. Hoarse grunts and a faint hiss. Its tail bent at an angle. A squashed, startled face.

Pepper ran after it; back down the hall where the cat had scrabbled under the kitchen table. 'Hey,' she said. 'Come here.'

The cat turned to look at her. There was a bit missing out of one ear. Ribs showing above a droopy belly. Big paws. Matted grey fur like a threadbare carpet. It hissed again. Pepper stepped backwards and the cat galloped past her, back down into the low room and jumped out of the window.

It was too dark to see where it went. Something roared and thumped. The river. It sounded like it was in the room. She closed the window, then knelt on the deep ledge and looked out. Dark humps of grass, the mass of all those trees. One tiny light in the distance. Her breath steamed on the cold glass. There was a quivering wail from outside. Was that what an owl sounded like? She had never heard one before. A shape moved down by the river – her mother. But then the lights clicked on and she heard her mother close the front door, take off her coat and stamp her shoes, saying: Where are you? The lights are working now.

In the kitchen, her mother opened cupboards and drawers. 'There's got to be something we can eat,' she said.

Pepper sat at the table wrapped in a blanket, which smelled like someone else's soap and biscuits. Outside, the sky was very dark and there was a single star among all the murky clouds, like a peephole that looked out into space. If she tipped back and concentrated on the star, it felt like she was getting sucked right out there. She tipped further and further. 'What doesn't make sense,' she said, 'is how space is supposed to go on for ever and ever,' and her voice sounded higher and different to usual.

The fan heater they'd found rattled loudly. The fridge was back on and there was a sour smell coming from it. Her mother didn't go near it. She didn't look over when it shuddered, stopped, then started up again. She didn't look at anything; not the papers, or the bits of plastic and wires, or the notes stuck all over the walls. She kept her coat on and stared into the cupboard.

Usually they would have unpacked by now. Her mother would be running the bath, the bathroom filling with steam and lavender. She would be saying things like: this is exactly right, I've got a feeling about this place, I think it's going to work out. Pepper would have laid out her precious things in the room she was going to sleep in.

Her mother crouched down and opened a drawer. 'Nothing but bags of bird seed in here,' she said.

22

'I saw a cat,' Pepper said. There was still rain in her mother's hair, which made it look very dark.

'There must be about seven bags,' her mother said.

'In a room with thousands of books and pictures.'

Her mother stood up, then reached into the highest cupboard. She brought down a tin and a lot of dust. 'Don't go in that room at the moment, OK?'

'Why?'

'God knows how old these things are,' her mother said. She found the tin opener and opened the tin and poured it into a pan, then clicked something and a bright blue flame roared up. The kettle shook as it boiled.

'Why can't I?' Pepper said. Then tipped back again in her chair. Who cared anyway, they wouldn't be here very long.

Her mother spooned coffee into a mug and it came out in fat lumps. She drank two huge gulps while it was still steaming. She made Pepper a cup, weak and with lots of sugar. It tasted dusty and of burnt meat but it warmed her insides. The windows fogged up. Pepper leaned her head against the table and when she woke up the kitchen smelled of familiar cooking smells and there were butter beans in tomato sauce, soft biscuits to dip in and a bowl of tinned peaches. Her mother could make a feast out of anything. When she cracked eggs there were sometimes two yolks inside.

'Finish these,' her mother said, pushing her bowl over.

Pepper shook her head. 'You eat them,' she said. 'You haven't eaten very much yet.' Although her stomach growled. Her mother left the bowl right there in front of her, so in the end there was nothing to do but eat the rest of the peaches. Her mother was watching her very closely; sometimes she did that and Pepper hated it, so she tilted her face up and dropped the peaches into her mouth one by one, like a bird eating orange fish. The windows shook and wind shrieked through the gaps. A drop of water splashed onto the table. They both looked up and saw a dark patch spreading. The lights flickered.

'I forgot what it was like,' her mother said quietly.

There were crumbs and a bean on the front of Pepper's shirt. Her head drifted down onto the dusty table and she sneezed, her nose dripped and she wiped it with the blanket. The lights flickered again and rain hurled itself against the windows as if it was trying to get in. She had to stay awake, there was something she needed to ask, but the blanket warmed to a fug of breath and body heat. She found the butter bean and ate it.

She hardly remembered being carried upstairs and put in bed. More blankets heaped on top. Drifting in and out of sleep, she swam up from a dream where everything kept moving, nothing would stay still, a tree turned into a cat snarling. Her feet were cold from sticking out of rucked sheets. It was completely dark, as if the whole world had disappeared. No fuzzy orange glow, no car lights sweeping across the walls. She must have called out because her mother came in, still dressed, and rubbed her arms and talked to her.

'I couldn't find the key,' Pepper told her.

When she woke again she was alone and it was still dark. She sat up and looked around the room, could just make out a small chair, a mirror, bare walls – where was the picture of the silver mountain, where was the yellow clock? Then she remembered. No white birds cooing softly downstairs. Only a branch thumping against the roof. Blue covers with gold stars on. She turned over and tucked herself back under. The bedsprings crunched. A lump in the mattress where her shoulder needed to be. She kicked and turned. Back through the hall, there came a sharp, sweet smell, very faint, moving through the rooms.

5

GAS. THE WHOLE PLACE stank of gas. Ada checked the hob, paced down the hall, then back into the kitchen again. Draughts kept the gas moving, so that at first it was stronger in the kitchen, then by the front door. Too tired even to yawn, head numb as if stuffed with reels of wool. The gas moved again. She followed it through the kitchen and into the larder with its empty shelves and slate floor. Squat orange bottles lined up against the wall. A faint hissing sound.

'Don't do that,' she said. She shut the door. After a moment realised she'd shut herself into a tiny room full of gas. Opened the door again, and the small window as wide as it would go.

The connector tube from the oven was crumbling, attached to one of the bottles with an elastic band. She turned the gas off, took off the tube and worked out the kinks. But when she went to reattach it, she saw there were two taps that looked exactly the same. Rain pelted through the open window. Which one, which one? She knelt down and studied them as if they were something holy that might yield answers. Must have fallen asleep for a second because she jerked awake with the tap digging into her cheek. Cursed all identical things. Left the gas switched off and the tube dangling.

She went back upstairs to check on Pepper, who was sleeping in Ada's old bedroom. Her fist clutching the duvet, which was the blue one with stars, Ada's favourite. She used to count them over and over in the night. She went past her mother's bedroom without looking in. Paused at the door of the spare room, saw the crooked and rusting camp bed folded in the corner. Went back downstairs. Heard the river's boom as it muscled forward. There was an armchair in the corner of the kitchen and she sat down among newspapers and crumbs. The fridge wheezed. After a while, she curled her legs up under her, pulled over a blanket and put her head down on the chair's musty arm. The clock sometimes missed a tick – tick, pause, tick – and she found herself waiting for it nervously, like someone waiting for news.

She woke with a tender neck and crusty eyes. Hips stiff as a swollen door. She still had her shoes on, bits of grass and grit stuck to them. Couldn't think where she was for a moment, and then realised the blanket she'd draped over herself was her mother's long brown coat: mud-splashed hem and tissues in the pocket. It was early and still dark and raw. She folded the coat carefully and turned on the heater. Filled the kettle from the tap. The water smelled like ditches; it always tasted foul after heavy rain. She broke off some granules from the block of coffee in the jar. There was an eerie lack of noise. No rain battered against the windows, no branches knocked against the roof.

There were piles of empty tins everywhere. Bottles of milk behind the armchair, gone thick and dark like treacle; brown-rimmed mugs hoarded under the table. No idea what her mother had been eating. Where was the bag of bread, the potatoes ready to be fried, the tins of corned beef and sardines? Where were the tins of baby potatoes, which she would spear out with a knife one by one? Nothing but the husk of a carrot in the fridge. The freezer stuffed with uneaten meals, all labelled with someone's neat writing: *Don't forget to turn off the oven at the end Pearl*. And heaps of bills – all overdue as far as Ada could tell, even though her mother had always paid up the day any bill came, despite struggling for money. She had once swapped a coffee table for four steaks and a can of petrol.

Uneasy thoughts brewed up but Ada pushed them back down. Thirteen years. She pulled the plug on the water in the sink and scooped out fat from the plughole. It reminded her of making lardy cake – mix handfuls of fat with yeast, soak dried fruit. She had always found something calming about listing recipes: the careful methods and ingredients. Knead dough with oil, simmer onions with butter, get disgusting grease off fingers.

But thirteen years. She had planned to come back, but one thing after another, the years rolled. Scrabbling for a new job every six months, nothing permanent, hauling boxes and bags to towns further and further away. And she had tried, hadn't she? Working up the time and money to visit, then getting notice that she had to leave her flat, or getting stranded halfway there on a bus, snow piling softly around the wheels. And then Pepper. Suddenly too exhausted for the difficult phone conversations – her mother never the one to ring, saying she didn't know the right number, what address was Ada at again? Her voice irritable and faraway. It had seemed better to wait until things were calmer, more settled. Always thought there would be more time. And finally, when her mother had agreed to visit them instead, when she'd said she would definitely be there this time, Ada had waited hours at the station before giving up, Pepper clutching her hair and shouting, goose! whenever a train sounded its horn.

Ada stacked up the dirty plates and turned on the tap. No hot water.

27

There had to be a boiler by now, there had to be. She looked in the larder, went up to the bathroom to check, then came back down. Opened up all the cupboards. There was the yellow mixing bowl; she ran her hand around the edge but it felt strange, the pattern indented rather than raised like she remembered. And when she picked up the green vase her mother used to cram wild daffodils in, it was plastic, not glass.

Through the windows came thin grey light. Mist low on the grass like thick ribbons.

There was a rustling noise and Pepper came into the kitchen dragging her duvet. 'It's cold,' she said.

'I know it is,' Ada said. She wrapped Pepper up tighter. 'I was just going to turn the heating on.'

'You've got creases on your face,' Pepper said. She looked around the kitchen. 'Where's the TV?' she asked. 'When are we going to the shops? I want to eat breakfast and sit in the bath.'

'We'll go to the shop later,' Ada said. Toast, she should make toast. But of course there was no bread. An image of her mother appeared: standing on tiptoes to light the grill with a match, then watching the blue flame roll across it. Looking like one of the herons that she had loved so much. Knees poking out of thin trousers – the grey ones she always wore. Solitary, wrapped in her own stillness. And the only time Ada had heard her sob it was a harsh, krrching sound.

She found a box of cereal and poured out two bowls. It was soft and stale, lurking at the back of the cupboard for God knows how long.

'Why's that all broken under the table?' Pepper said, cramming in spoonfuls of dry cereal like she hadn't eaten for weeks.

'It's a radio,' Ada said. Taken apart but not put back together. Not that it had worked very well anyway – there wasn't signal for anything in this valley. After an hour of fiddling you might find a dim babble of voices, a wavering cello.

Pepper slid down onto the floor to look. 'But whose is it?'

Ada took a deep breath. Hadn't yet told Pepper the whole story. 'I told you about the woman who died. This is her house, remember?' Praying Pepper wouldn't go on about skin and teeth again.

'She left her radio behind,' Pepper said. 'She left the chairs, the table, the books, the pictures, the . . .' She whirled around, looking for something else to list.

Ada said shhuusshh, otherwise Pepper could list all day.

'And her shoes and her coats,' Pepper said quietly, so Ada wouldn't tell her off.

'Remember I told you that I knew her a long time ago? Well, we lived here.' Ada took her bowl to the sink. She knocked her head on the low beam that went across – something she'd never done before.

'*You* lived here,' Pepper said. 'You lived here together? Like us living together?'

Ada nodded.

Pepper jammed a spring into the back of the radio. After a moment she said, 'You didn't cry.'

The bowl clattered into the sink. Ada ran the tap but the water stayed stubbornly cold. 'Help me find the boiler,' she said.

But there was no boiler. She went through the hall and into the living room. Saw the wood burner and stared at it.

'What is that?' Pepper asked.

'It's instead of a boiler,' Ada said. The old back boiler hidden in the wall behind it, which powered the heating and the hot water. It had to be fed wood all the time, like a greedy pet. A mean-looking thing. Always going out on the coldest day, the fire cement cracking, the chimney not drawing. Her mother out chopping wood for hours, the sound of it echoing like gunshots around the house.

'I want to burn something in it,' Pepper said.

'We need to get wood,' Ada told her. She had never lit a fire in her life. Her mother never let anyone else touch the thing. Where did she get wood from? There was no time to be messing around with the fire, but it was only going to get colder. And she couldn't stand the thought of freezing baths and showers for either of them.

'And her lamps and her shelves and her ceilings,' Pepper chanted.

Out into the weather. The roar of the river. Cobwebs slung like hammocks in the hedge. The smell of bonfire and wet soil. Long grass soaked her shoes. Nothing in the vegetable plot except mushy weeds bowing to the earth, something sodden and green that may once have been a potato. In the shed, swallows' nests festooned the beams. Old paint pots, their lids splashed with the blue of her bedroom, the yellow of the bathroom. The axe and saw were leaning against the wall but there was no wood, not even a twig for kindling.

Ada went back out of the shed. Mist hung over the valley like an awning. A sense of quiet and space, or constriction, depending on your opinion. The town was almost an hour's drive in the other direction. To get to the nearest houses you had to walk up the lane, along the road for fifteen minutes and then across two wide fields. The shop was further out on the edge of the busier road. She had spent a lot of time here daydreaming about escape, circling places on maps – places where things happened, where the big news wasn't another pub brawl, or a tree falling onto someone's house, or a jackdaw that stole people's jewellery and sold it on for a profit. Or something. A lonely place. And she didn't want the same loneliness for Pepper, who was outside the shed patting a tree stump like it was a horse.

'I've got a job for us,' Ada said. 'We have to find some wood to burn, but only small branches.' She didn't want to do any chopping.

Pepper dragged a branch over to the pile. 'Now we won't freeze like those other people,' she said.

'What other people?'

'The ones where the price went up too high.'

Too many evenings eating dinner in front of the news – Pepper suddenly concerned about forest fires, unemployment, taxes. They would eat ice cream straight out of the tub, watch the old Western that came on and then fall asleep with their mouths open, as if astonished. 'No one will freeze,' Ada told her.

'Someone will,' Pepper said, morbid and logical as always.

Soon they had a big pile. Ada thought about all the times she had listened to her mother going on about the expense of wood, the difficulty sourcing it, when it was all down here, free. She put a bundle of smaller pieces in Pepper's arms and took the heavier ones herself.

Inside, she found matches and balled up some of the old newspaper from the kitchen. It spluttered but was soon roaring. Ada laid small sticks over it, then bigger twigs, and finally two fat bits of branch. She closed the stove door. The fire spat and pinged against the glass. The glow got fainter and fainter. A second later, the fire was smeeching, a stench of acrid soot as smoke leaked out of the vents. A lot of smoke. God, there was a lot of smoke suddenly. It poured out and filled the room with a terrible bitter smell. She flung the windows open, coughed, then fled.

Pearl's car was small and green and dented, rust in the wheel arches, a leaking roof. Ada brushed the wet leaves off it. The sealant round the windows crumbled under her fingers and the doors stuck before opening with a jolt. But Luke had said it was working.

She settled Pepper in the front and double-, triple-checked the seat belt. Then got in herself, cursing the fact that you had to drive to get anywhere in this place. She was used to buses and walking, pavements, trains. No one knowing who you were and asking things.

'My seat's wet,' Pepper said. She lifted herself up and there was a dark patch on her trousers.

The number of times Ada had gone to school trying to hide a wet patch. 'Sit like this,' she said. She jiggled the gear-stick and put the key in, waited a moment before turning it. The engine spluttered then stopped. A burning smell and a glimpse of smoke in the wing mirror. She tried again. Her hands left clammy marks on the steering wheel. 'It's not going to start,' she said. She thought of the narrow roads and corners that went on forever. And felt relieved.

'But how will we buy food?' Pepper said.

Ada tried once more and the car griped but the engine turned over. 'OK,' she said, 'OK.' Tried to get a feel for the pedals. Jesus, which was which, the brake and the clutch? She crawled forward slowly and turned onto the road. There was a tractor coming in the other direction. A flash of red, a horn bellowed, the crush of hedge against the car as Ada squeezed against it.

Pepper hunkered down in her seat. 'Will we die?' she asked.

'We won't die,' Ada said. Hoped she sounded convincing.

There were branches all over the road, puddles that were inches deep. The car jerked when she changed gear. Once it stopped dead, but thankfully only sheep that saw and frowned. There were enough potholes to make the car bounce. But, finally, the shop. She pulled in, her heart clamouring, and smiled at Pepper, who stared back without blinking.

A man came out of the door just as they were going in – a tall man wearing a brown jumper, green boots. His hair a coppery colour. He held the door open, inclined his head, there was some mix-up with whose arm went where and in the end Ada had to duck under his.

Then he was gone. It struck her that she hadn't washed yet and was wearing the same clothes she'd slept in.

In the shop there was a whirring heater, notices for lost dogs, cars for sale, a room to rent. A stack of fishing rods and nets in one corner, a shelf full of those scratchy woollen blankets, Thermos flasks, maps. A wall lined with empty shelves, a few tins, soap, plastic washing-up brushes. A chest freezer with a motor that thumped, the insides coated in deep ice, empty except for a bright pizza box and a few grey shapes of meat. There was a shelf for comics, a tied bundle of newspapers underneath. On the counter, two sad-looking loaves and a jar of pink lollies.

Mick, who owned the shop with his wife, looked up at Ada and then went back to talking to another man, who was propped against the counter. Mick's grey hair was pulled back into a ponytail and he rubbed his cheek slowly as he talked. Very small teeth, which gave his jaw a caved-in look. 'The car jackknifed in the road,' he said.

'I heard the deer ran straight out,' the other man said. His nose was hatched with blood vessels. He got out a tissue and blew it.

Ada took a basket from the pile. Tinned peaches, tomatoes, chickpeas. Rice. A box of cereal. Milk. Firelighters. Matches. Three withered onions from a basket – there was hardly anything fresh. Instead, tins of baby carrots, peas and potatoes. A vacuum pack of beetroot. A tube of garlic. She looked over at the counter and saw that Mick was watching her. 'Do you . . .' she said. 'Is there any more fruit, or any veg?' The shop was a lot smaller than she remembered.

'There's plenty out,' Mick said.

The other man said, 'Supermarket opened a while back. Edge of town. About forty-five minutes' drive.' He stared at Ada. 'You still singing with that group?'

'I only did that once,' Ada said. 'With the school.' She had no idea who he was.

She felt Pepper tugging at her arm. 'Can we?' she asked. She held up two apples, both bruised, one with a mushy hole bored out. Mick was watching so she couldn't say no. They went up to the counter and she picked up the least-crushed loaf of bread. But still a dark burn spread over the top of it.

Mick rang in the amounts for each item. He watched Pepper, who was sidling with her back to the wall to hide the wet patch. 'Is that your kid? She's not going to steal anything is she?'

'The car leaks,' Ada said, as if that explained anything. She looked in her bag for her purse, didn't see Pepper glance at Mick, then gently knock a packet onto the floor.

'Mine does that,' Mick said. He took the last tin out of her basket. When everything was rung in it came to a small fortune. 'And I took it to the garage and they said it's water coming underneath when it rains. Does that make any sense to you?'

'I don't know,' Ada said.

'Yeah, it makes no sense to me either.' He scratched his cheek and it made a rasping sound. 'Listen,' he said. 'Sorry to hear about all that with Pearl. But I've got her milk bill here, bit overdue.' He checked in a notebook and rang in the amount. Ada felt herself grow hot; it was six months of milk at least. 'Good for the teeth,' her mother always said. Except her teeth had always been weak and wobbled like old gravestones.

Mick took the payment. 'I'll keep you down for the milk delivery,' he said.

She shook her head. 'We won't be here long.' She lifted down the bags, which Mick had packed too full, tins on top of the bread. He always used to be out the back watching TV: antique programmes – cackling when people paid too much for junk.

Mick seemed to know what she was thinking. 'She's gone,' he said. 'Five years ago now. In her stomach. The dog knew before me. Took to following her everywhere.'

'Dogs'll do that,' the other man said. He drummed his fingers on the counter. The worn leather of his hands.

'The dog knew before me,' Mick said again. He rasped at his cheek. There was a collecting tin on the counter. 'Collecting for old Edwards, remember him? He's had a few problems, asking everyone if they want to contribute.'

'I don't know who he is,' Ada said.

'Edwards,' the other man said loudly.

'I don't know who he is,' Ada said. But she felt in her pocket and put in a handful of loose change and crumbs. 'Wood,' she said quickly, so they wouldn't check how much she'd put in. 'Do you know where I can get some wood?'

'Well,' Mick said. 'You're in luck actually. I've got some round the back. I was going to hang on to it myself, but I'll do you a deal. Seeing as you need it quick.'

They followed him round to the back of the shop, where there was a heap of fat mossy logs.

'I suppose I could do you a couple of bags for thirty,' he said.

She nodded and thanked him. Drew out her purse once again.

'And what about kindling?' he asked. She'd be needing some of that, wouldn't she? He had some good cheap stuff if she was interested. He loaded up the bags and swung them into the boot of the car, then pocketed the money and gave a small smirk. He went back into the shop without any kind of goodbye.

Take a sour git and leave stewing for thirteen years.

'He knew who you were,' Pepper said. She stuffed a hunk of bread into her mouth.

By the door, the billboard for the local newspaper said: PACKAGING FACTORY TO CLOSE. FARM FIRE NO ACCIDENT. TREE FALLS ON HOUSE.

She swept out the stove and emptied the ashes, the lumps of charred wood and newspaper. Laid down two firelighters, then kindling on top. The flame flickered and grew. She stacked up the wood next to the fire – it felt good and heavy. Maybe now she could get back to what she actually needed to be doing. The sooner out of here the better. The flames roared. She put on a bigger piece of wood. The flames shrank, licking tentatively at the sides. Then they disappeared. She got it going again with another match and the flames leapt up then shrank back. The wood smoked. What was she doing wrong? Why would the bastard thing not just bloody . . .

6

SO GOOD TO HAVE her feet in the water. Soothing the sore bones. A root gripping her leg but no matter. Silt in her pockets. The river spread out around her, grey now and calmer, thin mist hanging either side like curtains. Two leaves dipped under. A branch turned slowly in the water. The water finding its way around rocks. The rocks slowly chilled. Her hands blue, her back numb, couldn't remember when she'd last felt warm. How long had she been here? Hours or years, it was impossible to tell. And her feet in this intolerable water, making the bones sore. Another leaf was dragged under. Nothing but mist and water, mist and water . . . What was that? Something rustled, there was a sound like breathing. Pearl sat up straighter, felt the tug of the root on her leg. It was nothing, just the river rushing to keep its appointments. But was there someone? She sat very still and listened. Nothing. No one rustling but her.

She stared for a long time at the river. It looked familiar . . . the bends, the rocks, the trees. That rotten stump. Slushy rapids like river soup. She racked her brains, felt the clack of small stones. It did seem familiar for some reason but it couldn't be the same old river, it would be ridiculous if it was the same old river – back where she'd always been. She watched a feather float past. She couldn't still be here, could she? When she could have ended up anywhere. The feather tipped and then sank. She leaned forward and caught it, a grey, bedraggled thing. 'Am I still here?' she asked it. The feather crumpled and stuck to her drenched skin.

Now where was she again? She had lost her trail; it was easy to lose the thread of it. It was hard enough trying to keep herself together. Ah yes, that was it: trees everywhere. Trees like brown dye dripping. She spat out a mouthful of river. Pulled a weed out of her hair. The water moved in slow circles, winding itself in loops. Twigs and feathers piled up in drifts. Pearl tangled up in them. Stuck in the lull of it, a root wrapped around her leg, weed in her shoes, going nowhere.

Gulumph. Gulumph. The river circled and sang out bass on the rocks.

'Shhh,' Pearl said. 'Shut up for a second.' Water soaked into her boots, ruining them probably; her favourites, her absolute favourites, well, they were alright, she had never liked them really. But for God's sake why still here, of all places? She kicked at the weeds. Another rustle. What was that? Somebody coming? Nothing. And now her feet were all wet – how had that happened? The moss sodden and her clothes sodden and no one to pass the time of day. It had always been lonely with nothing but this river. Nothing except the river's chatter. Although sometimes a slippery knot of fish fighting against the current. And once a whole flock of sheep washed down like rising loaves.

The water turned dark. Shadows came and went. So did the wind. The moon appeared, floated, and then left, appeared, floated, and then left. As if some idiot was switching a lamp on and off.

Pearl hunched on the rock at the edge of the river. Skin the colour of water, hair the colour of water. No reflection but the water shifting. Sodden bones. Staring down at the liver-coloured stones. God, it was boring and cold. Her feet endlessly tugged by the current. Everything dripping. A crap situation. She scowled at the water, watched it peak, then ruck up like an old carpet, then turn smooth as poured glass. It could never make up its mind – never just one thing or another, always moving, always changing. She sat on the rock and her thoughts peaked and rucked up and turned in circles.

Something glinted. At first she thought it was the water but it was further away than that; it looked like a light in a window. What was it – a house? It had slipped her mind, but of course it was the house – there was the house behind her, she could see it through a watery blur. Vague memories of the long hallway, the kitchen with its wet-leaf smell. Or was that just her, smelling of wet leaves?

She watched the house carefully. The river lightened again. The light in the window disappeared. Pearl heaved herself up and put her feet in the water. She took a step towards the grassy bank. Then another. But her feet were so heavy and her leg was tangled up in the weeds. She tried again, slopped water everywhere, but couldn't move any further. She shook her head, wrung out her sodden sleeves and sat back down on the rock. Still stuck in the place.

The river moved in bulky ripples; behind it, the wet kaleidoscope of trees. The woods were so deep and sometimes there were hoarfrosts so thick in there it was as if the whole world had grown . . .

7

FEATHERS, AND THEN A few small sticks fell out of the chimney. Ada had avoided the fire for a few days but now she rattled the grate; a stiffness in her back from sleeping on the camping bed, the metal like a trap about to spring. Every night she'd had restless dreams with hot water in them: running for a train and when the doors opened hot water pouring out, heavy clouds louring and then hot water pouring out. Her dreams always straightforward rather than cryptic, like someone saying, very slowly: now are you sure you understand what needs to be done?

What she needed was a bath and to wash her hair, which was matted and lank, like those greasy clumps of wool she used to find snagged on the hedges around here. She had almost had it all cut off once, but on the bus the woman sitting next to her had touched her hand and said: whatever you're about to do, it's a big mistake. She had got off the bus and walked home.

The wind rattled the chimney and sent down a clatter of grit. Another feather rocked down. Her mother had done this day after day, year after year. Somehow made it look easy. Although once, Ada had seen her kneeling in front of it saying: you keep me tied, don't you? Not angry so much as surprised, striking a match and letting it go out so she could inhale the spent smoke, eyes closed and face tilted, like a connoisseur. She always cleared her throat before she talked, as if having to force words up that were trapped somewhere. And she started pretending to be deaf. 'What?' she would say. 'Sorry?' Cupping her ear. Avoiding questions. She wouldn't answer the door if someone knocked; she would walk straight past the ringing phone. But could still make out the peep of a kingfisher if a window was open.

'We've run out of bread,' Ada would say, leaning round the door of the study.

'What's wrong with your head?' Her mother wouldn't look up from the desk. A clock's innards spilling out.

'Bread.' Ada would shake the empty bag. 'Bread.'

'Pass me that screw would you? It keeps rolling off the table.'

'Pardon?' Ada would say. 'What?'

It went in circles like that. It went in circles like that a lot.

'There's something sticking out the chimney,' Pepper said. She still had her coat on, her hair specked with mist.

Ada slid the metal cover off the flue and felt around. Got in past her wrist before hitting something solid. Remembered herself at five, watching a man help a cow give birth. Sleeves rolled up to the elbow. 'Who's in there?' she had asked. 'Who is it?'

She took her arm out. 'It's blocked,' she said. 'The whole thing is blocked.' Didn't her mother used to sweep it out every year? Worried it would poison them in the night, smoke them out like foxes; the thought of danger bringing out the glint of drama she harboured – she would turn a near miss into a collision, a twinge into something chronic.

41

Ada put on boots and went outside. There were sheep in the distance wrapped in mist, the trees wearing mist as scarves. The light curdled like old milk.

There was definitely something sticking out of the chimney. She found a ladder in one of the barns, more rust than metal, uneven legs. Dragged it out, the legs jarring on stones, and looked up. It wasn't a tall house but now the roof seemed to yawn up and away.

'Did you used to sleep in the bed I'm sleeping in?' Pepper asked.

Ada leaned the ladder against the house. 'I've got to climb up there,' she said.

'I'll do it,' Pepper said. 'It's easy.'

'It's not easy,' Ada told her. She looked up once more. The horrible sensation that everything was tipping forwards. And she wasn't even on the bloody ladder yet.

The first rungs bounced under her feet. Ten steps up she realised she'd forgotten to ask Pepper to hold it steady. Went back down slowly and showed her how to grip the sides.

Her heart clanged like the rungs. She paused, then kept going. Felt the ladder tilt, looked down and saw Pepper staring off to one side, only one hand on the ladder. 'Oi,' Ada shouted. 'Concentrate on this.' Add Pepper if you want to plummet to your death.

The wind seemed to pick up as she went higher, dragging her hair across her eyes. She made the mistake of looking down again. God it was high and the concrete yard glared below. The trees a swathe of dusky orange, like dim lanterns.

At the top, she had to lean forward to see into the chimney, hands scrabbling against the roof. There were a lot of tiles missing; something else to add to the list which kept growing and growing. There was a mass of sticks clogging the chimney. She tried to pull one out but tipped, swung sideways, somehow grabbed the ladder. Pepper called something, her voice a thin waver. But Ada couldn't look down. She clung hard to the ladder, mouth dry, swaying like a pendulum on a broken clock.

The ladder shook. 'Can you put your right foot down a step?' a woman's voice called up.

Ada groped with her foot, but her leg stretched down and down without hitting a rung. 'I can't,' she said.

The rungs clunked. 'Here,' the woman said. A hand gripped Ada's ankle and guided it onto the rung below. 'Now the other foot, OK?'

They went down slowly, rung by rung. And then there was the bottom. Beautiful solid ground. Pepper desperate to tell her, the little git, that she'd seen the cat again; it had run right past the ladder and round the back of the house.

The woman took the ladder down and folded it. 'Where does this go?' she asked.

'I'll take it,' Ada said, but Judy – she had realised halfway down that it was Judy – carried it back to the shed herself.

'There's this,' Pepper said, holding out a white dish. She shoved it into Ada's hands, stared at Judy for a moment, who shifted and pushed at her sleeves, then ran off in the direction she'd said the cat had gone.

'I brought you something,' Judy said. She watched Pepper running. 'It's nothing much, leftovers, you don't have to eat it or anything.' Her russet hair was cut short and clumpy. A kitchen-scissor job. Red cheeks, her eyes squinting even though it wasn't bright. Her body stockier, something taut in her folded arms. The colours were all washed out of her clothes, mended seams on her jeans. Wellies with an ankle line of mud.

'Up there,' Ada said, pointing to the roof. 'I'm sure I would have been able to, if you hadn't come.'

Judy pushed her hair out of her eyes. Which had almost rolled. 'I could use a cup,' she said.

Judy's boots left slices of mud along the floor. Ada put the kettle on. Still the last residue of panic flitting around her body. She made a pot of tea and got out cups. A gaudy purple one for herself and gold for Judy. All her mother's things either tacky or practical, no middle ground between a garden fork and a plastic chandelier. She heaped two sugars into Judy's.

'I cut down on sugar,' Judy said. 'For the teeth.'

Ada nodded. She tipped the cup away and poured another. The tea bags rose up in the pot and then sank.

Judy gulped scalding tea and poured more. The gold cup held carefully in chapped hands. 'I heard you were back,' she said.

Ada looked around the squalid kitchen. She pushed a pile of catalogues out of Judy's way – outdoor clothes: gloves with leather pads, cheap tweed like shiny granite. 'Just until this place is sorted out,' she said. She stood at the edge of the table. 'How long have you been back?' There had been a few letters, stilted and formal, neither of them good at writing, then after a while, no letters.

'I'm not,' Judy said. 'I'm not back.' She pushed her sleeves up higher above her elbows. 'I never left. I wanted to come to the funeral, but Dad got a problem with his stomach, we had to take him to the hospital, turned out there was a pseudo cyst in there.'

The funeral. Ada took the pot and filled it again. 'A pseudo cyst,' she said. Didn't that just mean no cyst?

'He's living in town now,' Judy said. 'Had to sell the bungalow, pay for his residential bills. They let him take his sound system but not his fish tank. They don't allow pets. I told them that if a fish escaped it probably wouldn't be able to terrorise other residents. They said: how did I know?' She stopped and looked at Ada. 'I guess you won't remember the fish tank.'

'I remember,' Ada said. They would scatter bright food pellets and watch them sink.

'They said I should buy him curtains with fish on instead. And I did.' She shook her head. 'And a duvet.'

Ada swallowed the gritty dregs in her cup. The kitchen clock went, tick, tick, pause, tick. 'Mario,' she said. 'There was a fish called Mario.'

'There was never a fish called Mario,' Judy told her. 'They were all female.' She picked up one of Pepper's gloves and smoothed out the wrinkles, then dropped it on the table and scraped her chair back. 'I should look at your chimney while I'm here.'

There were the cold remains of the fire. The feathers like decoration. Judy knelt down and put her arm in. 'What I thought,' she said. She showed the black twigs and feathers. 'Some old nests in there. Good job you didn't light a fire or the whole thing might have caught.' She started pulling out tangled handfuls.

'I can do it,' Ada told her. She got out a bin bag but there was nothing to do except hold it open while Judy stuffed twigs in. They ripped holes through the plastic. Lichen flaked like old paint. In one handful, a few broken pieces of egg shell.

There was a gold band on Judy's ring finger that was loose and slipping over her knuckle.

'Are you in town now then?' Ada asked.

'I'm up at the farm,' Judy said. She nodded towards the window as if the farm was just outside it. 'We've got the whole thing just the two of us now.'

Ada pushed the twigs down so that more would fit in. 'You and Robbie?'

'Of course me and Robbie,' Judy said. She took the full bag and tied the top. 'Of course me and Robbie.'

Judy and Robbie had been together since they were fourteen. It was his family's farm. He had dropped out of school as soon as he could, always working, always out from dark till dark. Ada remembered mucky overalls, oil, a tired slump to his jaw. The smell of beer. And his night terrors: Judy describing how he would jerk upright in bed, shouting, fighting the sheets. Judy had spent most of her time at the farm, although she'd never liked it. It was the cows, she said, the way they looked at you as if they were planning something, biding their time.

'But why are you?' Ada said. Judy looked at her and frowned. 'I mean, the cows.'

Judy leaned further into the stove. 'What about the cows?'

'Remember when they chased us? And they were in a circle.'

'I don't remember that,' Judy said.

'They circled us,' Ada said. Their wide faces had pushed in close, sides shunting against each other like rocking canoes.

Judy pulled out more tattered feathers. A ditchy smell and gloopy leaves. 'Cows never do that.' Grit clattered in the grate like hailstones. 'There can't be much more of this,' she said.

'Cows always do that,' Ada told her.

The wind sounded louder in the chimney now. Judy scooped out a handful of grit. The smudges under her eyes were almost violet. A few grey hairs in her parting like frayed wire. So she had been stuck here all this time. Ada thought of all the places she'd lived in over the years. The town with the sculpture of a horse, the house where the woman next door grew huge pumpkins. Or was that the same place?

46

Moving on whenever she had to: when rents went up, when landlords decided to sell, when neighbours in cramped flats made so much noise she didn't sleep for a week. When things didn't work out as she had expected.

They filled four bags with old nests. The bags bulged and warped. 'I think it's OK to light now,' Judy said. She put her head right in to check. Soot trickled down onto her hair, but no more twigs or feathers. She got up and prodded a log with her boot. 'Where did you get these from?' she asked.

'The shop. Yesterday. Mick did me a deal on them.'

'How much?'

'I don't know,' Ada said. 'Twenty.' She lit the firelighters and watched as the flames jumped. But they started to dwindle as soon as they got near the wood. She jabbed at them, adding small bits of kindling like offerings.

'The wood's crap,' Judy said. She knelt down and poked at the fire. 'Mick's screwed you over with this. The pieces are too big and they haven't been seasoned. Look how damp they are. How much did you say you paid?'

'He said it was good stuff,' Ada said, heard her voice become whiney. 'He put it in the back of the car for me.'

'Mick's like that,' Judy said, shrugging. 'He'll charge anyone double if he thinks he can get away with it. One price for tourists, another price for locals.'

An odd lurch in her chest. 'He knows me,' she said.

'Wood takes six months to season. At least. I'll get someone to drop some in as soon as possible. I know a few people. A big load of it, it's cheaper that way,' Judy said. 'Tide you over until you leave.' Her voice was gruff but had always had a chime to it, like a bell hidden somewhere. Her arms folded across her chest. Smeared in

47

soot. They had once watched an eclipse together and had burned so badly they had to be covered in thick cream. A week later they had peeled their skin off in sheets.

'Hopefully sometime next week OK?' Judy said. Then she was gone, leaving the front door thunking in the wind like a rolling bucket.

Ada stirred a pan of pork and apples, decided to throw in a heap of blackberries that Pepper had left on the table. See how it turned out. She went into the lounge, along the hall, then back into the kitchen, sure she could smell melting solder – but it was so faint and then it disappeared.

She called Pepper for dinner. Heard the door to the study creak open. 'What were you doing in there?' she asked.

'Nothing,' Pepper said. She dipped her finger in the pan and licked it.

'Do you want to help stir?'

'Nah.' Pepper dipped her finger in again – no cooking for her unless it meant stealing huge spoonfuls.

The sauce turned dusky purple, almost grey, and was watery, like it had been wrung from an old cloth. Definitely needed to thicken. 'Could you find the cornflour in the cupboard?'

Pepper pulled out packets and boxes. 'Which one?'

'Try and read what it says,' Ada said. Stirring the sauce, keeping her voice light.

'That one,' Pepper said, pointing to a packet of dried soup. When Ada shook her head, she tried again. 'That one.' This time a box of stock cubes.

'What does it begin with?' Ada asked. She used to be able to do it.

'See, see, it begins with see,' Pepper sang frantically, shoving a bag of coffee at Ada. 'Did I get it right?' she said.

Ada took the bag, wished for the thousandth time that someone would tell her what was best to do. Then she nodded and said it was right. Switched it for cornflour when Pepper wasn't looking.

'He had grey eyes like me, didn't he?' Pepper suddenly asked. 'My dad?'

'Grey eyes?' Ada said.

Pepper opened her own eyes wide and stared.

'No,' Ada said. 'I mean yes.' The memory of him fading each year. What to tell Pepper? That she remembered a birthmark shaped like an anchor on his hip; a lisp in his voice when he was tired? That he had once electrocuted himself on her oven, filling the tiny kitchen with the stench of singed hair, and how he had cursed, then laughed magnificently, then cursed again?

'But before you said they were blue,' Pepper said.

Ada mixed cornflour into a paste. The lights flicked off, then back on again. 'Did I?' she said. 'I guess I meant that sometimes they looked grey and sometimes blue.'

'I see,' Pepper said slowly.

The fridge juddered. The sauce thickened, wrinkling like wet paper.

Pepper picked out a mushy blackberry. 'I would have eyes that sometimes looked red and sometimes looked black,' she said. 'Like blood. Like my eyes were full of blood.'

Where did that come from? Once again she was off and skittering away.

8

THE MAN WHO BROUGHT the wood had on a dark red jumper and his hair was the same colour as the wood: bright brown, almost orange. His bottom teeth were crooked. 'Shep,' he said to the dog in the back of his truck. 'Stay there Shep.' He carried an armful of logs into the shed and stacked them up against the wall.

Pepper skulked up to the truck and offered the dog her hand, which he sniffed, backed away from, then butted his head into, whining. He had curly fur like a sheep and a flat, mournful face. One of his eyes was blurry. There were a million dogs called Shep – she would have called him something better.

Her mother came out with two mugs of tea, the steam racing up into the air. Her cheeks were red in the wind and she had a red scarf tied round her hair. The man watched her as she walked across the yard and put the mugs down inside the shed.

'She's scared of dogs,' Pepper told him.

In the back of the truck there were hammers and bits of metal, paint tins, a folded black sheet lifting in the wind. Pepper ran her finger along the edge of a box full of carved wooden shapes.

'You can look at those if you want,' the man said.

But Pepper stepped back and picked at her lips. The shapes were only interesting when she wasn't meant to touch them. And if she looked at them now she would have to say something nice about them, it would be expected of her, and that should be against the law.

There were piles of soaking leaves everywhere that smelled like banana skins. Her mother's voice floated over: 'Sorry, no you. Gloves. Hopefully not very long.'

Shep barked suddenly, a furious yapping, and he stood up in the truck, rigid and quivering, staring at something in the distance.

'Shep, stop it,' the man called. 'Relax old buddy.'

Pepper looked around but there was nothing. After a moment, the dog turned a circle and lay down, twitching a leg out and an ear.

She drifted in and out of rooms, trying to imagine her mother here, growing up. She had never thought about her growing up before and she couldn't picture it, especially not in this house, which was so cobwebby and strange and far away. There was no TV, no people in the street to watch from the windows. No smell of cars or fish and chips. No shops to stare into, no parks full of sandpits and pigeons. And when it rained it was grey and sharp, rather than yellow. And when it got dark it was like the house had been wrapped in black paper.

But she found things. A small waterproof coat, a tin of pencils in her mother's old bedroom, a purple scarf, a necklace with half a silver heart dangling on it, a bottle with a candle stuck in. A set of measuring spoons and a creased recipe book with an orange cake on the front; she had seen her mother make that cake before. She found a clay bird with a chipped wing, painted black and white and with a splash of red. It had three wobbly letters on the bottom. She took it to her mother and asked what it said. *A D A*. 'Did you make it?' Pepper asked.

Her mother sifted through a pile of paper. 'Do the taxable assets exceed the annual limitations?' she said. 'I don't even know what that means.' She turned the page over and asked for the calculator.

Another day, Pepper glimpsed the cat running past the front door. Dark rivulets of rain on its back. She went out and clicked her tongue. The cat stopped and looked back at her. 'Come on old buddy,' she said.

'Gurmunuw,' the cat said. It tilted its head to one side. Then it turned and bolted through the long grass.

And one day, rooting around in the garden, she found something red among a patch of plants with brown leaves. A mushy strawberry, all the plants wilted and dead but somehow this one strawberry left behind. She ate it in the cold drizzle, juice trickling into the corners of her mouth and down over her chin.

The study door was stiff when Pepper pushed it. The hinge screeched and she stopped, listening for her mother. She could hear her upstairs in the bath, talking to herself like she sometimes did, the faint splash of water and the taps rattling – she would have run the water so hot there would be a red line around her waist.

Pepper went into the study and clicked on the dim light. She touched the books, the notebooks full of lists, the broken watches and silver chains. There was a dusty bird on the desk that stared at her. She touched its body. It was stiff but it didn't look dead. She reached up and took down a box of photographs. These were what she wanted to look at. There were no pictures of any people. Instead, there were three brown birds under a bridge; a flash of bright blue above the water; a swan with its head tucked under its wing; a magpie; crows flying round a field. On the front of one of the books there was a drawing of a tall grey bird with purple bits on its wings and a black wisp on its head. She had never seen a bird like that before and she looked through the whole box of photographs but couldn't find a picture of it.

There was a camera on the shelf; an old, chunky one with a brown strap. It was heavy. She held the camera up and looked through it. All she saw was a black square. She clicked the button but nothing happened. Click, click. She shook it and tried again. Click. Nothing.

A night of heavy rain which left the trees dripping. Water pooled on the front step and some of it came in under the door. Her mother was going to the shop but Pepper didn't want to go – it was always cold and the man that worked there, Mick, watched her and tapped his long fingers on the counter. Also, she felt a faint pang of fear whenever she thought of being in the car.

She was meant to stay indoors but everything looked varnished and bright after the rain, so she put her coat on and went outside, then came back in and slung the camera over her shoulder.

Through the sopping grass and down towards the river. It was wide and brown today, and it rippled and churned. There were deep creases when it went round rocks and a hollow, clunking noise. It looked strong, like a muscle. When she threw in a stick, the stick didn't float on the surface – it got dragged under, as if something had reached up to grab it. She walked along the bank and there was the bridge she'd seen in some of the photos – it had rusty railings and a broken plank in the middle. She made herself stand on it. The river roared under her feet. She crossed the bridge and the trees thickened in front of her. They were almost bare now – their trunks were silver and they tilted upwards and there was a path going through them. Pepper looked back at the house, then walked up into the wood.

The noise of the river and the noise of the trees were the same. They both roared and thrummed. Twigs and leaves rained down. The ground was slippery and smelled rich and there were wide gullies of water that she had to jump over. There were coppery leaves everywhere, and plants dying back to a dusky colour, and a pile of sawn branches that had orange insides bright as lamps. There was a shiny black beetle that looked blue close up, mounds of horse poo, piles of pine needles that she poked until ants came out.

The wood increased ahead of her; below, the river swung in and out of sight as if a door was opening and closing. Something flitted across a branch and she fumbled with the camera but the bird had already gone.

The tilting trees made her dizzy. The path branched and she turned right without noticing. Mud and leaves caught in her boots. Fat drops of rain fell through the branches and landed on her arm. There was a wigwam up ahead, made of branches that had been tied together at the top. A sweet wrapper glinting at the entrance. She looked inside. A dusty floor, lots of small footprints. She put her foot in and made her own prints, then kicked the sweet wrapper into the ground.

The path branched again. Pepper stomped on with her head down. Old grudges bubbling up: that boy who said there wasn't room for her to join his club, the teacher that forgot her name, that lowdown group of girls who told everyone she had a bad disease. That girl who seemed nice at first but then swatted a bee straight out of the sky. The stupid boy who wouldn't go into the park with her because he was scared of pigeons. Her father. That sour-smelling man on the bus that sang romance songs to her and made everyone stare.

A branch cracked behind her and she spun around. The path veered downhill and she couldn't see the river. There was a clump of mushrooms on a tree, wet and salmony, folded over like ears. White mushrooms blotched with grey. Brown ones with dark frills. A branch cracked again. She turned round and started walking back, too fast, her feet sliding on leaves, the camera bouncing against her chest. The path forked. Both ways looked the same. Her breath was ragged in her throat. Her heart clattered and there was a hot feeling in her eyes which she tried to rub away. A small bird flapped above her. She fumbled for the camera but it was too late. 'Crapping hell,' she said.

'You've left the lens cap on,' a voice said behind her.

She stiffened and turned round slowly. It was Luke, the man who had driven them to the house. 'I meant to do that,' she said. She looked away and wiped at her eyes with her sleeve. Waited for him to carry on walking down the path.

'Heading back, are you?' he asked.

Pepper pretended to be very interested in a particular tree. She crouched down and examined it. 'Not yet,' she said. But when Luke shrugged and carried on, she waited a few moments then followed behind, leaving a long gap between them so that he wouldn't know she was there.

Luke kept his hands in his pockets and didn't skid once. He whistled something slow between his teeth. He was wearing a shirt and tie under his jacket even though he was just out walking. His skin was very brown and creased, like a cloth after polishing shoes. After a while, he stopped. 'Give us that camera a minute,' he called back.

She stayed where she was and held the camera tight.

'Don't be a moron about it,' he said. 'I don't know much about them, but I can show you how to take the lens cap off at least.' He came over and showed her, then twisted the lens so things looked clearer. 'I think this is the focus,' he said. 'Do you know what that is?'

'Yes,' Pepper told him. You needed it for school and she didn't have any.

'Have a gander through him now,' Luke said, passing her the camera.

She looked and saw crispy lichen right in front of her face, even though it was on a branch above. Then a mushroom on the ground, bronze and sticky. She prodded it with her foot.

'I wouldn't touch that,' Luke said.

'Why?' She reached towards the mushroom.

Luke kicked at a pine cone. 'It's a death cap,' he said. 'Liver failure, chronic pain. It would be a slow death, maybe take a couple of weeks.'

The mushroom gleamed like a coin. Pepper aimed the camera at it and clicked the button.

There were roots all over the path and Pepper tripped, sprawled, tripped, sprawled. She tried to catch up with Luke. 'Are there big grey birds here? By the water?'

Luke seemed to be listening for something. 'Hear those trees creaking. Takes me back to being on the boats that does. The noises the sea could make – no one else would believe it, sometimes like an engine, sometimes chalk screeching on a board. Thinking maybe I could write something for the newspaper. But I don't know if they'd want it. Probably no one would want to read something like that.' He turned to Pepper like he wanted her opinion.

'No,' she said. 'They probably wouldn't.' It was important not to lie.

Luke stumbled over a root and mud splashed up Pepper's leg. 'Yeah,' he said. 'Maybe you're right.' The path levelled and he stopped and said something to a boulder, except it wasn't a boulder, it was a man leaning over a wide bend in the river wearing a grey coat. There was a boy sitting next to him. They both had fishing rods in the water and there was a net and bucket. Inside the bucket, three dark fish.

'Not much today Clapper,' Luke said.

'Nah,' the man replied.

The boy stared at Pepper and she stared back. He had very neat hair, like he had just combed it. A pair of thick glasses that he pushed up his nose.

'That's Petey,' Luke told her. 'Lives with Clapper. He's about your age I'd say. This is Pearl's granddaughter.'

Clapper didn't look up. 'Yeah,' he said. 'Down at the house.'

Luke looked once more in the bucket, then carried on along the path. Pepper followed. When she turned back to look, Clapper was watching the water carefully and his hands were very steady.

The ground turned sandy and there was the bridge in front of them. 'There's lots of birds next to that,' Pepper said. 'In the photos.'

Luke nodded. 'Pearl used to wade out into the water. Sometimes squat for hours, waiting.'

'I could do that,' Pepper said. She should have been back before her mother, but she could see the car already parked next to the house.

'No one's stopping you,' Luke said.

As they went over the bridge, purple clouds rolled closer and rain came down in a torrent. Pepper's nose ran over her lip. Her waterproof crumpled against her skin like a leaf. She looked over the railings and saw someone sitting on the far side of the bank. It was raining so hard that whoever it was blurred into the rain. Pepper glanced at Luke but his head was bowed towards the ground. When

Pepper looked back, the air was so full of rain she could hardly see three inches in front of her face. Huge drops splashed down, soaking everything, and Luke was too slow so she ran over the gravel, up the steps and into the hallway, where the saucepan caught the rain as it came through the roof.

9

PEARL ENDURED THE RAIN all night. The kind that wore away at her bones. Battered, huddled on her rock, each drop seeping in until she was doused.

The rain filled holes in the road; it filled flowerpots to the brim. It filled the blocked gutters of the house and spilled over – dark, shiny water mixed with leaves and soil. It churned the fields to mud and when the fields couldn't take any more, it ran down in wide gulleys to the river. The river rose by a foot.

Then, slowly, very slowly, it stopped, as if someone was turning a stiff tap. Leaving behind sallow light, roads and roofs lacquered with rain. The ground pulpy and bruised as an old peach.

The river was up around Pearl's knees and flowing fast. It was choppy and brown as dishwater. She got down off the rock and stood in the water, leaning against the current. The weight of it knocked into her legs and she staggered, managed to get her balance, then started to wade towards the bank. Halfway across she stumbled and plunged her hands in to steady herself. The water rushed on, grabbing anything – sticks, rocks, weeds – and dragging them with it. Breaking up leaves, spitting and guzzling. Trying to do the same with her. She braced herself, then stumbled again on clumps of roots. She gripped them and clung on, managed to get one foot on a rock, another on a root, handfuls of mud and stones, and then she was at the top of the bank, hauled out in the long wet grass.

She lay there for a long time. Water ran off her and pooled on the bank. After a while she knelt up and blinked away silt. The river pulled at her legs and her feet. 'Get off,' she said. She shook her foot. 'Bugger off for a minute.' The river roared and jostled at her but she kicked at it and stood up, her wet bones buckling. She lurched and water sloshed in her ears. Told herself to get a grip and took a step through the grass. It was difficult, her legs heavy and bowing but she moved slowly away from the river. The wet ground made it easier: the wet ground and the wet grass and the damp air – everything drenched with water. Water brimmed up from the ground to meet her and mist clung to her sleeves and hair. She saw each droplet, like tiny stitches in a blanket.

And up ahead, through the mist, she saw the house. Still ugly, still looking like it was about to collapse. But it wouldn't collapse – battered by wind, flooded, cracked; always mended. There were the seams of repaired plaster, the nailed-down tiles, the patched-up corrugated roof. The wood reinforced with brick. Guttering lashed on with wire. A tough place, like a ship leaning out. She took a step closer. It was so wet, so dark, so isolated – how had she ended up here? She moved closer. A light came on in the upstairs window. The curtain moved. The river roared; there was no getting away from it. Impossible to shake off. She could feel it pulling at her, the cold working its way in. Sometimes, on a freezing night you could hear the creaking echo of the glacier it used to be. Cracking its bones. The river reminding itself.

But she tried to shake it off; she tried to make her way towards the house. It was easier to move in the mist, as if she were extra drops of water; the air and water curdling. Actually, it was easier to crouch down, where the mist was thicker. She got down on her knees and crawled, feet and hems dragging, hips shuddering. There were the front steps and the door above them. But the mist thinned a few metres away from the house. She tried to crawl just a bit further . . . she could almost reach out and touch the steps.

There was the light again. Pearl looked up, thought she saw a blurred shape moving past the window. The curtain moved. She strained to see but her eyes were murky and useless. Something moved, a hand pressed against the glass. The mist crept around Pearl's knees. Then the light clicked off and the house was dark again.

Pearl lingered at the edge of the house, trying to remember. Why here? Why by herself? It wasn't what she expected. What she needed to do was to go back over it – it was important to try and work her way back to the beginning. Dredge something up. Her thoughts were foggy, they kept scudding away over stones, but she remembered a few things. What it had been like, near the end. Stuck in the house on her own. That was it: she had been stuck in the house for God knows how long and it had been boring, it really had, what with her staying in bed all hours, and sitting still for hours, her hands on her knees as if she was old.

And it had happened suddenly, as far as she could tell. One moment chopping up wood for the fire, and the next, struggling to do it, struggling to lift the axe. The routine of it slipping along with her hands: how to work the vents, how to sweep the ashes, how to strike the match against the box.

She wouldn't let anybody in the house. She slept in the chair in the kitchen, nothing but her old brown coat to keep her warm. A rattly little snore in one nostril. 'Now for one thing,' she would sometimes say to herself. And: 'I suppose I should be getting on with it.' But she would just stay sitting there, staring at the wall. Maybe she would listen to a mouse skittering. Sometimes a breeze would come in and scatter bits of paper and envelopes, and, startled, she would turn and watch them flap down onto the floor. It would remind her of something, and she would get up and wander around the room, looking for something. 'That isn't it,' she would say. She would fumble through piles of papers, open the kettle and peer in. She would reach up and feel along the top of a cupboard and then in her hand there would be ropes of dust and a twenty-pound note. She would smooth the money out carefully and then roll it up and put it inside a mug. Yes, that was it; she would put it inside a mug and then later she'd take it out again and hide it under the telephone. Or do something ridiculous like put a newspaper in the fridge, guarding it jealously from no one.

She could picture herself now, those last few months. Wandering around the house as if she were lost, tapping on walls, moving a book from place to place, picking up a watch and staring at it as if there was something she should be doing with it. Sometimes going to bed in the morning and getting up in the middle of the night; eating bread in the dark, sleeping through a whole day. Calling out names . . . although whose, she couldn't quite recall. Sitting still as a rock in the chair but her mind surging. An image, a word, a sentence sometimes rising to the surface out of the din, sharp as a watch pin. 'There you go then,' she would say. 'There you go.' Over and over.

Not acting like herself at all. Her mind a tangle. No idea what she had been thinking. It was almost impossible to recognise herself, like seeing her face through a murky mirror.

She needed to go back further than that. What she needed was to try and cast her mind back further. But the ground slurped at her feet and the river roared and tugged. The air stank of rain and bonfires, the mist thinned, rainwater ran down towards the river. She slipped and raked her fingers against the wall. The mist lifted. Her thoughts sloshed and dripped and tangled and the river dragged at her; back over the grass, back over the mud and the stones.

She had tried to put on a chair as a jacket. The memory jumped out at her like a slap in the face. There she was: struggling in the kitchen to put a chair on, convinced it was a jacket. One arm under each side. The rungs digging in. Her back arched over. She could hardly bear thinking about it. Putting on a chair. She had always been a fool, she knew that. But a chair. Pearl shook her head. She could almost laugh about it now. Looking back she could almost laugh about the whole thing.

10

THIS WAS THE DAY's routine. Up in the raw early morning to get the fire going. A few fading embers from the night before that needed coaxing with kindling. Now Ada knew how to work the vents, how to pile up soft and hard wood so that it would stay burning all day. The house warming up grudgingly, the radiators popping, the water tank clunking like old lungs.

Then: strip wallpaper, rub down splintering paint, scoop filler into cracks. Pull up desiccated carpets and scrape horrific gunk from between bathroom tiles. There were the coffee stains on the armchairs – ring after ring, like planets. There was the table with the shorter leg, which her mother had sawn off so it would fit through the door. There was the satin lamp, found for sale outside someone's house and reeking of cigarettes whenever it heated up. Halfway through a job she would remember the stack of paper-work: bills, legal forms like battlements to fight through. 'Huh?' she would say. 'Whose declaration of *what*?' Put down her pen and go and empty the brimming saucepan in the hall. Sit at the kitchen table again and see one of her mother's shoes under a cupboard, a spider clinging on with delicate legs. The power would flicker and she would go outside and mess around with the fuse box. She would start filling bags with empty jars and then see a door hanging off its hinges.

She made marmalade cake and soup with carrots and ginger; trying to replace the smell of damp with cooking smells. But still: damp shoes, damp clothes, the dank smell of river. The leak in the hall splitting the ceiling like the crust of a loaf. She found a silty smudge, like a handprint, on the outside of the kitchen window and a small pile of stones on the front steps.

The table was strewn with paperwork and half-empty cups. Ada got up and stretched and rubbed her neck. 'Pepper?' she called.

It was a midweek afternoon. The wind blustered and brought squally rain. A dirty bonfire smell and, in the distance, clouds bulging yellow and purple.

She went out into the hall and saw that the door of the study was ajar. Pepper was kneeling on the floor. There was a camera in front of her and a book open with some kind of diagram. Her mouth puckered up, finger tracing the drawing. When she looked up and saw Ada, she shut the book and pushed the camera under the desk. Then went over to the curtains and wrapped herself up in them.

Ada picked the camera up and put it away. 'I told you not to touch these,' she said. Pepper lost interest in things quickly: games and books broken, ripped, left outside in the rain. Which was why school was such a struggle. Teachers phoning to say Pepper couldn't concentrate, that she had pushed or bitten. Making enemies instead of friends. Pepper fuming and red-faced, refusing to speak. And finally a letter saying that it would be beneficial, mutually beneficial, for her to have some time out, while the school tried to find a more suitable arrangement.

'I didn't break it.' Pepper's voice muffled with curtain.

'I know. But stay out of this room, OK?' Ada never used to come in here. Instead, she would linger by the door, peering in to watch her mother mending jewellery or studying a bird book. She could remember every little thing: the orange light coming through the scratchy curtains, the metallic tang of solder, the stuffed jackdaw on the desk. Shelves crammed with books, cameras, lenses, binoculars. Her mother out for hours looking for birds. Ada dragged along, crouching in freezing grass to watch a nest in the riverbank. Or wait silently for kingfishers. Or watch while her mother pushed through hedges looking for blue eggs. But more often, she was left alone in the house. Time and time again her mother pulling on her boots, her jacket, regardless of rain or sun, and disappearing down to the river, or striding across the edge of the moor. Coming back with a camera full of pictures but not much to say. Her moods as stark and unfathomable as craters on the moon. Although once she had taken up the jack-daw and waltzed with it around the room.

'I saw someone out there,' Pepper said. She wiped her nose on the curtain.

'Don't do that, you varmint,' Ada said. But she leaned closer to the window and looked out herself, because twice she'd had the feeling that there was someone outside, watching the house. Never anything more than rain-soaked windows though, and being unused to a house so remote.

She touched the stuffed bird, stroking it with her finger. A few dusty feathers fell off its chest. It was her mother's place. It always had been. Her river, her trees, her birds. Ada glanced at the wooden box. It was where she'd want to be.

At the shop a few days later; a basket full of tins and cereal, the least-burnt bread. There was Judy coming towards her.

'I was talking to Robbie,' Judy said. She put her basket down between her feet. 'He thought we should invite you over. For dinner.'

Ada looked in the fridge for butter. Couldn't mistake Judy's reluctant tone and felt the same herself. Imagined an evening of stilted conversation and felt a pang for their old selves, crouched down comparing scabs and belly buttons. 'What day did you have in mind?' she said.

'I don't know, sometime next week maybe, or the week after that,' Judy said.

Someone called over to her from the counter: 'I must show you the new mullions at some point Judy.'

'Definitely keep me posted on that,' Judy called back.

'I could ring you about it, closer to the time,' Ada said.

'We don't have to decide anything now,' Judy said. She waved to someone who had just come in.

Ada held the cold block of butter. 'What's a mullion?'

Judy raised her eyebrow in a perfect arch, suddenly looked thirteen again. 'I have absolutely no idea,' she said. She picked up her basket. 'Is the wood OK? I told Tristan to bring you properly seasoned stuff. He should have done it for a good price.'

'He's gentle, isn't he,' Ada said. 'Generous I mean.' She studied the butter carefully. 'Fair. He was very fair. With the wood.' Thinking of his bright hair, the way he had picked up an old swallows' nest in both hands and moved it carefully out of the way of their feet.

*

Saturday morning and rain washing over the windows. The gutter overflowing in heavy splashes.

Ada came downstairs slowly. There was a sprinkling of plaster on the bottom step. She looked closer, saw faint scratches in the wall and brown marks on the carpet, almost too small to notice. They were dry and gave off a rusty smell. Two sharp pains squeezed out of her chest, like notes out of an accordion. She got a wet sponge and scrubbed. The bottom of the stairs . . . she looked up at how steep they were, how slippery the wood was. The handrail was too high and loose. But her mother could stride over the precarious stepping stones in the river, pitying anyone who turned back. Ada scrubbed harder but the marks wouldn't come out.

The phone rang. She couldn't place the sound for a moment. Followed it until she found the phone on the floor further down the hall.

'Ada? It's Val, from the pub.' Her voice was scratchy and forceful, like an old record. 'I didn't think you were going to answer for a minute.'

'Blood,' Ada said. She looked at the sponge. 'I was trying to get blood out of the carpet.'

'That's simple m'dear. Have you got a bar of soap? Ordinary soap that you use in the bath. Scrub that into it, leave it for a while then rinse it off. Better than all the fancy chemicals they sell. I used it to get the squid ink off all the sheets and towels in the guest room. Came off in seconds, that did.'

'The squid ink?'

'It was a guest, didn't think much to the establishment apparently. But listen. We're short on people to work today. The girl I normally use seems to have gone down with some sort of sickness or other. Weak immune system. I tell her to drink orange juice, eat soup with chicken in it, but no one around here listens to me. And I thought you could step in.'

'At the pub?' Ada spoke slowly.

'Tonight. Five o'clock. Cash in hand. You know the ropes – you used to work here sometimes didn't you. Nothing's changed except maybe the waitresses. Got a new chef a few years ago. Oh and the dishwasher packed up. But you'll pick it up.'

The money would be good, pay off at least one of those bills. Or get someone in to repair the leak. 'But where would they have got squid ink from?' Ada said. 'Did they bring it especially, just in case?'

At half past four she strapped Pepper into the front seat and drove to the pub.

Val hadn't said if she was waitressing or prepping food, so she had no idea what to wear. She had clothes from some of her old jobs: a striped T-shirt from a shoe shop, a green fleece from a garden centre. An overall she probably should have given back, from packing up boxes of Christmas lights one summer. None of the jobs had lasted – couldn't abide touching people's feet, didn't know the difference between mulch and compost. On reception at a hotel, she would unlock rooms for people that had locked themselves out, then an hour later would be called to unlock the same room again – the guest blaming the door. They always blamed the door.

'Why are we going?' Pepper asked. 'Are you going to drink whisky and fall asleep?'

Once. That had happened once. 'Are you going to drink something fizzy and run around the room?' Ada said.

Pepper scowled. 'I don't do that any more.'

Ada squinted against headlights. 'I'm just covering someone's shift,' she said.

'But I fought you said we weren't living here,' Pepper said.

'Thought,' Ada told her. 'I *thought* you said we weren't living here.' Where was the pub anyway? Usually you could hear music blaring and engines revving in the car park by now. A teeming, sweaty bar, raucous laughter, more often than not someone outside pissing against a wall.

The road narrowed and the hedge scraped against the windows. There was the pub up ahead, low and whitewashed. No sign or name. And hardly any cars. A statue of an angel looking down at a bilgy pond.

'Stay close to me in there,' Ada told Pepper. She pushed the door open. A blast of hot air hit her face. A radio bawling old jazz. The room was almost empty; just a man in a checked shirt and cap standing at the bar. Guns, antlers and copper pans hanging on the wall. A plastic holly wreath with faded berries.

'Ada.' Val came out from the kitchen, both hands stretched out as if she were about to embrace her. But she dropped her arms as soon as she got close. She was doused in perfume, and her pale hair was held back by a pink fabric rose. She was wearing a sweatshirt and jogging trousers. 'Look at you,' she said.

She stared at Ada's face until Ada put her hand up to her cheek. 'What?' she said. 'What is it?'

But Val was already looking down at Pepper. 'You look a lot like your grandmother,' Val said.

'We put her in the river,' Pepper told her.

Ada settled Pepper at a table in the corner. 'Stay here,' she said. She laid out paper and a pencil and straightened Pepper's jumper. Then followed Val into the kitchen, which was small and smoky and stank of oil. There were dirty pans stacked in teetering piles next to the sink, a man in a stained apron hunched over them, cleaning out a bowl like he was beating eggs.

'Howard. This is Ada. I told you about her. She's working tonight. Howard.'

The man beat the pan a few more times before he turned round. 'Yeah,' he said. 'Could you pass that scourer?' He looked about fifty, with threadbare hair and deep rings slung like hammocks under his eyes. He was wearing yellow trainers and a necklace of wooden beads. There were purple scars and burns on his hands and wrists.

Ada passed him the scourer, which had crumbs and milk skin stuck in it.

'I saw your brother yesterday,' Howard said to Val. 'He was asking about you.'

'Don't talk about that crook to me,' Val said. She picked up a handful of potato skins and threw them at the bin. Most of them went on the floor. 'Right.' She clapped her hands together. 'I'll leave you to it.' And she went out of the kitchen.

The radio buzzed out static. Ada turned the dial to clear it.

'Don't touch that,' Howard said. 'It's the best you can get in here.' He swiped a cloth over one of the pans.

After a while, Ada cleared her throat and asked if there was anything she could do. Howard gestured towards a pot of something that was bubbling too fast and a chopping board with garlic heaped on it. The knife was blunt and Ada hacked at the ends of the cloves, then peeled them. There wasn't a garlic press anywhere so she started cutting them up into the smallest bits that she could.

'Wait.' Howard rushed over and shielded the chopping board with his body. 'These are going in whole. I don't want bits all mixed up in there.'

Ada's face felt hot. 'I didn't know,' she said. But who wanted a whole boiled clove in amongst a thin stew? Probably tried it herself

71

at one time or another – she'd started cooking whenever her mother forgot, or when she couldn't stand the thought of more instant rice. She'd used whatever was lying around, learning what would taste good and what wouldn't. Not pasta cooked with vinegar – one of her earliest disasters.

Howard tsked and ripped up tough spinach leaves, which creaked in his hands. 'How many tables have we got?' he said.

There were four people at a table by the door. No one else for food, except for Pepper in the corner. Ada felt a small shock – the last time she'd stepped out of the pub kitchen she'd been twenty-one, serving a rowdy table. Now there was her daughter, swinging her legs. She had a glass of orange juice in front of her and a newspaper, which she was ripping a hole out of with her teeth.

'More than usual,' Howard grunted when Ada told him.

She found a notebook and pen and went over to the table to take the group's orders. 'My grandad said the whole valley was cut off for two weeks in January,' one of them was saying. When he paused, Ada said: 'Can I get you anything? To eat?' She realised they didn't have menus and she went to look for them by the till, where they used to be. The man standing at the bar leered at her. He looked familiar, maybe someone she'd been to school with.

'We don't have menus any more,' Val said. 'It's just the usual stuff with chips. Some kind of special that Howard puts on. Maybe a couple of lasagnes in the freezer.'

Ada recited the list to the group. 'And the special's a garlic and spinach stew. You can have that with rice.' She took their orders back to Howard.

'We don't have any fish,' he said. 'You'll have to go back and tell them. No fish.'

'You said anything with chips,' the man at the table said. 'You hear

72

chips, you say fish.' He looked around at his group and they all nodded agreement.

'I know,' Ada told him. 'But maybe you hear chicken too. Is chicken OK?'

When Howard was sorting out their orders, Ada took a bowl of stew over to Pepper.

'What is it?' Pepper asked. She poked around with her fork, then ate some. The fork clattered back down. 'It's horrible,' she said, pushing the bowl away.

Ada hushed her and took a forkful herself. The overall flavour was sulphur and scorching. 'It's nice,' she said. She worked something gristly around in her mouth.

'You eat it,' Pepper said. 'I will be fine.' It was her old trick, to sit looking sorrowful and resigned when something hadn't turned out as she wanted it to. A long-suffering expression on her face.

'I'll get you something else,' Ada said. Back in the kitchen there was smoke and cursing. She took out heaped plates to the group. Didn't hang around to ask if it was OK.

Again, she saw the man at the bar looking at her. Jake, that was his name. At eleven, she had planned their whole future together. Something about his long eyelashes, or the marble collection he had. There was no way of avoiding him, so she went up and asked how he was.

'Can't complain,' he said. His front tooth was broken. 'How about yourself?'

'Just trying to sell the house at the moment,' she said.

Jake flexed his hands against his high stomach. 'I've got a new truck, out there,' he said. He inclined his head at the door, swayed slightly.

'Good,' Ada said. 'It's good to have a truck.' She nodded for a long time.

Jake stared with red-rimmed eyes. 'You're a beaut, aren't you?' he said. 'Why don't we go out there? You can see it if you want.'

'God no,' Ada said. She took a step back. 'I mean, I think I saw it already. The new truck in the car park, right?' She examined an empty pint glass like a detective searching for prints. Halfway back to the kitchen she heard him ask Val who she was.

Howard was leaning against the worktop, massaging his heart. 'It's not good for me,' he said. He gestured around him. 'A stressful environment.'

In Greenland they would bury seabirds and dig them up when putrefied. A way of preserving food for winter. Travellers had written about trying to eat it and Ada imagined them looking exactly as Howard did now: harrowed. When he wasn't looking, she reached over and turned down the roaring burner on the stew.

'It's all these customers,' Howard went on. He opened a packet of crisps and slipped two into his mouth. 'They're not from round here generally. You get a lot of people buying up houses, staying a couple of weeks every year. They expect certain things.' He breathed noisily. 'I heard you were going to sell your place. I know someone who's interested. Yeah. Likes the look of the place. By the water. Reckon he'd take it off your hands quickly enough. I'll put him in touch with you if you want.'

'Have my phone number,' Ada said, writing it down quickly. The estate agent had reported no interest whatsoever.

Pepper came into the kitchen, scuffing the floor. 'Who likes the look of what?' She peered into the chest freezer.

'The house,' Howard told her.

Pepper jabbed at feathery ice. 'Those people want you to go out there,' she said. 'They're not very happy.'

74

When Ada went out to the bar, the group were stern. No, they didn't want anything else. No, they just wanted the bill.

'All OK?' Howard asked. He rubbed his heart.

'All fine,' Ada said. 'They just wanted to pay.' Shook her head at Pepper, who went back to picking at the ice.

No one else came in for the rest of the evening. Ada washed the dishes and swept onion skin off the floor. Rearranged the fridge so there wasn't raw meat next to cheese. Howard was at the bar drinking. Val barking advice on everything from his health to his haircut.

Ada fixed herself and Pepper a plate of sandwiches and they both pulled the crusts off and left them at the side. A clock chimed the half-hour, then the hour. Wind rattled the windows. Uncanny how quiet the pub was – like an abandoned fairground – whorled stains on the floor, broken chairs. Ada touched one of the old guns on the wall, thought of all the times it must have been pulled off and aimed with beery intent.

'When did it get like this?' she asked Val. 'So quiet?'

'Quiet?' Val said. 'It's no different than it always was.' As if the change had been so incremental she'd hardly even noticed. She sipped a cup of tea. 'Pearl came in,' she said. 'About a year ago. I gave her a drink and dropped her back in the car. Walked all the way up here. I think she wanted some company.'

'Company?' Ada said. Her mother had never wanted company in her life.

Val shrugged and opened the till. 'Here's your money sweetie. I'll give you a bell whenever we need you again, OK?'

Ada was so relieved to be going she found herself nodding. It was only when she was back in the car that she realised what she'd agreed to. The heavy feeling of getting embroiled.

75

11

THE DIAGRAMS WERE LIKE mazes. Pepper knelt on the floor in the study and squinted down at them. At first they'd made no sense, but slowly she was working things out. How to fit on a bigger lens. Which lever to move round after she took each picture. How to adjust what Luke had called the focus. Everything fitted together and then the satisfying click when she pressed the button.

It had been raining forever. Sallow days, like something woollen left on the line too long, its colours rinsed out. The trees smeared into wet air. There was no going out but the woods and river looked different every day and she kept watching them from the window, not wanting to miss anything.

She turned the page. It was late afternoon: just on the cusp between light and dark. What her mother called *dimpsy* even though Pepper had never heard anyone else call it that. It was hard to see the next picture and when she looked up it had suddenly gone very dark, the sky turning the same green as boggy water. The wind knocked against the house. Lightning lit the sky like an X-ray, showing the pale bones of the trees. Pepper stood in the window and watched, remembering her own bones showing up on a screen when she'd swallowed that bit of metal which was stuck in her chest.

There was a low rumble of thunder. 'Come up here and watch,' her mother called down.

The house stank of wet paint and Pepper could taste it in the back of her throat. She went upstairs and into the room her mother was sleeping in. The wind shook the window. 'I got born in a storm,' she said.

'Just after,' her mother said. She was holding a paintbrush with cream paint on it, the same boring colour the walls were anyway.

'And the nurse said I cried louder than all the thunder.'

Her mother picked out bits of brush that had stuck to the wet paint on the wall. 'I don't think she did. All that woman talked about was her apple tree; how she had crates of apples all over her house that were rotting.'

'Louder than all the thunder,' Pepper said. It was better to be born in a storm than just after one.

They leaned against the window and watched. Huge thundery booms and gusts of wind. White sheets of lightning. The reflection of the rain rippled over their skin. The thunder was right above their heads – it sounded like the sky was cracking. More lightning, then more, and Pepper didn't want it to stop, crack after crack of thunder. But there were longer gaps in between now, and the thunder was quieter, the lightning flashed less bright. She willed the storm to come back but the clouds moved apart, the sky turned grey again and the quiet was almost too much to bear.

'You can do some painting if you want,' her mother said. She turned away from the window and went back over to the wall.

Pepper pressed her forehead against the cold glass. The paint was sour in her throat, the horrible rasping of the brush against plaster, just so that man could come and see if he wanted to buy the house.

'It's not going to be for much longer,' her mother said. 'OK?'

A shivery feeling rushed over Pepper. She covered her ears, la la la. If only the storm would come back. She closed her eyes and then opened them again. The sky was the same old grey and the wind had calmed right down. She went over to the wall and stood in front of the bit her mother was painting.

'I've got to get this done,' her mother said.

Pepper stayed where she was and when her mother tried to lift her she made herself as heavy as she could. It was easy: all you had to do was go completely slack and imagine your legs were made of the heaviest metal in the world, whatever that was.

'You're a bloody lump.'

'You are,' Pepper said. 'You are.'

Her mother tried to move her again. 'Stop being boring,' she said. She touched the paintbrush lightly against Pepper's cheek.

Pepper clutched at her face. 'My eye,' she said. 'I can't see anything.' She staggered around and bumped into the wet wall, then she lay down on the floor and covered her face with her hands.

Her mother sighed and went over to the window. She tucked her hair behind her ears, tucking and tucking over and over. There was the faintest rumble of thunder in the distance.

Pepper stayed on the floor and watched her mother from between her fingers. They both knew she was faking it. After a while, Pepper went over and stood next to her. Very close but not touching.

'Maybe we should play the hiding game,' her mother said.

'We probably should,' Pepper told her. Already running through her mind where she could hide. She always found the good places.

78

She had hidden in the loft of one house and stayed there all afternoon – her mother hadn't even known there was a loft. And another time, in another house, she'd balled herself up in a deep drawer with a sieve on her head. Her mother was terrible at hiding. She would stand behind a door that had glass panes in it. Or she would hide in a curtain with her feet sticking out.

'You go and hide,' her mother said. 'I'll count here.' She covered her eyes and started to count slowly.

Pepper ran out of the room and stopped, looked left, then right. Panicky laughter bubbling up. The house sprawled in front of her. She looked back at the bedroom then ran, skidding, along the corridor. Went halfway down the stairs then tiptoed back up, hand over her mouth and snuck into the bathroom. Looked around and heard her mother saying she was coming. It was too late to find somewhere else so she stood in the bath and pulled the curtain around. Hunched up, her shoulders shaking and her stomach all tight and sloshy.

Her mother walked past, paused outside the bathroom. 'Muuhhuuuha ha ha,' she said in the deep scary voice. 'I'm going to find you.'

Pepper stuffed the shower curtain in her mouth but still a squeaky laugh came out. Her mother came into the bathroom and stopped. Then she pretended to give up and leave the room but at the last minute she turned and pounced on Pepper, who shrieked and thrashed around in the curtain, the shower dribbling onto their shoulders.

'Your turn,' Pepper said. 'Your turn now.'

'OK,' her mother said. 'Are you wearing shoes?' She checked Pepper's feet but she was only wearing socks. 'There's water and gritty stuff all over the hall.'

'Come on,' Pepper shouted. 'Let's play.' She stayed in the bath and counted. Maybe peeked a bit. One, two, three, four. Miss a few, one hundred. 'Ready or not,' she called out. The first thing she did was whirl right round to check her mother wasn't hiding behind her. Which had happened once before. Then she ran downstairs and checked the kitchen. Everywhere was quiet. Through the hall and all the downstairs rooms, pouncing on a coat that she thought had moved, pouncing on a curtain. Up the stairs and back into the bathroom, snatching back the shower curtain. Nothing. Under the beds in each bedroom. Down into the kitchen, across into the lounge, the study. 'I know where you are,' she called out, but minutes passed, then more minutes. She started upstairs again, looking under beds, flinging open wardrobes, but the house was quiet and she stood at the top of the stairs looking down. 'I know where you are,' she said softly, but she stayed hovering at the top of the stairs listening for any . . .

12

SHUFFLING, CRAMMED IN THE cupboard under the stairs between a mop and an ironing board. Ada heard Pepper go past the stairs and down the hall into the kitchen. 'Got you,' she said, and made a crashing sound. Ada stifled a giggle. Her palms sweaty and her stomach jittery. Just like when she was a kid hiding from Judy. Pepper went back upstairs and the shower curtain rattled on its plastic rings. 'I know where you are,' she called. For a tiny person she made the floorboards creak like trampolines.

Ada moved so that the mop handle wasn't sticking into her back. The wall was cold and damp. Bits of limey paint flaked off. Pepper was laughing so much she was practically hysterical. But upstairs, stabbing at the wet paint with her finger, her face had suddenly become Pearl's – the furrowed brow, the way her eyes darted when she was looking for a way out of doing something. Like the time Ada had come back from school and reminded her mother that she needed a costume for the next day – they were doing a play and the costume could be anything.

'Anything,' her mother had said. She'd looked around and then unhooked her coat and hat from the peg. 'Wear this.'

'What would I be?' Ada asked. She put it on and the hat fell down over her eyes.

'I don't know,' her mother said. 'A scarecrow. I'd have to find some straw from somewhere, maybe take a handful from the Jamesons'.'

But Ada shook her head, said no, she didn't want to be a scarecrow.

'Well, what then?' her mother said. Pacing, grabbing lampshades and colanders and putting them on Ada's head.

'A witch. I want to be a witch.'

'That's a bit obvious, isn't it?' Pearl hung the hat and coat back up and stared at them for a long moment. Then she went into her study and closed the door. There was no sound for a long time, then something thumped, there was a lot of rustling. Hours passed. Ada cooked spaghetti and grated in cheese but her mother didn't come out to eat. The sound of a bottle clinking. Ada went to bed and lay awake listening. Something ripped, her mother murmured, 'Go in there you bastard needle.' One of the girls at school said her mother had sewn a white fur cloak and crown. Another girl said her father had spent all week making something out of colourful wool. At a school fete, someone had pointed to Pearl and asked Ada if she was her grandmother, and Ada had nodded. She lay in bed and listened. The thumps and clinks went on all night.

In the morning her mother held out a heap of bin bags and pins. A sagging bin-bag hat. A bin-bag dress with torn sleeves. Looked at Ada carefully as she tried it on. 'It's not too bad, is it?' she said. She put in another pin so that the waist was tighter and then smoothed the plastic down over Ada's back.

'It's just right,' Ada told her. She put the costume on over her uniform and walked slowly up the road to meet the bus. Then, just as the bus came round the corner, she pulled it off and pushed it into the hedge. Told her teacher that she had forgotten to bring anything and was cast as the schoolgirl, watching the robots and fairies rampage over everything.

There was a noise outside the cupboard and Ada held her breath. The door creaked open and there was a wedge of dim light. Any second now Pepper would burst in shouting, got you, got you. But the door shut again. The floorboards upstairs creaked. Ada pressed herself against the wall and felt water dripping. Water splashed onto the floor by her foot. Her leg was cramping up and she stretched it out.

Her leg touched someone else's leg. She sucked in her breath. Could hardly see anything in the dim cupboard. Another splash of water on the floor. 'Pepper?' she said. But she could hear Pepper at the top of the stairs. More water dripped down. There was a gritty pool by her feet and a scattering of small stones. A musty smell, like soaking clothes that couldn't dry, wet leaves, standing water.

Outside the door, one of the clocks chimed and Ada jumped. The mop clattered to the floor.

'Shhhhh,' a voice whispered. The familiar sound of a throat being cleared. 'You're going to ruin the game.'

Rain drummed on the roof. Pepper's footsteps stopped, then came slowly back down the stairs. The air was so thick and wet it was hard to breathe. Water dripped onto the floor. 'I know you're here,' Pepper called out. Her voice was trembly and thin. She came closer and the cupboard door opened. 'Found you, found you,' she said. She pushed herself into the cupboard, breathing hard and fast.

Ada climbed out slowly. She turned at the door and looked back; saw nothing but the mop and the ironing board, a damp box and a pool of water on the floor. Which she mopped away carefully.

13

WHO WAS IT? THEY definitely seemed familiar, but she had been in the house alone, hadn't she? Yes, now that she looked back over it – back past the chair and those final tangled months – she had been in the house alone for years. But at least more herself, whatever that was.

Those were the years when the work started to dry up. Pearl dusted off her desk and her tools. Told herself that it made her eyes sore, it paid about as much as a kid's paper round. Less probably. The tools bankrupted her, the mechanisms fussy and arthritic. But she took to rubbing her thumbs over her index fingers until the skin turned shiny. Wanting to do something with her hands.

Snapped bracelets, brooches with broken pins, rings that needed resizing. Other people's precious things. But less and less of them. Maybe one small package came through a week, then every month. The jewellery shop that used her to clear their backlog closed down. Replaced by a pharmacy – a window display of breast pumps and hair dye, the smell like a sweetshop and a graveyard.

But now and again there would be work and she would lean over her desk fitting chain links together, soldering clasps. Relishing the technical language: filigree, fob, locket bail. Completely opposite to the way people spoke about the things they sent her. 'I couldn't do without it,' they would say. 'I don't know what I'd do if it stopped working.' Even though it was only metal for Chrissakes. It was only bits of metal – melted and worked into casings and twists. And it was only stones – dead trees and animals subject to so much time and pressure that they buckled, turned unrecognisable. What happens to everyone, she thought.

She wore trousers people donated to charity shops – cord ones and probably men's from the way the crotch bagged out. Possibly made her look like a pillock, but they were hard-wearing; she hardly ever had to wash them. She rolled the legs up and stuffed them into boots. She wore the same jumper every day each winter, because she loved the dark green colour and the soft wool around her neck. She wore shirts loose enough to cover her slumping belly and chest. Her skin determined to turn her into someone else, someone with pouchy cheeks and eyes, and a dry, pale mouth.

She was sent a watch to fix. It had a silver strap and gold engraving. Some heirloom or other. She spent weeks on it, the stiff gears like her stiff hands. Her fingers were calloused, seared from years of working with metal. Always the comforting smell of oil on them. The watch's workings were delicate and Pearl took her time: cleaned them out, greased a new mainspring, fitted the parts carefully back in. She sent it off and then a note came back saying that the spring had been put on the wrong way, so that it had jammed. The mechanism busted and they would not be sending her any payment, and she was lucky that they'd decided not to take it any further.

She should have written back. She should have phoned them up.

But instead she made excuses: her handwriting was illegible and getting worse; she hated using the phone, everyone sounded like a stranger, even people she knew very well. Her own voice echoing back, nasal and uncertain. And if it was so bloody precious they shouldn't have burdened her with it in the first place.

The bilberries came out and she gorged on them until her mouth was stained black.

She felt a twinge in her back and knew that it was her liver – something awful, something rare and awful. She told him about it – who was it? He always seemed to be there, sitting at the table with a mug of tea, and when she came in he would look up and nod, and then get back to whatever he was thinking about. He had a dent in his nose, waxy hair, a lilt to his voice like someone patiently working through a conundrum. What was his name? Luke, that was it. Always there, and if he wasn't, she would be restless for some reason, unable to just settle down and do something.

'Your liver isn't at the back,' Luke told her.

Pearl sat down next to him and gulped at his tea. He never bothered making her a cup. 'My kidneys then,' she said. She scooped the cat up and put him on her lap, fussed its ears and said something mortifying like, 'There you go fluffy face. How about that then, eh?' Pressing his grizzled body into her chest, kneading his back. Somehow slipping into the habit of coddling the thing, speaking to it like it was a baby.

'Did you hear about the fire at the shop?' Luke said. 'A spark from the oven apparently. Although Mick put it out straight away.'

'I might have heard something,' Pearl told him. But Luke was the only person that she learned any news from. He was brimming with stories of the place. Of the man from a farm a few miles away that got his arm stuck in an antique hare trap – had to get the thing cut off with a saw. Of the plans to build a bigger road, the kind with four lanes, a few miles away. The price of milk, the price of petrol. Of the fact that Mr Jameson had crashed his car into a lorry, but the interesting thing was his passenger. Not Mrs Jameson. And those stories trailing into stories of his days on the boats. Of icebergs like cathedrals, of the sun so hot it was like a cage over you. He had seen a tornado pick up cows. He had picked a coconut and drunk the milk, which was actually more like water. 'Don't rub it in,' she would tell him. But she liked to hear about the birds he had seen: flamingos, pelicans. Showy birds, he said, and not as good as the ones on the river.

Months passed and nothing to mend. Pearl paced and looked out of the windows. The car's tyres were going flat – she barely used it except to go up to the shop. She hardly went out except to walk along the river or up into the woods. The world seemed vast and difficult; much easier to stay put; there was more than enough here that she had to do. But whenever she heard a car go past, or whenever a door creaked open in the wind, she would stop what she was doing and listen. Always looking out for someone . . . Who was it? It would come back; it would come back to her any minute now.

She sold a few things she didn't need: the TV, an expensive copper pan, a leather travelling case with buckles.

A package arrived with a ring to be resized. A wedding ring which needed five millimetres adding. A bride with fat hands. Pearl ordered a piece of sizing stock to match the metal, then when that came she laid everything out on her table, cut the ring and heated it. That was the part she liked – it had to be exactly right. Too much heat would damage it, too little and it wouldn't bend in the right way. She knew the exact moment, could feel it when the metal gave. Then pull the ring apart and solder in the stock. When it cooled she buffed it up, wrapped it, and sent it back.

She ate so many ramsons that her skin reeked of garlic.

'Your advert's gone out of the paper,' Luke told her. He spread the local pages out on the table and pointed to where her advert used to be. Right next to the birth notices, a photo of a baby with a creased old man's face.

'What do you think would cause a twitching eyelid?' Pearl asked.

'Why has your advert gone?' Luke said.

'Maybe something in the brain, do you think?' Like a faulty mechanism that needed refitting.

'I'm going to ring them up.' Luke went over to the phone and picked it up.

'Don't do that,' Pearl said.

'Tell me why it's gone then.'

'Because the editor's an arse,' Pearl said. 'He put the price up.'

'How much?'

'It was too much.' She bent down and worked her fingers through the cat's fur.

'How much?' Luke said.

'I don't remember,' Pearl told him. 'Twenty, I think.'

'Twenty more for the year? That's not much,' Luke said. 'What with the price of paper going up, ink, printing, electricity. Twenty's not that much.'

'It's a rip-off,' Pearl said. She looked at the newspaper again. Couldn't quite believe that her advert wasn't there. But she could just ring up again, she could always just ring up at any time and get them to put it back in.

The river flooded and the bank crumbled, as if something had come up and taken huge bites out of it. Mushroom rings appeared every morning. The trees turned orange as torches.

She saw a mass of flocking starlings, the patterns they made like the way water moved. She wrote down the observation in her note-book, *mur, murms*, her pen hovering over the paper. Couldn't think of the right word. A little slip that she barely noticed at the time, a precise description reduced to *murmurs*.

And God forbid either of them ever admitted it, but it was getting harder to hike the long distances. Neither of them wanted to stray too far from the house, always using the river as a marker. First, Luke would slow down and she would press on ahead, then it would switch. Urging each other on. Who could spot the heron first, who could identify the migrant bird blown in by a storm. Who could read the weather to see what they had coming. Tired and stumbling but not wanting to admit it. They both knew the particular scratches of hawthorn and gorse.

But one time, Luke fell. He was up ahead and she heard a strange cry and then he was down, his foot twisted into a rabbit hole and his ankle completely gave out. Bruised, maybe broken. They were miles from anywhere. The moor turning bone-coloured as the light went.

'You'll have to leave me here while you get someone,' Luke said.

'Nah,' Pearl told him. 'It'll get too cold.' A hollow feeling spread through her chest. There wasn't a path that she could see and daylight was disappearing every second.

'You don't need to worry about me,' Luke said.

'I'm not worried about you. Why would I be worried about you?'

Luke put his foot down and crumpled again. Pearl wondered for a moment if she could carry him but he was not a small man. She looked in his bag. There was a blanket, a bar of chocolate, some crap book about a detective chasing a killer. And there were hollows in the granite that the weather had carved out. She lowered Luke down gently, sat next to him and pulled the blanket over. They ate the chocolate. Just their backs touching but she woke up with her head

89

on Luke's chest and a sheep pissing right next to them. It was a better night's sleep than she'd had for a long time. Which was probably because of the cold, the way it slowed the heart right down.

The phone rang and someone asked when their ring would be returned and she told them she had sent it back already.

A strange pain in her eye, a throbbing feeling. Sure for a whole week that she was going blind but it didn't happen.

Sometimes Luke didn't stop by for days. And then he would turn up and eat all the bread and drink all her milk. Sit for hours in the kitchen. Pearl would keep to her study, pretending to be busy. She would straighten out her books, take down boxes of photos then stack them up again. Waiting for Luke to come in and find her. In the end, she would have to go into the kitchen for something.

'Listen to this,' Luke said. 'This bloke at the pub was talking about people digging up metal and things on their land. Precious stuff. Apparently there's a lot around here. Someone found a load of coins. And they reckon my garden's got something in it.'

'So?' Pearl said.

'I should have a look, don't you think, see if there's something there.'

'Dig your whole garden up?' Pearl said. 'Just because someone told you there might be a coin in there?' The lines around Luke's eyes and mouth were deep and dry. He shrugged and put his hand on the back of his neck. Pearl picked at her lips. In a few days she would ring him, in a few days she would say that maybe they ought to have a dig around and see what they could find.

A package came and she tore it open. It was about the size of a ring box. Already imagining the hot metal, what type of stone she would have to reset. But it was a sample of washing powder. She threw it down on the table. She sniffed it. She washed her clothes with it. They came out cleaner so she switched.

She ate as many hazelnuts as she could find in the hedges.

Then one day a woman turned up holding a locket with a broken hinge and insisted that it was mended straight away. It would be difficult for her to come back and collect it, and no, she didn't want it posted; hadn't Pearl heard how much stuff was lost in the post?

'I'll have to push all my other work back,' Pearl said. She took the locket into the study and looked at it through a magnifying glass. There was a tiny photograph of someone in there. The hinge worn from too many openings and closings. She glanced at the woman, who was watching intently, then fumbled with the locket, dropped it, picked it up again.

'Be careful with it,' the woman said.

'I know what I'm doing,' Pearl told her. She looked in her drawer, couldn't think what she needed, then remembered hollow wire and hinge pins. She laid them on the table. The jewellery saw, the soldering iron. The woman started to cry. A quiet, watery noise. Pearl opened a drawer and stared into it. The woman didn't stop crying. Pearl went over and patted the woman's arm with her fingertips. 'There,' she said. 'There.'

'I don't know what I'd do without it,' the woman said.

Pearl put the jewellery saw away and got out pliers. Her hands shook. She wiped them on her thighs. She felt very tired. She took a breath and cut into the locket.

She could ring up about the advert and get it put back in any time she wanted.

A persistent ache in her fingers that turned into sharp pains. She couldn't hold a mug of tea, she couldn't sleep. 'It's nothing,' she said to Luke. When he finally drove her to the hospital they told her it was the tendons, something in them seizing up, stiffening, pulling her fingers inwards towards her palm.

Someone brought her food in labelled boxes, with instructions on how to heat it up. The one with the frizzy hair and the kind face. Who was it? Always talking about the farm. A smell of grass about that one, wind-whipped skin. Feeding the cat as if Pearl might have forgotten.

The phone rang but she didn't answer it.

The blackberries came out in their millions.

Sometimes, on a cold day, Luke had to hold her mug so that she could drink. Sometimes she could slot a cog into the back of a watch and pinch a delicate clasp together. Sometimes they both just sat on the sofa, Luke's blanket over their knees, listening to the river. Luke had his thoughts, whatever they were. He would plonk down plastic bags of food that he'd brought over, make hot drinks one after the other. The food and the cups stacked up because he was not her housekeeper and never would be. He tucked the blanket around her when it fell off. He told her she was a grumpy bastard. He told her he should just leave her to it then. He said he had his own things to attend to. He opened the front door but she heard him come back and sit at the table in the kitchen.

There was something she was meant to ask him about, something about his garden, something she thought they should do together, but it kept slipping her mind. She listened to his small sounds. She moved her fingers slowly, waiting for something to mend.

14

'I NEED TO GET paint today,' Ada said. 'And new brushes.'

'I'll come too,' Pepper said.

The wind had risen in the night, elbowing down the chimney and putting the fire out. They had woken to a freezing house and the kitchen window flung wide open. A plate had smashed and Pepper had a splinter in her foot before Ada could tell her not to go near it. Had to heat a needle and ease it out; hard to find amongst the grime and dust and scuffed heel.

'I'm not getting it from the shop,' Ada said. Just so Pepper knew she wouldn't be able to pick up any sweets or bird ornaments or anything else that she kept going on about.

The tiniest pause. 'So?' Pepper said, shrugging.

'It's from a place that Luke mentioned. It sells paints and stuff further down the valley.'

But the car wouldn't start. At first, she thought the wind was drowning out the engine noise, but after a while she realised the engine wasn't going at all.

She sat in the kitchen with her coat on, drumming her fingers on the table. The man Howard mentioned, Ray, had phoned yesterday and said he'd come over in the next few days to look at the house. But the walls were only half painted, half-filled boxes everywhere. She glanced at the cupboard under the stairs. Drummed her fingers faster.

'It's a long walk,' she told Pepper, who ran ahead, her coat streaming out.

Following the main road would be easiest, but cutting across the moor would be quicker. Ada walked up the lane and turned onto the road, past rumpled puddles and strewn branches. The sky was clear blue. The wind sloughed off the fustiness of the house. She undid her knot of hair so that the wind could tug at it. Thought again of how keen Ray had sounded – as if the viewing was just a formality to go through. She swung her arms. It had all been a lot easier than she'd imagined; she had come back, she had done what needed to be done. Dipped her toe in without being dunked right under.

After a mile they climbed a gate into a field and followed a track which sloped past a dry-stone wall. The field turned to tussocks and gorse as it edged onto the moor, the ground boggy and splashy. Everything was merging colours: greens, greys, rich browns like a horse's back. The maroon of dying bracken. Red water welling through peat.

The path climbed uphill over jutting granite. Pepper stood behind Ada and pushed her up with both hands. 'You're heavy,' she said.

'Don't rub it in,' Ada told her. She leaned back so that Pepper was pushing and pushing but not going anywhere.

'What would you pick out of no toes or no fingers?' Pepper asked.

'How am I meant to choose out of that?' Ada said.

'It's the game, you have to.'

Ada raked handfuls of hair out of her eyes, then stopped and tied it back up tightly. It was always so much windier up on the moor. 'I don't know. No toes.'

'That's what anyone would say,' Pepper scoffed.

'OK. What would you choose out of eating kidneys or that maggot-ripened cheese I told you about?'

Pepper thought about it for a long time. 'That is a very good question,' she said eventually. 'A very good question indeed.'

The path stopped at the top of the hill. Not even a sheep track going down the other side. Ada scanned the moor but it looked blank; identical in all directions. And yet her mother had just walked across, as if following some kind of inner compass or map. Which Ada definitely did not have. She had taken Pepper to a park with a maze in it and got trapped in there for two hours.

Clouds loured in the distance. 'Is that the spinster over there?' Pepper asked.

'I don't know,' Ada said. Why didn't she know? She looked over at the hunched and misshapen rock that Pepper was pointing to. 'Spinsters made their own living spinning wool,' she said. 'So they didn't have to get married.'

'Spinster, shminster,' Pepper said, not listening. She looked down the hill and then hurtled head first, hair sticking up like chopped hay.

Ada watched her run, then starting picking her own way down, braced and stiff, ankles squelching in bog. The wind was freezing but sweat dribbled down her ribs. Her knees ached and there was a twinge in the side of her back. This was why she never exercised: she only ever felt decrepit when she was doing something active – day-to-day she felt fine. She rubbed her back, stopped looking down for a moment and stumbled on a root, twisted and fell sideways onto the sopping ground. Not gracefully.

Pepper stood over her. 'You almost fell on poo,' she said. She squatted down and tugged at the tough root. 'It could have happened to anyone,' she said kindly.

Ada sat up and moved her foot around. The sooner off the moor the better. A drenched, barren place, especially in winter. Although now that she looked closer, there were things she'd never noticed before: a thin tree with pink and orange flowers, a bush full of sloes. On the ground there were lichens like crochet, tiny purple flowers, yellow mushrooms like thimbles.

'Did I make a stupid noise when I fell?' she asked. Pepper nodded and did an impression. Ada threw a bit of sheep poo at her, then got up slowly. When she was five, walking across the moor with her mother, she'd thought the shiny black lumps were liquorice – at least she wouldn't make that mistake twice.

Pepper bent down and picked something up – it was a sheep's skull, gnarled and sallow, one snapped horn and two worn teeth. She held it up to her face and growled.

The wind pushed clouds and fog down from higher ground. At first Ada could see twenty metres in the distance, then ten. The landscape blurred and thickened to wet grey.

'Put your hood up,' she said. She stopped and looked back the way they'd come. 'Stay on the path, OK.' But there wasn't a path any more. Nothing but fog all around, wet yellow grass and mud under their feet, pale granite showing through like bone.

Pepper glanced up from under her hood. 'I want to go back home now,' she said.

Ada took a few steps forward. Out of the dim fog she saw a tree, bent over by the wind like a streaming flag. Was that the tree her mother had always saluted, a way-mark for the path ahead? She went towards it, looking for a stone wall, and almost stumbled against the remains of a wrecked hut. 'I think I know where we are,' she said. Home. Pepper had called it home.

Pepper went into the hut and stared out of the empty window. 'Did you used to walk here?' she said. 'Before?'

'Sometimes.' Ada circled the hut, remembering a broad path leading down to the road. Fog galloped down the hill.

'Did you used to see this house?' Pepper asked. Then she pointed at a rock. 'Did you used to see that?' She swung the sheep's skull on her finger. 'Did you see this?'

There wasn't a path. There were probably hundreds of these old wrecks dotting the place. Ada paced around it once more. Nothing. She was about to turn back the same way they'd come, when she saw shorter grass, a footprint in mud, and glimpsed the path through banks of fog like a causeway through the sea. She turned and saluted the tree – realised too late that it was actually a fence with a snagged bin bag flapping on it.

The moor turned back to fields and hedges and a car went past on the road in the distance.

'Look at all them birds,' Pepper said.

'They're crows,' Ada said. There was a flock wheeling around a group of bare trees like leaves in the wind.

'Not crows,' Pepper said. 'Ru, rok.'

'Rooks?'

'Rooks. Lots of birds today. Those little grey ones. And a starling. And a magpie. And one with black under its head and red here.' She pointed to her chest.

'When did you see all those?' Ada asked.

Pepper shrugged. 'I don't know. Just around.'

Ada stopped at the gate and looked back. Thought about those little yellow mushrooms and flowers. But in the fog, the moor was an empty blur; like a face in the distance you don't recognise until you get close enough to see the scars, the crinkles, the way the bones slope.

The house was on its own next to the road. It had a blue door and a withered tomato plant with a few hard green tomatoes on it. Ada knocked and waited. A dog barked. She knocked again. The dog barked louder and then ran out from the back. Ada stood rigid as it skidded and weaved around her legs. 'Good dog,' she said. 'Bugger off.' Dogs were like the worst drunks – lunging at crotches then pissing over other people's shoes.

'It's Shep,' Pepper said. She crouched down and wrapped her arms around the dog's head.

A voice called out and then Tristan came round from the back of the house, brushing dust off his hands.

'You,' Ada said. 'I mean paint. We're here to buy paint.' She knelt down and tried to clean Pepper up, who was daubed with mud.

Tristan watched her. 'You look like you came right across the moor,' he said.

Ada rubbed her hands over her own face, felt grimy streaks down her cheeks.

'Shep's licking my feet,' Pepper said.

Tristan showed Ada a shed stacked with paint and tools. Wood shavings heaped on the floor like shorn hair. She chose two tins of cream paint and a brush and paid him. The skin on his hands was split and calloused. He locked the shed door and said he was just about to head up to the cafe and Pepper butted in saying she wouldn't be able to make it back home unless she ate something right now, so could she come too? And Ada felt the same herself.

His truck stank of wet dogs. Mud dripped off Ada's boots, her hair matted like felt. When she was six, a supply teacher had told her class

98

to draw pictures of their souls. Hers was a tangled mass of felt-tip that sprawled off the page. 'Your soul seems to have spilled onto the table,' he had sighed, and gone to get a cloth to wipe it off.

The sign outside the cafe said 'Brake for Hot Food'. It was a pebble-dash bungalow at the top of the valley and the main road snarled past. She and Judy used to go there sometimes to drink milkshakes and had once slipped out the back to smoke a cigarette Judy had found – both of them hacking like unsettled swans.

Inside there was a heater clanking and the smell of burnt crumbs. A couple dressed in creased wedding clothes, their small daughter in a ballerina tutu.

The plastic chairs creaked when they sat down. Pepper put the skull on the table. Tristan took his coat off; underneath he was wearing a thick red work shirt and khaki trousers. Freckles on his hands and throat, glints of orange in his hair. Put Ada in mind of the moor's colours. His bottom teeth were overlapping, his skin chapped but smooth along the tops of his cheeks. Younger than Ada had first thought. He nodded at the waitress who came over with a pad and pen.

'Alright Tristan,' she said. She was about forty, with a bored drawl and a clip like a shooting star in her hair. 'What are you having?'

'Coffee,' he said. 'And have you got any of that special left?'

She nodded and wrote something down. Looked at the skull for a long moment, as if it was next in line to order.

'Coffee for me, too,' Pepper said. She slipped off her chair and went over to the counter to study the trinkets for sale.

The waitress flared her nostrils. 'Anything to eat?' she asked. She glanced back at the till, where two men were waiting, blowing steam out of their mouths like cold horses.

'We'll all have the same,' Ada said. Outside, the fog had thinned and the sky was a wan green. The waitress brought over their coffees, thick as gravy with a rainbow sheen.

Tristan dropped sugar into his mug and stirred it with his finger.

Ada's jeans tightened as the mud dried. She wiped at her cheeks with the back of her hand. Felt something gritty crunch on her teeth. Silence apart from the clatter of plates. Spoons clinking against cups. She wiped her face again. 'Luke told me where to go to buy paint,' she said.

The coffee left a gleam on Tristan's lips. 'He tries to help me out. Recommends me for decorating work, carpentry when it comes up.' His voice was deep, almost hoarse.

'Your house. It was always empty when I was growing up.'

'They put it up for rent a couple of years back. Saw it when I was driving past.' He kneaded his right leg. Something stiff about the way he walked on it. 'But they're thinking about moving in there themselves soon, the owners.'

The sky turned mirey. A few silver rain streaks on the window. Ada gulped her coffee, glanced at Tristan, drank some more. 'I've got someone coming to look at the house. That's why I needed the paint quickly.'

Tristan reached over and touched the sheep's jaw so that it clacked.

'So it shouldn't be more than a few weeks now.' She stopped, realised she'd been addressing the skull.

Tristan was studying the hinge of the jaw. 'They come down and look at the place now and again. Trying to make up their minds.'

The waitress brought over napkins and cutlery and a basket of sauce sachets. Ada took a packet of ketchup and tore bits out of the corner. Her stomach gurgled.

Tristan leaned back in his chair and looked around the cafe. 'This is a good place,' he said. Seemed not to notice the buzzing strip lights, bleary floor, frayed wires behind the counter. He pointed at a blackboard that said: 'Cake, Chips, Pheasant'. 'A few weeks ago that said: "Oysters". From the estuary. Best thing I've eaten. You probably used to have them here all the time.'

Ada grimaced and shook her head. She couldn't abide oysters. The same went for radishes and those weird crackers made out of rice – each one you ate made you hungrier and hungrier.

'I only had them once before, in Canada, near the mountains, except they called them prairie oysters there,' he said.

'Prairie oysters.' Ada glanced at him. 'You know what those are, don't you?'

Tristan spoke like he moved: slowly and carefully. He rubbed at his jaw. 'I thought I did,' he said.

The strip light above them fuzzed. 'Where would the oysters come from? It's up in the mountains. No sea.' She stirred her coffee for a while, trying to think of a delicate way of putting it. 'You ate bull's balls,' she told him. Fried in batter probably, with plenty of sauce as a disguise.

He breathed out slowly. 'Well,' he said. His lip twitched, either going to laugh or say something else, but he stayed quiet. Folded his hands across his stomach. After a while he said, 'Now I'll tell you something.'

Ada leaned forward, thought he was going to tell her what was floating around in their drinks.

'Your house is tipping.'

She slopped coffee onto the table. 'No it's not,' she said.

'That's what I've heard. And if it is, the whole foundation would need to be reset.'

There was a bellow from behind them. Pepper and the girl in the tutu suddenly scrapping. 'Get off it,' Pepper shouted. She bit at the girl's hand. 'Put it back.'

'I didn't do anything,' the girl shrieked.

Ada jumped up and dragged Pepper away, one hand under each armpit, as if rescuing her from drowning.

'Horrible thieving sod,' Pepper said. 'I saw it first and she hid it in her shoe.'

The girl's parents glared at Ada as they carried their daughter out. She was licking her injured hand. Something silver sticking out of her shoe. 'She is a sod,' Ada told Pepper. 'But Jesus, who do you think's going to get in trouble if you carry on biting, you or me?'

The waitress came with heaped plates. 'Three specials,' she said. A strong meaty smell and onions, fried potatoes. They all looked down at the food. 'It's the pheasant,' she said, 'like you asked for.'

'It's good,' Tristan said. Caught Pepper's eye. 'Good fighting food.'

The meatballs were earthy and full of herbs. Rain lashed against the windows. The waitress came back and smiled smugly at their emptying plates. 'It's the chef's family recipe,' she said. 'For when everyone has pheasant they want to get rid of. You might find some bits of shot left in there,' she said. 'Meant to tell you earlier.'

Pepper's fork clattered down.

Tristan heaped up a huge bite. 'My sister gave up meat,' he said. 'She's only eleven but she won't have any of it.'

'Eleven,' Pepper said. 'That's not very old for her to be your sister.'

'I'm twenty-four,' Tristan said, as if that explained anything.

Pepper thought about it. 'I'm six,' she said. Then pointed at Ada. 'And she's thirty.'

Ada pushed her food from one side of the plate to the other. 'Thirty-four,' she said.

'Thirty-four,' Pepper announced. She worked her tongue around in her mouth, then coughed and spat out shot like a good hunk of tobacco.

15

AT THE SHOP THERE was a china bird with a chipped beak, a box of maps with tattered corners, a basket by the door with a few crusty vegetables. Pepper would look in and find carrots with two legs, a swede with a withered and fuming face.

Mick always watched her. After a while he would call over: 'Why aren't you at school yet, eh?' He would dig deep in his ear with his finger like he was scratching his brain. 'Going to get in any more fights?'

Pepper would hold the swede up so he could see his own resemblance.

Mick would blink, shrug and gesture to a crumb on the counter, pause, then flick it onto the floor. Slowly, to make sure she got his meaning.

The power went out and everything was strange colours: yellow candles, the cold glow of a wind-up lamp. The gas flame in the oven turquoise and roaring.

Rain drummed on the roof. Her mother baked a thin cake and rolled it up while it was still warm, then let it roll back flat to cool. 'It will remember how to do it now,' she said. The smell of the matches she blew out was like birthdays.

Pepper always got in the way when her mother cooked, so she went upstairs and lay on the camping bed. There was a fabric bag under the slats. It had a label with something written on it. 'P' 'e' 'a', something then something else. Inside, there was a watch, a cardigan, a gold ring, three small pins, the tiniest screwdriver, a ball of tissues, and a delicate brass button with engraved swirls, which fitted exactly in the middle of her palm. She put everything back in the bag but kept the button in her pocket.

Early morning, the sky tinged orange in the distance but grey as a sucked mint in the valley.

Pepper walked over hail that crunched like broken glass. It was getting colder. The feeling that things were hardening, preparing themselves. The river was flinty and made a plunking noise, like someone was throwing in rocks. She held onto the camera and looked for birds, her eyes getting used to noticing particular movements: a wren darting, blackbirds rootling in leaves, the rich brown bobbing of a dipper.

There was someone sitting further up the bank and Pepper circled over slowly. Luke said you shouldn't disturb anyone that was fishing, but if she could just see some more of those coiled fish.

'What the hell?' The person turned round. It was an old woman with her legs dangling in the water. She had rolled the arms of her jumper up to the elbow and underneath, her skin looked pale, almost blue, like cold milk in a bottle.

'I thought you were fishing,' Pepper told her. She turned to go.

'Ha,' the woman said. 'Wouldn't get anything in this stretch. Nothing but midges here, maybe a few skaters. And a heron very early.'

Pepper stopped. 'A heron?' she said. 'Is that one of those tall, grey birds?'

The woman put her hand in her trouser pocket and felt around. Water and bits of hail leaked out. 'Where is it?' she said. 'I had it in here.' She looked in the other pocket and then on the grass around her.

'It will be somewhere you don't expect,' Pepper told her. Like her glove, found that morning snagged on a piece of wood by the fire.

'It's only a bit of metal,' the woman said. 'I suppose it's only a bit of metal.' But she kept looking in her pockets all the same.

Pepper stamped her numb feet and walked along the bank looking for a good place to take a picture. There was a peeping noise and she looked up and scanned the river.

'Kingfisher,' the woman said. 'It'll be further up there, eating a fish probably. I'll show you.' She got up, clambered down the grass, into the water and started to wade.

Pepper followed along the top of the bank. But the trees thickened, the path veered away from the water. There was a muddy slope in the bank, below it purple shingle lapped by ripples, and she hesitated, remembering for a moment how her mother had stiffened and gripped Pepper's hand when she had first seen the river. And Pepper did stiffen, but she scrambled down and sloshed into the shallows. Freezing water seeped through her boots. The current dragged at her with every step. Roots humped and tangling. A metal pipe trickled sludgy run-off. Moss garlanded rocks and suddenly a deep pool, where she stumbled and plunged one arm in. A cold shock of water, the back of her nose stinging. Under the water, stones wavered green and coppery as old coins, they changed shape, swelling and shrinking as the water moved.

Up ahead, the woman had slowed down and was running her hands over the water. She picked at bits of wet, mossy stuff. Pepper splashed over, and the woman turned round to look. 'Why are you following me?' she said.

Pepper stopped. 'The kingfisher. You said I should follow you.'

The woman kept touching the surface of the water with her fingertips. It looked springy, like the water was bending, but when Pepper tried it her hand went straight through. 'Maybe there was,' the woman said. 'But it's miles away now.'

'You said I should follow you,' Pepper said. Her cold toes cramped up inside her boots. The familiar heavy feeling, like she had swallowed cement. Turning her into someone hard, who didn't care. She turned and stumbled over a stone, holding the camera up so it wouldn't get wet.

'What's that?' the woman said. 'What've you got there?'

'Nothing,' Pepper told her. Tried to make her voice savage.

The woman looked at it carefully. She seemed to be talking more to herself. 'It's just light,' she said. 'Just light hitting chemicals and producing a reaction. But it's more than that. It captures something, pins it down, something so brief you almost wonder if you really saw it.'

Pepper stopped wading and glanced back, checking to see if the woman was making fun of her. For she had put into words exactly Pepper's own jumbled and peculiar thoughts.

Every afternoon she saw Clapper and Petey walking along the road behind the house. She would stand and watch from the window. One day Petey looked up and saw her and she ducked behind the curtain. The next day he looked up and nodded, neat and solemn,

106

pushing his glasses up his nose. The day after she waited and waited but they didn't walk past. She went outside and stood in the road and then they came round the bend, too late for her to move so she pretended that she was looking for something in the hedge. They were carrying something big and yellow over their shoulders.

'He won it in a raffle,' Clapper said. 'Up at the school.'

'It's a canoe,' Petey said. He had a string of cracked conkers around his neck like war trophies.

Clapper put the canoe down on the road. 'We should let the maid sit in it,' he said.

Petey frowned and considered. 'I suppose we should,' he said.

'Where are the paddles?' Pepper asked. She sat down on the plastic bench.

'Stingy bastards,' Clapper said. 'I didn't even notice it didn't come with any paddles.'

She left out food for the cat but it didn't want any of it. Not bread. Not rice or cut-up bits of sausage.

'Coo, coo,' she called softly when she saw it running across the yard. The cat didn't even turn round. She followed it through the long grass, which still had bits of frost in it that hadn't melted.

That woman was there again, standing on the riverbank. The river rushed past, choppy and brown. The cat stopped and stared at the woman, then arched its back and its tail got fluffier. But it took a few steps forward, placing its paws carefully and quietly in the grass as if it were creeping up on something. Then its mouth went stiff and it made that quavering, scolding noise Pepper had heard it do before.

'Don't be stupid Captain,' the woman said. The cat's ears went back, it crouched very low, then bolted across the grass and into the next field.

Pepper dug her foot into the ground. 'Where does that cat live?' she asked. Praying the woman wouldn't say it was hers, or someone else's further down the valley.

'He belongs up there,' the woman said, pointing at the house.

Pepper turned and looked back at the house. 'Up there,' she said. Water welled silver in her bootprint and the river glinted. 'Up there,' she said again. She wiped her nose on her glove. 'It certainly is cold today,' she said.

'What are you talking about that for?' the woman said.

Pepper shrugged. 'I'm trying to make conversation.'

'Oh,' the woman said. '*That.*'

'This is what you have to do. I say, whereabouts do you live and what do you do for a living? And then you tell me. And then I say it's cold. And then you agree. And then I say I hope the road doesn't get ice. And then you say you heard the road will get ice. And then I say—'

'Christ,' the woman said. 'Why do we have to say all that?'

'I don't know,' Pepper said. She held onto the camera strap. 'Do you think there will be ice?'

'Of course there will,' the woman said. She looked at the camera. 'What aperture have you got that set to?'

'I don't know.'

'What shutter speed?'

'I don't know.'

'What film's loaded in there? Look there, what does it say?'

'It doesn't say anything,' Pepper said. She opened the compartment. There was nothing inside. Her chest got a sharp pain. 'I think the film fell out somewhere,' she said. She pretended to look all over the ground.

'You forgot to put one in,' the woman said. 'You dappy mare.'

'Nobody told me!' Pepper shouted. She looked in the empty compartment one more time and tried to remember all the things she'd taken pictures of but she couldn't, they were lost, and she couldn't even look for them because they had never really existed.

That evening, Luke turned up, hovering in the doorway carrying a plastic bag. 'You mentioned I should come round sometime,' he said to her mother. He had fixed the car for them and the engine didn't rattle any more.

Pepper checked the pots to make sure there was enough food for someone extra.

Luke stood by the kitchen door, eyes glancing around uneasily. He knocked his head on the stooping ceiling and jerked whenever the lights flickered. 'You mentioned I should come round,' he said again. He looked awkward and strange in the small kitchen.

Her mother got him to sit down and she piled his plate with food. Which Luke picked at and moved from one side to the other. One foot jangling under the table like he was trying to press on a brake. In the end, he pushed his plate away and leaned back. 'Smell is taste,' he said. 'Can't have one without the other. But I imagine that was proper.'

'How about coffee?' her mother said quickly. She got up and filled the kettle.

'Why can't you taste?' Pepper asked. She licked the last sauce from her plate.

Luke touched his crooked nose. 'Have you ever walked into a glass door?'

Pepper paused mid-lick. 'No,' she said, watching him carefully to see if he was making it up.

Luke got up and put one, two, three spoons of coffee in his cup, then talked with her mother about boring things, so Pepper stood next to the heater and tried to see how long she could keep her hands on the hottest part.

After a while, Luke came over and hunched over the heater, gulping at his thick coffee. He made his voice low. 'Heard you've been fighting,' he said.

Pepper scowled and picked her lips. 'So?' she said.

'See that scorch mark on the floor there?'

Pepper looked and saw something round and black in the corner.

'And see this?' Luke lifted his trouser up and showed a silvery mark on his ankle. 'Your mother did that. Wasn't meant to be cooking with alcohol but she wanted to make something flame in a pan, as far as I can remember. Dropped the hot oil. Curtains went up in seconds. I had to stamp it out before it spread through the whole house.'

Pepper stared at her mother, who asked what they were whispering about.

There was mud under Luke's nails and Pepper asked him why, had he been digging? 'Ah.' Luke shifted, turning uneasy again. 'Just been trying to find something out is all.' He cleared his throat, then rummaged around under the table and brought out the plastic bag, which was full of camera stuff: lenses, a small folded tripod, spare rolls of film.

Pepper had to go and get the camera even though she had sworn never to touch it or think about it again. She fitted a lens on slowly. She zoomed in on her mother's backside.

Luke looked away and pretended not to notice.

When Luke had gone, she heard something scratching at the door and there was the cat sitting on the steps. Hail gleamed in his grey fur. She clucked softly with her tongue. The cat looked away and yawned. 'Come on,' she said. 'Come on.' She patted her knees. 'Come on Captain.'

The cat slipped round her legs and ran into the kitchen. Paced the room, rubbing cupboards and jumping up on the counter and the sink. She tried to lift him down but he kicked and lashed out and broke a glass into a hundred pieces.

'Shhh,' she said. She picked up the bits of glass carefully and put them in the bin. Scolded the cat, but not too much. Rolled the brass button for him to chase but he slunk under the table and licked his paw. His tongue rough and pink as a wafer.

'Go into the lounge, it's freezing in here,' her mother said, coming into the kitchen.

Pepper glanced at Captain. One paw over its ear and then the other. 'In a minute,' she said.

'There's a cat under the table,' her mother said.

'I told you. I told you there was a cat.' Pepper crouched down and stared at him. 'You belong here, don't you Captain,' she said.

'What did you call him?' Her mother crouched down too and looked closely at the cat. 'Jesus, look at him, he must be at least twenty.'

'He has to stay here now,' Pepper said. 'Doesn't he?' She went under the table with Captain and touched his tail. He flinched and whipped round, yellow eyes glaring. Pepper crawled back out. Her own cat to look after. She called him and patted her legs.

The cat stayed under the table washing.

16

ANOTHER SHIFT AT THE pub – turned out that Val's waitress was off sick permanently; the blues or the brittle bones, Val couldn't remember which.

Howard frantically prepared a pasta sauce, sweat dripping into his ears. Chopping mushrooms and boiling them into a gluey paste. A few drinkers at the bar. Tristan propped up on one elbow. Val haranguing him about all the work he was doing – shouldn't he be easing up a bit now that it was winter, looking after himself better? Although if he insisted on working himself into the ground she had a problem with a piano that was blocking a door she wanted to open.

Two customers for food: one who sent the meal back, and the other, Luke, who ate stoically, working his way through like it was a job that needed doing.

Tristan was walking along the road. He pressed against the hedge to let the car past, shielding his eyes from the lights.

Ada wound down the window. 'Do you want a lift?' she said.

It was a rare clear night. The sky stripped back to stars. On the cusp of December and a smell so particular to this place: the tang of frost behind the mulch and dank. And there was frost: the first glints as it laid itself down on the grass.

She drove slowly, the headlights picking out beer cans in the hedge, a pair of gleaming eyes.

'You missed the turning,' Tristan said.

'There's a quicker way down here,' Ada told him. One of those roads with grass down the middle, the car shunting from pothole to pothole.

Her clothes smelled of singed onions and grease. She changed gear, the car jerked, revved, then shuddered over a cattle grid.

Tristan held his leg steady then flexed it at the knee. Saw her looking over at him. 'It's worse when it's cold,' he said.

Ada looked back at the road. Luke had told her about Tristan's leg – how he'd broken it years ago in a hiking accident somewhere so remote he'd had to walk on it to get himself to the nearest town. 'It gets pretty cold here,' she said.

Tristan looked out of the window. The lane widened and there was a sprawling farm ahead. 'I worked on that place,' he said. He sat very still but suddenly words poured out. How he'd restored all the staircases, the beams; stripped back panelling and discovered a stone fireplace. A bread oven in a wall that he'd researched, found out how it worked. It was all there already, he said. Just waiting for someone to find it, work it up. He rubbed over his knuckles as if he was polishing them.

'Did they like it?' Ada asked.

Tristan didn't turn to look at the house as they drove past it. 'They only use it for summers,' he said.

Mud turned to tarmac and the lane joined up with the road. The moor stretched out behind it.

'You've got bits of mushroom in your hair,' he said. He reached over, his fingers above her ear.

'Mushrooms are only the fruit of something much bigger,' Ada told him. 'Not a lot of people know that.' There was Tristan's house in front of them. 'Here we are,' she said.

'Here we are,' said Tristan.

And on to Judy's. To pick up Pepper, who had begged not to come to that wretched place with the bad food.

Ada had paced. Picked up the phone and put it down again. Picked it up once more. In the end she dialled quickly and Judy picked up.

'I've got your dish here,' Ada said. 'From the casserole.'

There was a pause. 'That was a plastic dish,' Judy said. 'You can keep that, or throw it away.' She tapped the phone to clear the static.

'I think the static's on my phone,' Ada said. Both of them tapping like they were exchanging a secret code. In the end Ada had just blurted it out. 'Can I ask you a favour?' she said.

She turned up the steep track and parked outside the barns. No idea how Pepper would be; the scene in the cafe hadn't been pretty. And another incident lingered in her mind: Pepper pretending to one babysitter that she was allergic to milk and her heart was about to stop. The poor girl ringing in tears saying Pepper was lying on the floor and wouldn't move.

The corrugated roofs reflected a sliver of moon. The yard was strewn with husks of cars. The smell of silage and pigs and manure. The kitchen window threw out orange light. Ada hovered outside, looking in, until Robbie glanced up from the sink and saw her.

The kitchen was full of the same bright clutter she remembered from Judy's bedroom – now free to reign over a whole house. A blue dresser stuffed with recipe books and manuals: how to cook pasta, how to repair a washing machine. Four knitted hens and a bowl of buttons and nails. Woven baskets. China ornaments. Geraniums. Rag rugs, multicoloured and fraying at the edges. Jars crammed with dried flowers and bits of oily machinery.

'Look what I did,' Pepper said. There was a sheet of cardboard on the table with dried pasta shapes stuck to it. 'It's you.' A ghoulish and distorted face, one eye falling off, a mass of pasta curls. Choose green spirals for the most flattering representation of your mother's teeth.

'I think she captured something,' Judy said. She switched on the kettle and the kitchen filled with steam. 'We weren't sure what to do, then I remembered us making those pasta things.'

Pepper had stopped doing pasta pictures when she was four, but Ada didn't tell Judy that. She squeezed Pepper's clammy hand – she must have been fighting to stay awake for hours.

Robbie stayed by the sink and ducked his head towards Ada, wrists scalded from the hot water. A few more creases across his face, more weight around his belly.

'Robbie said I could help check the animals,' Pepper said. 'Didn't you?'

Robbie swept his arm over tired eyes. 'I did indeed,' he said. They went outside. A gate creaked, their hushed voices moving from barn to barn. 'Why is that cow sleeping?' they heard Pepper ask.

'She's a funny thing,' Judy said. She gave Ada a mug of hot gingery stuff. Sat down, then got up again and came back with a bottle of whisky. She poured some into both mugs. 'Robbie won't let you take her back. He goes crazy over anything small. I almost have to prise the newborn animals off him.' She stopped and looked down at her hands. 'The daft fool.'

They both blew on their drinks. Ada sipped and coughed. 'I'm not used to this any more,' she said.

Judy took a drink. 'Me neither.' They both shifted on their seats. The TV flickered blue on the walls. There was an aerial photograph of the farm by the door – the farmhouse tiny among the patchwork of green and yellow fields.

'Jake Trewin,' Ada said. 'I saw him at the pub, a few days ago.'

Judy raised her eyebrow. 'Let me guess – he asked you out to his new truck.'

'I almost went at first. I thought he just wanted to show me his new truck.'

Judy choked on her drink. 'That truck's ten years old,' she said. She coughed again then glanced at Ada. 'You should have gone. Asked to see his marbles.'

The shelves in the oven pinged as they cooled down.

'You're probably the first woman he's seen in weeks who's under forty,' Judy said.

Ada tore at her ragged fingernails. Vowed once again to stop, then tore at another piece. 'Not much under forty.'

'God, don't say things like that,' Judy said. 'Five and a half years is a long time. We could do a lot in five and a half years. We could probably tunnel through a prison wall or something.'

'Or learn to play the harp,' Ada said.

'Ha. I was at the optician's the other day and she said to me, Judy, you have a deficient blink. You're going to need to practise blinking eight times a day. And I said: I have to practise *blinking*? There go my dreams of learning Mandarin. And then I cried.'

Ada leaned back against a knitted green cushion. The TV flickered pictures of a rocket going into space. 'You and Robbie,' she said.

'What about it?' Judy said. 'What I want to hear about is you, off gallivanting.'

Since when did Judy say things like off gallivanting? Ada thought about it; a few fleeting relationships, a few awkward situations with people at work. All messy, all things to extricate herself from. 'I went out with someone from work. He talked about his wife the whole night. How she liked to rake leaves. It relaxed her. He talked about leaves a lot. I told him to go home and work it out.' Ada picked at the edge of the cushion. 'I hate raking leaves. They always get impaled.'

'Maybe that's what she found relaxing,' Judy said. She traced the lines on her hand as if she was reading her own palm. Outside, a shed door banged and a cow groaned. Judy sat up, listening. 'One of them's ill at the moment,' she said. Her face was suddenly creased and tired.

'Are you sure you—' Ada said, but then the front door opened and Pepper and Robbie were in the hall stamping off their boots, Pepper saying that she would pay him seventy-five pounds for that beautiful horse with the limp and the punky hair.

Ada glugged down the last of her drink and stood, slightly woozy. Saw Judy do the same. 'We're not used to this,' Ada said.

'No,' Judy said. She sighed deeply, like a pair of bellows. 'We're not.'

'Come here Cooptin Schmooptin,' Pepper said. 'Come here my cherry.' The cat stared at her then jumped onto the windowsill and mewled. 'Get down!' Pepper said. 'Get over here.' She picked him up and he thrashed at her.

'Christ, be careful,' Ada said. 'His claws were really close to your face.'

'Sit on my lap Captain,' Pepper said. She sat down and patted her legs.

'Maybe he should just go out,' Ada said. Dreading telling Pepper they wouldn't be able to take him with them. Thank God she'd got bored of the cameras already.

'Cats are supposed to sit on people's laps,' Pepper said. She thumped her legs.

'He's not used to it,' Ada told her. The cat was a stray her mother had found and taken in. She'd ignored him most of the time, let him come and go as he wanted. There was a feral look about him – his embattled tail, bite marks on his ears that had healed to hard ridges. Something desperate in his eyes.

Pepper thumped harder on her legs. Ada went over and held her fists, rubbing her thumb over until they relaxed.

The cat jumped back onto the windowsill.

A few days later someone rapped their knuckles against the door just as Ada was taking a blackened tart out of the oven – she'd tried to improvise custard but it had gone tits up – burnt on top and sloppy in the middle.

When she opened the door, frosty air wafted in, acrid smoke wafted out. There was a man on the front steps. 'I've come to look at the house,' he said. He had a drooping face and a small, worried mouth. Short, thick hair, cut so evenly it looked like a new carpet. He was wearing a sweatshirt that said *my brother went on holiday and all he bought me was this lousy sweatshirt.* 'I'm Ray, spoke to you on the phone.' He stuck out his hand, which was pale and very cold, a dirty silver ring on one finger.

Ada tried to sweep the smoke out of the doorway. If she'd known he was coming she would have made bread. Wasn't it bread that was meant to sell a house? Or was it apple pie? Definitely not scorched and raw eggs. The smoke alarm started screeching and she took the battery out. 'I meant to test this anyway,' she said and was startled when Ray barked out a wheezy laugh.

They went into the kitchen. There was silt all over the floor again, a pool of water under the sink. She suddenly realised how poky and cluttered it was – Ray had to bow his head to look out of the window.

'You've got a nice outlook,' he said. 'Trees and all that, people like trees.' His shoes were pointy and polished, as if they were part of a completely different outfit. 'It's not the prettiest building out of context, but people like water. Not me personally, although I have to drink about two litres a day.' He ran his hands over the wall, glancing at the pictures.

'He hasn't taken his shoes off,' Pepper said. She hung behind Ada's legs, almost tripping her up.

'It doesn't matter,' Ada said. She threw a tea towel over the cake, kicked something sticky and grim under the table, maybe a hairball the cat had left.

'You can't live here if you don't like water.' Pepper crossed her arms.

Ray kept his hand on the wall. 'I wouldn't live here myself,' he said. He squatted down and looked at a brown mark near the skirting. 'Surprised if this place hasn't flooded in the past. It'll whack up insurance I suppose.'

'I don't think it's flooded,' Ada said. She heard a noise on the stairs, like someone stumbling, but when she glanced round the door there was nothing there.

'Be surprised if it hadn't,' Ray said.

'But who will live here?' Pepper asked.

In the living room, Ray went straight over to the stove. 'This just for heating in here?' He straightened the logs with his foot.

Before Ada could answer, Pepper jumped in. 'There has to be a fire all the time. Otherwise you get freezing water and the radiators don't get hot.'

'It's not as bad as it looks,' Ada said. She explained how the back boiler worked; then shook her head at Pepper and swiped at her to make her go away. Pepper slunk back but didn't leave the room.

'You could put that in a museum,' Ray said. An ember flared on the carpet and went out.

Round the rest of the rooms downstairs. Ray giving out sidelong looks, the skin between his eyebrows puckering like tacked cloth. A heavy feeling in Ada's ribs with each step. How little she'd actually done – she could see it now. The house a wreck and still her mother everywhere: overflowing boxes, hoards of photos, her coats and boots waiting by the door.

Halfway up the stairs, Ray slipped and grabbed at the handrail, a low yelp in the back of his throat. He palmed his bristly hair. Stood looking out of the upstairs window for a long time before he turned round.

Ada started to speak, stopped, tried again. How to describe the particulars of the place? The way the wind bawled through the loose windows, the smell of soot and smoke from the chimney, the continuous whump of the river, like a heartbeat. 'There's three bedrooms,' she said.

Ray nodded and glanced into each room but didn't go in. In the bathroom, Pepper had been for a pee and hadn't flushed. The lid left up and the bowl bright yellow. Pepper sniggered.

Ada clenched her hands. Hot and panicked as a trapped moth. 'It's messier than I would have liked,' she said. 'But if I just had some more time.' Imagined a lifebelt on choppy water, fingers punting it away instead of gripping on.

Ray nodded. 'Not sure it's exactly what I had in mind,' he said. He kept staring at the toilet until Ada went in and closed the lid. 'I'm not sure it's exactly what I had in mind,' he said again. His voice flatter, like a battery losing charge. He went slowly down the stairs and stopped at the bottom to straighten a tilted frame. 'Nice picture,' he said. He plucked at the neck of his sweatshirt as if searching for a collar to turn up against the cold.

Ada slumped against the closed door. Less than ten minutes had passed. She listened to Ray's car door thump and the engine start up. Behind her, she heard footsteps clumping up the stairs, a rattly cough and then the creak of someone sitting down on a bed. Her mother's old bedroom; Pepper messing around in there again. The bedsprings screeched. Ada ran upstairs and opened the door hard, anger suddenly coursing through her. 'Why were you being such a—' she said. But the room was empty, just a thin edging of frost around the window, and a crumpled dent in the mattress as if someone had just got up and left.

A bath. She needed a boiling bath filled to the brim. Sickly smelling bubbles, skin stained red with heat. She lay back in the water, dunked her head under into the thunderous quiet. When she came back up, Pepper was there, undressed and covered in goosebumps. She slipped in, her toes digging into Ada's thighs.

This had always been their routine, ever since Pepper had been a baby: red-faced and howling and needing soothing. When Ada was so exhausted she didn't know what else to do, when her eardrums had felt like they were about to split, and the smell of milk and sick and dirty plates was too much to bear.

Pepper splashed water up the wall. Gurgled a watery song.

Their skin wavered – pale green and warped. Sheets of steam rose up. Ada wanted to stretch her legs out and close her eyes. Pepper asked her something but she pretended not to hear. She dunked back under and water pressed into her ears like hands. No sound except her heart clattering, the water humming, the pipes clanking and shifting through the house.

17

BACK IN THE HOUSE and her nerves as brittle as the frost. Knees crunching, aching teeth. Ice inside the letterbox, ice under her nails. But she was definitely in this time. Clinging onto the frost on the grass, on the windows, where the river couldn't jostle her about. And her thoughts easier to get a grip on; not swilling around so much, a kind of grainy edge to them and everything suddenly much quieter, much stiller, as if the clapper in a clanging bell had been pinched between two fingers.

Pearl listened. A bed creaked upstairs. 'Who's there?' she said. She went through the hall, paused for a moment at the stairs and looked up at them. All that time wasted being scared of driving, of poisonous fumes from the fire, and in the end it was stairs. She shook her head – no point dwelling on all that now.

She made her way slowly down into the study, then went straight over to the desk and opened the top drawer. Where was it, where was it . . . There. An envelope with photographs inside. She fumbled through, her fingers white and stiff; dropped them and watched as they scattered over the floor. A day's worth of pictures. The light shifting from dawn to twilight. Nothing extraordinary, hardly any birds in them, but the ones she'd kept separate, the ones she used to look through from time to time.

She had been up early as usual. Boots on, coat buttoned up to the chin. February giving over to March. Wind bristling, huddling snowdrops, water still grey and stunned from the cold. She spent a long time finding the right spot – the correct angle of light, complicated colours, something to frame the shots with in the background. Then she set up the tripod, selected a lens, attached it and set the aperture and focus. And then waited. And waited. She blew on her fingers and stamped her feet. Took a few shots of the rusty sky reflected on the water, another of crusty lichen. Blew on her fingers again. The day billowing out in front of her like a pegged sheet.

Why did she do it? After all it was always a trial, what with the cold in winter that made her face so stiff. Or clouds of midges in summer, the devils biting her wrists and eyelids. Rain wrecking everything. Wind knocking the tripod over. Difficult to go for a piss without at least some of it trickling down her leg in the hurry to get it over with before some walker came along.

But she knew why. She could remember exactly why, even now. For the way that time seemed to slow down and stretch, measured in the river's ripples rather than by clocks and mealtimes. For the invisibility. For the hush. To forget. To make some sort of record – but of what she wasn't sure exactly. To notice things she wouldn't otherwise have noticed: dragonflies hunting, the patterns of light, the specific way that water poured over a dipper's back. There was that thing she had read once: would a tree falling in a wood make a sound if there was no one there to hear it? She used to turn that over in her mind, felt that somehow it related to her. But always ended up irked because Christ, there was no knowing one way or the other was there?

She had a picture in front of her now, on the floor of the study. A wren at the edge of the shot, scurrying into the bank. That had been taken mid-morning. The wren had darted out and she'd snapped it. A small moment, worth all those hours of waiting.

At midday she'd eaten a tin of baby potatoes, another of sliced pears.

And then there was a noise behind her and someone came through the long grass making a racket. Human sounds always seemed harsher after a few hours by herself – the croaky breathing and rustle of clothes. 'Have you seen my dog?' the man had said. He was wearing those shiny waterproofs that walkers wore, and a grey knitted hat pulled down to his eyes.

'No,' Pearl told him. She stared through the lens, waiting for him to go away.

'She ran over this way,' he said. He looked down into the water. Called out the dog's name, which was something stupid like Trudy or Rebecca. 'She's got an infection in her leg.' He paced up and down the bank, his breathing panicked.

Pearl looked up from the camera. Resigned to it now. She stumped up the bank and towards the trees to look for it there.

It took an hour, a precious hour. The light changing. She heard a kingfisher flying down the river – it would have gone straight past the camera. She circled a bramble thicket and there was the wretched dog sniffing the ground. Pearl stiffened as it loped up to her and wiped its nose on her leg. Had never trusted the things, they moved too fast, impossible to know what they were thinking. 'OK,' she said. 'You have to come here now.' The dog didn't follow her. She hesitated then felt for a collar and ended up pulling the thing back the whole way. Said, 'Here you are then,' and thrust it at the man. But he kept saying thank you, thank you, as if she'd done something worth mentioning and in the end she'd had to mumble something about the light and move herself upriver out of the way.

The last few shots showed the afternoon seeping away; the sky turning the dark blue of costly ink. A bright leaf like a star, a bedraggled feather. There had been a heron, she remembered that clearly, standing by the bank for almost an hour. But she'd given up taking pictures of herons a long time ago. None of them ever came out right. Herons hardly ever moved – there was always too much time. She'd get in close and adjust the settings, then reframe the shot, readjust the settings, trying to capture it perfectly. But the pictures always came out blurred or tilted or with her own shadow sprawled across them.

There was a noise in the house. Pearl looked up from the photographs. Footsteps. A floorboard creaked. She stayed very still. Then footsteps again, on the stairs this time. Pearl got up very slowly. 'Who is it?' she said. She stood in the doorway and looked out, just glimpsed something moving away down the hall. Her hands clenched and bits of frost dropped to the floor.

She followed. Down the hall and towards the living room. Looked through the doorway. Saw the tattered rugs, the mildewed sofa. Brown stains on the walls like the sepia on old maps. That terrible purple lamp – what had she been thinking? And the table with its legs practically sawn off. Pearl stepped into the room. The cat was curled up on the chair like a threadbare cushion. His ears twitched. He opened one eye and stood up, back arching, then jumped down and stalked straight past her. Not even a glance, the disloyal sod.

There was someone kneeling in front of the fire. A woman. She opened the stove door and poked at the embers. Smell of soot and wood smoke. Pearl moved a little closer. Her clothes steamed in the warm. Frost melted off her boots and her hands. Found herself scowling at the fire like at an old enemy. It had always been her responsibility to keep the fire going, to tend it so that there was enough heating and hot water. It was a burden but at least it was something she could do, something to show that she . . . yes, she had kept the house warm at least.

She watched as the woman leaned over the fire. Caught the profile of her face. It was funny, if she squinted the face reminded her of something. It was a lovely face, round and smooth and pale. Two bits of mottled pink high on each side. A darker scatter of freckles. What was it? Something familiar. Pearl dredged back . . . it was before all those years by herself, before all that . . .

The woman turned and blinked. The poker gripped in her hand. A log slipped in the fire and flung sparks against the glass.

'You're back then,' Pearl said.

Because that was it. Those photographs. That was the day Ada had left. Pearl had finished up just as it was getting dark, packed the camera back in the case and walked home, holding the tripod over her shoulder like a rifle. Opened the front door and heard Ada upstairs, opening her wardrobe, brushing her teeth, some kind of urgency about it. A packed bag at the bottom of the stairs.

She'd put the tripod down and called up that she was back. 'Why is there a bag down here?' she said.

'I'm leaving today, remember?' Ada called down. 'I told you. That job came up. Temporary, six months.'

Pearl went into her study and sat at her desk, listening. A cold feeling beginning to spread up from her feet. She had forgotten the date, thought that it was a week, maybe two weeks, in the future. Imagined some dreary town far away. She got up and listened by the door, but there was no sound upstairs. She went slowly up the steps and out into the hall. The front door was open and the bag had gone. She felt weak and leaned against the wall. Thought, well, that's that. Thought, I was eating tinned potatoes. Felt in her pocket and touched the button that she kept there, for luck or comfort or just out of habit. Her hands too warm and then too cold.

Ada came back in, cheeks crimson with the cold; holding a scarf she'd left in the car. 'Don't leave the door open,' Pearl told her. 'All the heat will go out.' She went upstairs and helped carry down the heaviest bag, offered a lift to where the bus stopped on the top road.

'Judy's picking me up,' Ada said.

There was nothing to do but carry the last bag down and put it with the others at the bottom of the stairs.

The clock ticked very loudly.

'What are you going to do?' Ada asked. 'This evening?' She crouched down and fiddled with the zip on her bag.

Pearl shrugged. 'I've got a new batch of prints to go through,' she said. But why did she say that, when she knew she was just going to sit in the house watching it get dark?

Ada nodded. She looked towards the door. 'I made you something,' she said. 'It's in the oven.' She was tall, her hips just beginning to widen, tangled hair falling across her eyes. Her daughter, lingering there in the hallway. Pearl felt shrunken and tired, a sort of dryness in her skin that wasn't just from spending too long out in the cold wind. She thought of all the months, probably years, that Ada had spent planning this: her escape. Circling jobs and flats in newspapers, sending out applications. Waiting by the door to catch the replies as they were posted through. Pearl saying nothing, enduring Ada's desperation to avoid getting stuck in the place.

Minutes passed. The smell of cooking from the kitchen: slices of potato and onion and apple just the way Pearl liked it. And it had been wonderful; when she ate it later it was wonderful. She had eaten the whole thing.

A car beeped outside and Ada jumped but didn't turn round. She leaned down towards Pearl, brushed against her dry cheek. Pearl could feel Ada's heart racing, or maybe it was her own.

'See you soon, OK?' Ada said.

Still they waited. The cold draught. The car idling outside the door. Pearl slipped a rolled-up twenty inside Ada's bag. Then opened the door because if she didn't no one would. Said what she said when she was setting up a picture, when the image wasn't aligned, when she just needed to refocus the thing so that she could see it properly. 'There you go then. There you go.' Watched the closed door for a long time.

18

ADA STAYED KNEELING IN front of the fire. The wood sputtered and condensation streamed down the glass.

'It's going to go out,' her mother said.

'I know how to do it.' She fed in another piece of wood, which charred at the edges like overdone bread.

'You'll smother it,' her mother said. She came closer and her clothes hissed. The sound of stones clacking together, a frosty chill. Some kind of restless energy, as if water was banking up before spilling over.

Ada dropped the poker and it clattered on the hearth. Picked it up and dropped it again. Fed in more kindling. The flames rose tentatively, licking at her fingers. She closed the stove door. Watched the flames gutter and bend before she turned round.

Her mother was small and bedraggled, a slight hump curving the top of her back. Thinner hair, the same dirty white as weathered paint. The damp curling it into feathery clumps. Deep lines around her mouth; her skin translucent, almost blue – pulled taut over her cheeks but folding and puckering under her jaw. Her jumper was covered in frost, her trousers dank and clinging to her thin legs. And her hands: gaunt and knotty with swollen knuckles. The bones showing through and stiff like cables. Her eyes were small and fierce as always.

She took a step closer and the fire sizzled. 'I suppose it'll be up to me to sort this out,' she said.

Ada turned back to the stove. 'I'm doing it,' she said.

'Christ, I never thought I'd have to see the bloody thing again,' her mother said. Her voice was hoarse and she coughed a rattly, watery cough. She was close behind Ada now, her knees crunching when she moved, specks of frost on the carpet.

Ada clenched her hands. 'Neither did I,' she said.

Then, a screaming clamour. The front door slammed open and Pepper shouted, 'Stop it. Get back here.' Her voice was frenzied. Ada got up and ran through the house. Turned back to look but there was no one behind her. The cat rushed past with something in its mouth, galloping so fast it snorted. A small bird, still flapping. The cat dropped the bird on the kitchen floor and it lay there trembling.

Pepper stood over the bird, her coat and boots on over pyjamas. When the cat tried to get near it she hissed and bared her teeth. 'It's a thrush,' she said. 'Look at its speckles.'

The bird arched one of its wings. Its feathers were matted together, browns and yellows tinged with cream. Its chest fluttered up and down. Pepper stroked it with her thumb. 'You'll be OK,' she said. She looked up at Ada. 'It'll be OK,' she said.

'It'll be just fine,' Ada said. She had got up too fast, felt faint and swaying.

'*Just* fine?' Pepper said. '*Just* fine?' The bird tried to lift itself up and she let out a howl and ran out of the room. The front door slammed shut.

The cat skulked around, low yowls in its throat. Stalking on the tips of his paws. He didn't take his eyes off the bird. Ada grabbed him round the middle and he fought to get away, wriggling his hips and back legs and kicking out. But she managed to get him pinned against her knees and she carried him through the hall. Had to take one hand away to get the front door open and he twisted and caught her leg with his claw. Freezing air came in, the grass brittle with frost. She shoved the cat out, put her foot in the way and closed the door before he could run back in. He whined and paced on the other side.

She went back into the kitchen. Her mother was there, watching the bird. Which was now up and flapping, lunging towards the sink, knocking into plates and mugs. 'You don't know what's happened, do you?' Pearl said to it. 'Inexperienced. Thinking of berries and not paying enough attention.'

The bird hauled itself up towards the shelves, wings flapping but its body listing. Ada moved slowly towards it and reached up to open the window, but just as she did, the cat jumped onto the windowsill outside and pressed himself against the glass. The bird knocked off a cup and it shattered on the floor.

Ada banged on the window. 'Get down,' she said to the cat. 'Piss off.'

'Let the bird out,' her mother said. 'There's nothing you can do about it now.'

The bird bumped against the window. Ada watched it. She watched the cat waiting. She went back to the front door and opened it and called the cat. Then ran back and flung open the window and nudged the bird out just as the cat bolted into the kitchen. She slammed the window shut.

The room was strewn with feathers and bird shit and bits of broken cup; a chair on its back that Pepper had knocked over. The cat growling and pacing. Cracks all over the walls, peeling paint. Damp newspapers and grit everywhere, half-filled boxes, her mother lingering at the edge of the room, her clothes rustling like the river lapping at leaves.

Ada leaned against the table and closed her eyes. 'What am I supposed to do?' she said.

Her mother picked a small stone out from between her teeth. 'Just get on with it, I suppose,' she said. She dropped the stone on the floor. 'You should clear up all this crap for a start.'

Ada went outside to look for Pepper. Found her sitting cross-legged on the shed roof, face stony and blotched.

'He didn't mean to do it,' Ada said. 'It's what cats do sometimes.' The sky was orange in the distance, the edges seeping into pale grey. A band of violet ridges running through it like furrows in a field.

Pepper stared straight ahead. 'He did mean to,' she said. 'I chased him away.' Her voice was flat and hollow, not even anger in it.

'The bird flew off,' Ada told her. 'It was OK.'

Pepper shook her head. 'It's over there,' she said.

Ada looked and saw a sad bundle of feathers on the ground. Shock, she guessed, more than anything else. 'Come inside. It's really cold out here.'

Pepper ran her finger over splintering wood. 'I hope Captain never comes back,' she said.

'Come down, OK? I'm going to make breakfast.' Ada walked back towards the house, listening for Pepper scrambling down off the roof, but when she got to the front steps and turned round, Pepper hadn't moved.

She filled the kettle and waited by the kitchen window. Pepper had done this before but she always came down after about half an hour – too cold or too hungry to stay outside for long. But an hour passed. The tinge of orange in the sky disappeared. Pallid clouds moved in. The water in the kettle cooled down. Ada made a sandwich and took it out to Pepper and held it up to her. 'Come inside and eat this,' she said. When Pepper shook her head, she left it on the edge of the roof.

Another hour went by. The clouds thickened. The frost slowly disappeared. The sandwich stayed on the plate. Ada stood by the window. The power snapped on and off. She leaned against the sink and closed her eyes. A sulphurous smell came up from the plughole. She pulled open the cupboard, got out the bleach and emptied half the bottle into the sink. Then she strode out of the door and over to the shed.

Pepper was shivering. 'Come down,' Ada said. She put her foot onto a wooden slat and hauled herself up so she was looking Pepper in the eye. 'Now.'

Pepper shook her head. 'I'm never coming down.'

Ada grabbed Pepper's arms and pulled her forward until she slid off the roof and onto Ada's chest, almost knocking the breath out of her; but she held onto Pepper's stiff and frozen body and lugged her into the house and up into her bedroom. Pepper stayed silent and rigid while Ada put more layers on her, wrapped her in a blanket and pressed a hot-water bottle onto her chest. She allowed a couple of mouthfuls of hot sweet milk to go down her throat before clamping her mouth shut, lying down on her bed and turning to face the wall.

*

The afternoon passed slowly. Pepper didn't come back downstairs. Ada picked at the cold sandwich and watched it get dark. She straightened the chairs and swept up the bits of broken plate. Frost grew back over the windows. She went to bed early, exhausted, but didn't sleep. The camp bed sagged and a spring snapped, making the whole frame lurch. She got up and checked on Pepper. She was asleep. Ada wrapped her up tighter and felt her chest to check she was warm. An owl called out. A branch scraped against the window. She lay back down. Couldn't get warm herself. She heard footsteps as her mother made her way around the house. Cursing and muttering, her cough like a troubled engine. The pipes pinged. The stairs creaked slowly, then the sound of something slipping, a faint cry, a dull thud. Then another cough from a different part of the house. Ada pulled the covers tighter.

It didn't seem like morning was ever going to come but at some point there was a shift. A glimmer of grey, which spread like the sky was being scrubbed. Ada's breath floated above the bed. Even the trees were shivering. As she watched, a distant flare of cerise appeared in the distance, like a pot of ink had tipped over.

The river boomed. She was suddenly starving. Gut-achingly starving; her insides hollow and cold. When she stood up her legs shook.

The kitchen was still strewn with matted feathers. She looked in the cupboards and the fridge but there was nothing she wanted to eat. A parched and papery onion. A tub of cream cheese floating in its own liquid. That jar of floury stuff with brown liquid on top, what was that? She took it out of the fridge and left it on the side to throw away. A few potatoes, a bowl of apples. Hardly any milk. All she had was half a loaf of stale bread. She took out a frying pan and lit the gas underneath it.

When the pan was hot, she cut a fat slice of butter, slid it off the knife and into the pan, where it spread out and sizzled. The kitchen filled with the smell of hot butter. Then she put in thick triangles of bread and fried them until they were golden on both sides, sprinkled on handfuls of sugar and let it cook to a crust. The windows steamed up and dripped. She ate the hot bread straight out of the pan, licking her fingers to get all the sugar.

19

THE BITTER THOUGHTS WERE like a balloon that got bigger and bigger but didn't burst. Pepper dwelled on them, picked at them, turned them over and over.

She went outside and looked at the bird. Something had dragged it down the grass to the edge of the field. One eye was open. Still the rich colours. It seemed to her that the bird was just the same as it had been before the cat had caught it. She crouched down and touched it. It was stiff as old twine. The feathers rumpled in the wind, which was raw and turned her fingers as stiff as the bird.

'I'm surprised nothing's taken that yet,' the old woman said. Pepper hadn't even heard her coming.

'The cat killed it,' Pepper said. She sucked at the welts on her hand, itchy and sore from Captain's claws.

'What did you expect? All cats are bastards like that.'

Pepper smoothed down one of the bird's tufting feathers. 'He wasn't meant to be,' she said. He was supposed to be her cat. She had tried to stroke him, and whisper things in his ear, and she'd filled his bowl so full it had spilled over.

The woman studied the bird. 'A buzzard will carry it off.'

'A buzzard?' Pepper said. 'A buzzard?' Her eyes and nose streamed in the raw cold. 'A buzzard?' she said one more time, and let out a harsh, barky laugh that startled even herself.

'What's the matter with you?' the woman said. She took a step forward and frost chipped off her boots. She looked windswept and messy and a wet tissue fell out of her sleeve and blew away into the river.

Pepper didn't answer. She picked the bird up in two hands and held it.

'For Chrissakes,' the woman said. 'If you're going to be like that you'll probably have to bury it.'

Pepper held the bird carefully. It was very cold. 'I think you're right,' she said. She went over to the barn, found a spade and dragged it back. It was heavy and the metal was freezing and banged against her heels.

'I wouldn't bother if I were you,' the woman said.

Pepper lifted the spade and tried to dig it into the ground. But the ground was hard and cold and full of stones. She scraped at the surface but couldn't get the spade to bite into it. 'It's bloody impossible,' she said.

'Put your foot on it and push,' the woman said. The cold air had turned her hair into a silvery web and there were droplets on her eyebrows.

'That's what I am doing,' Pepper said. Her fingers were red and purple. She scraped some more and it sounded like grinding teeth. She lifted and dug down, felt a sharp jolt in her shoulder, lifted and dug down again and pushed at it with her foot, but her foot slipped off and she cracked her knee against the spade. The spade fell on the ground.

For a moment she just stood and looked at it.

'It would be a good meal for the buzzard, feed it up for winter,' the woman said. 'And they'll be more thrushes in the spring – they nest in that hedge.'

'I won't be here in the spring,' Pepper said as she stomped away, leaving the muddy spade and the bird on the grass.

And every day the house got worse. Ice inside the windows like bumpy glass. Books curled and smelled like wet towels, doors swelled up and didn't shut properly.

Someone came to fix the leak in the hall but the next day it leaked in a different place.

The power chuntered. The radiators screeched and were only hot halfway up. And the worst thing: something went wrong with the cooker so that it wouldn't light.

'Why is this happening?' Pepper said. She had started wearing two jumpers and a hat indoors, which made her skin itch. She scratched her arms until they bled. She looked at the tins of beans and soup on the shelf, tried not to imagine eating them cold.

'There's gas left in the bottles,' her mother said, tipping them to one side. 'I can hear it.' There were tired circles under her eyes. When a door creaked in the draught she spun round as if she expected to see someone there.

Pepper ate slice after slice of bread until her stomach bloated and gurgled. She was supposed to stay by the fire but instead she stirred the saucepan of leaked water until it spilled, picked at rust on pipes, pushed her fingers into spongy plaster. The new paint wouldn't dry properly and when she leaned against walls it left smears down her back.

Judy came over and looked at the cooker. She touched the top of Pepper's head and her hands smelled like medicine because of the cream she rubbed in – to stop her skin cracking, she said. Pepper thought about the silver necklace in her mother's bedroom; she'd seen the other half in a drawer in Judy's house.

She sat on the kitchen floor, opened a cupboard and took out the little spice bottles. Something she used to do a lot. She opened each one and breathed in the familiar smells, dusty and exotic: the orange one like powdery sand, the spicy one that smelled of biscuits.

Her mother and Judy clanged the gas bottles and laughed quietly. Her mother said that people kept telling her Pepper should be in school. Her voice sounded different with Judy, something lighter in it, not so tired.

Pepper tipped out the balls of nutmeg and rolled them around her hand. Dug into her palm with the sharp black cloves.

On Saturday morning there was a soft knock at the door and it was Petey. Dressed in a blue and purple sweatshirt, a scarf covered with snowmen. A smart wool coat that hung off his shoulders and down past his knees. 'I thought I should invite you to play,' he said. He pushed his glasses up his nose with one finger.

Pepper stood behind the door and made it swing open and shut. 'Why?' she said.

Petey blinked and looked up at her from the bottom step, his body a dense, rigid square. 'I thought I better invite you,' he said.

Pepper stopped swinging the door. 'What would we do?' She could hear her mother doing something with the radiators, the metal pranging, the sound of air gushing out of them. Looked out at the freezing mist and frost – nothing but bare, spidery trees; the river; wet, wet grass.

Petey frowned and then turned and gestured into the distance. 'The usual things,' he said. 'The usual things people do.' He hunched his shoulders and started to walk back up the drive.

Pepper had no idea what those things were. She watched him for a second, then called into the house: 'I'm going outside.' Heard her mother say don't go too far, as she pushed the door closed and ran to catch up with Petey.

They walked along the road, staying on the verge. The grass was very long and there were lots of tall, brittle stalks sticking up. There was a clump of blackberries with furry mould all over them and a fat spider with gold stripes. Sometimes Petey would stop and crouch down and poke at something in the grass and sometimes he would find something in the hedge and put it in his pocket.

'What are you doing?' Pepper said.

'Collecting,' Petey said. He picked something up and put it in his pocket but didn't show Pepper what it was.

She picked at the dry skin around her mouth. 'Why are you?' she said.

Petey put his hand deeper in his pocket. Pepper followed behind, stopping when he stopped. She watched him carefully, the red marks his glasses made behind his ears, the clean nails on his fingers. He smelled like onions and soap. He was wearing grey school trousers and school shoes, which made her feel sick. She tried to see what he'd found. Her glove caught on a sharp twig and it ripped a hole. She clenched her hands. 'I won't be here much longer,' she said.

Petey turned up a lane with grass down the middle. He sniffed.

'It's not what I expected,' Pepper said. Her voice sounded very loud in the cold air.

Up ahead the road widened and there was a group of small houses that all looked the same, with patches of muddy grass and cars parked outside. Satellite dishes, aerials, washing drooping out on the lines. At the front, there was a set of rusty swings and a seesaw. Petey sniffed again. 'What did you expect?' he said. He chose a swing and sat on it but didn't swing.

Pepper sat on the swing next to him. She pushed herself high up into the air. Higher and higher, so that the frame creaked. 'What did I expect?' she said. But she just carried on swinging and couldn't answer.

It looked like there were bits of grit and glass stuck all over the houses. One of the doors opened and a man came out, whistling. He looked over at them and then called out: 'Alright kid. How's it going down at the house?' It was Ray, the man who had come over to see if he wanted to buy it.

Pepper slowed down on the swing. Her mouth felt dry, her hands clammy on the chains. 'People keep saying they want to have a holiday there,' she said. That's what Howard had told her Ray wanted it for.

'Really?' Ray said.

'Yes,' Pepper told him. 'You would be silly not to buy it probably.'

'Is that right?' Ray said. He got into his car and music blared out. He started the engine and pulled out onto the road.

Petey sat very still and upright on his swing. 'It would be a good place for a holiday,' he said.

'That's what I told him,' Pepper said. She could smell the swing's sharp, rusty metal.

'I would like to go there on holiday,' Petey said. 'Right down by the river.' He looked up at the window of the closest house and there was Clapper. They nodded to one another. Clapper was holding a mug of tea and sipping, the TV flickering behind him.

'You live here anyway,' Pepper said.

But Petey was looking dreamily upwards. 'Right by the water,' he said. 'Then I could look out of the window and see fish whenever I wanted.'

Pepper skidded her foot on the gravel so that she stopped swinging. She leaned in close to Petey. 'Have you ever had a pet?' she said.

Petey shook his head. 'I want one.'

'Yes,' Pepper said. 'But you get a thing and you think it will sit on your lap, or come and find you, or not kill anything, or stop you feeling lonely. But it doesn't.'

'I know it,' Petey said.

Pepper sighed and tipped herself backwards on the swing. Five was too young to understand.

'I got a fishing rod,' Petey said. 'And it was meant to be the best one and it was my birthday present and my Christmas present and it broke first time. And another time I had a clown at a party and he was meant to sing songs and be funny but all he did was eat all the food and steal my grandpa's watch. And they said a night-light would help me but it keeps me awake even more.'

They both sat in silence for a while. The swing's chains rattled.

'I hate clowns,' Pepper said.

Petey nodded. He reached into his pocket and pulled out a handful of wrappers and bottle tops. Rubbish that he'd picked up off the verge. The swing creaked as he got up and put the rubbish in the bin. He went over to the seesaw and sat on it and Pepper sat on the other seat. He was heavy and she got stuck in the air. Petey got off carefully. He pushed his glasses up his nose. He started to lift his end of the seesaw so that Pepper could go up and down. 'You are very light,' he said.

There was the sound of a car and Ray drove back in. He grinned and saluted Pepper and she gripped the seat and closed her eyes and felt, in her stomach, the world lurch up and down.

20

THE DEER WAS DRAPED over the table, back legs crossed delicately. No head, skinned. Burgundy and mauve, a silver tinge. Muscle, sinew, white seams of fat.

'Howard's off sick,' Val said. Something she hadn't mentioned to Ada on the phone. 'He was talking about his chest. Can you have a heart attack without knowing it? He wasn't sure. He's drinking bicarbonate of soda, making funny breathing noises.' She gestured to the deer. 'He usually deals with this kind of thing. Do you know how to sort it?'

Ada stayed where she was. 'Maybe Howard could come in for this,' she said. She leaned against the door and breathed out slowly. Her hands clammy, stomach tense and gritty. Couldn't deal with this as well. One of the deer's legs looked broken, the bone jutting out.

'I got it cheap,' Val said. 'It's been skinned and gutted.' Something sharp and irritated about her this morning, she kept glancing at the door to the bar. 'I thought there was a book about it here somewhere.' She opened and slammed cupboards. 'Knew I should have bought that computer, I could have looked up a diagram or something.'

Ada stayed by the door. 'I can't do this,' she said. She shook her head and turned to go. But then thought about the house: the half-filled boxes, the photos she kept finding scattered over the floor, the dubious oven, the leaks, the hours she would spend waiting, listening. She looked back at the deer. It was easy to see where some of the cuts would have to be made. Under the shoulder, across the ribs, the top of the legs. She tied her apron at the back. There was a saw on the work surface she hadn't noticed before and a knife which Val started to sharpen vigorously, scraping the blade hard and fast.

'I remember Howard talking about the saddle. Do you know what the saddle is?' Val said. 'I always thought he meant it as some kind of joke, riding the deer around or something.' Someone called her from the bar. She carried on sharpening. 'That'll be the tax woman,' she said. 'Coming over to check my accounts. And you know who works in that office, who would have put them up to this? My wretched brother, that's who. As if I would fiddle them.' But she looked uneasy as she put the knife down and went out of the kitchen, leaving Ada alone with the deer.

The flesh was marbled and sleek. Ada took up the knife and stood over the table. The shoulders, she knew she had to take off the shoulders. She held one of the deer's front legs up and ran the knife below it, felt muscle and sinew, saw darker red underneath. The knife was sharp but the handle was loose and quivered as she cut. The shoulder came off in one big piece. She did the same with the other leg. She'd expected a strong reek, something awful, but the deer smelled musty, of curdled milk, and fresh too, like dried grass. 'There you go,' she said as she cut.

Now the neck. She used the knife to slice as far as she could until she hit a thick wall of bone. The knife wouldn't go through it. She glanced at the saw and back at the deer. She picked up the saw and pressed it against the bone, drew it back and then pushed forwards. Licking her teeth at the splintering, grinding noise. Moved on to the meat either side of the spine. Almost lost a finger when the saw jerked over the ribs. Gradually reducing the body down. Cutting away at it, talking softly. Not words, just small murmurs and sounds, and the sound of the knife as it slipped between meat and bone.

The tap dripped and made a small pool in the sink. No voices from the bar. The kitchen cold and quiet.

Ada turned the deer over, cut the flanks near the bone and pulled them back, like undoing a coat. Left now with the meat around the spine, two muscly back legs joined at the end. There was a grainier feel to the muscle in the leg, a lot more meat. She worked the knife and the saw and the legs were off. Then the horrible task of splitting them down the middle. Which she did as gently as possible.

The door swung open and Val barged in, got out a cheap frozen pie and stuck it in the microwave. Ink stains on her fingers, a harassed look. She saw Ada looking and shrugged. 'No one will know the difference around here.' The pie came out grey and soggy and Val slapped it on a plate with a heap of potatoes and took it out to the bar. Butting the door open with her hip. The door swung shut again.

The pieces of deer on the table were still quite big; there was probably more she could do with them. Ada looked at the neck and thought it could be cut into rough chops. Steaks from the leg; what she thought might be fillets from the meat around the spine. Hitting a sort of rhythm, slicing the meat off the bone, picking off shin meat, cutting strips from the loin.

Sweat trickled down her ribs. Her hair was damp on her forehead and she brushed it away with her shoulder. Hours had gone by. She tied up the bag of bones for Val to deal with, then found a roll of plastic bags and divided the meat up into neat packages, wrote out white labels with the date on, found an empty shelf in the freezer. Something pleasing about finishing the job and parcelling it up. A relief. She sealed the bags carefully.

Ada untied her apron and washed her hands. Blood and gristle flecked up her arms. She washed the knife and the saw and swept bits of bone and trimmings from around the table. It was early afternoon. She was meant to be doing the evening shift as well — there was enough time to go back to the house, check the gas, try and make another start on the boxes.

But when she opened the freezer, she found sliced apples and bags of peas. In the fridge there was cream, wine, butter, a few soft carrots and half a swede. Potatoes in one of the cupboards, flour, a packet of crumbling stock cubes. She unhooked the apron and put it back on.

She took out a frying pan, a roasting tray and a battered orange casserole. Sliced butter and let it sizzle, added onion, then pieces of the finer meat and cooked it until the juices ran out. Added white wine, handfuls of frozen apple. A bay leaf. Spooned the mixture into a pie dish. In another pot, she braised the tougher meat, added hot water, tomato puree, stock cubes and red wine and left it to cook into a stew.

It was dark outside. She switched on the lights. Got out a bowl and made pastry, rolled it out and covered the pie. Put it in the oven and baked it. Added chopped potatoes to the stew. Fried the bits of meat she'd picked off the bone with more onion then layered it with potatoes, plenty of butter and the cream. When it came out of the oven it was golden and bubbling.

The window steamed up. A waft of good, rich smells. But she had cooked a lot of food, used up most of what Val had spare in the kitchen. She took off her apron and wiped over her eyes. Tidied up, listening for Val. There was no noise from the bar. She cleaned out the pots and swept the floor, then swept it again.

After a while the door opened and Val came in. She looked around the kitchen at the steaming food. 'What's all this?' she said.

'I just tried something out,' Ada said. 'A few things lying around so I used them. The potatoes going soft anyway and—'

'Stop whining about it,' Val said. 'I've got a couple of men out here asking what's cooking. Realised they were starving – I told them that's what happens when you come out for a drink over dinner time to escape your family. I've got my tax woman telling me she fancies a bite herself. So I need to go and tell them what there is.'

Ada told her what she'd made. Val went back out to the bar and a moment later she was back in again. 'Four orders,' she said. 'Pie and potatoes twice. One of the potato bake things. One stew. Have we got anything green to set it off?'

There was nothing but frozen peas, but Ada mixed in some extra fried onion and butter. She arranged a portion of each dish on the plates and garnished them while Val told her to hurry the hell up before it got cold.

Ada swept the floor once more, then dried up the last of the dishes. Stuck her finger in the stew and tasted it again. It definitely needed more pepper and less wine. And the potatoes were crumbly and grey as old snow. She strained to hear anything from out at the bar. Nothing. Then Val said something and laughter went up like geese.

She stood in the middle of the kitchen. Checked the oven was off – it was. Checked the freezer door was shut – it was. Caught a whiff of the bake and it reminded her of the dish she'd left in the oven when she'd moved away – she wasn't even sure if her mother had eaten it.

It got darker and darker. She switched off the lights and put her coat on, was just about to slip out the back door to the car park when Val came in carrying four empty plates.

Val looked at her. 'One of the blokes has booked a table for tomorrow night,' she said. 'A table of six. His birthday or something. The tax woman finished her plate and said no point scrutinising the rest of the accounts.' She carried the dishes to the sink and piled them up. 'I should try some myself. See what the fuss is about.' She took a big forkful of pie. Chewed it slowly. Her lips pursing like something had irritated them. 'Come in again tomorrow,' she said eventually. 'I'll pay you a bit more for the trouble. And write down anything extra you need.'

21

TYPICAL FOR ADA TO come back now, right in the middle of winter. Not a good time – what with the roads iced up and the house freezing; difficult to get anywhere, cooped up for days, the lights clunking on and off and plunging everything into such deep darkness that it was impossible to move without clouting your hip or your shin. A fretwork of cracks on their bones probably, like maps of the long winters.

Pearl would work out the finances, which always boiled down to the same thing: not enough money for the endless supply of wood the stove needed. So, two jumpers, two pairs of trousers, tie a hot-water bottle to your stomach, don't sit still long enough for chilblains to get you between the toes. But Ada never listened. She would sit for hours under a blanket, her feet sticking out, nose numb and red. She would run a bath when the tank was low and shiver in tepid water. She would cook a pie that took so long the gas would cut out halfway through, leaving them to pick at the crust, the middle gooey and raw.

One winter, when Ada was twelve, ice took over everything. Pearl chipped it away from the windows, brushed piles of hail from the steps, knocked frost from the car's wheels. A bracelet of icicles hung from the porch roof. Ada ducked under them when she went out of the door; she had grown three inches in a few months. A new habit of tearing at her nails, a lisp when she was unsure of what she was saying. Made it hard to hear her sometimes.

And they started to mishear each other a lot. Table slipped to ladle, flour slipped to fire. Pearl went to the doctors and got them to check her ears – skulking in at fifty-seven, worried about going deaf, sitting amongst the other mothers with their soft skin and perfect eardrums. She was given drops to soften any wax. Outside, the ice thickened. She bought a bag of cheap salt for the lane which turned orange and smelled like metal. It didn't stop the ice. She scooped up a handful and threw it at Ada and Ada shrieked and threw some back. Ada said it looked like someone had peed all over the lane. Pearl said, since when has your pee been orange? Ada said, my pee has never been orange. Pearl said, so why did you say it looked like someone peed all over the lane? Ada said, I said it looks like *orangeade* all over the lane. Pearl passed a hand over her ear as if she was pushing aside a curtain. She scraped the grit up with a shovel.

For Christmas she bought Ada a yellow mixing bowl. Ada bought her a glass photo frame wrapped in tissue paper.

The next winter it rained. At first it was a relief – every day was mild, grey, wet. The sky looked like wet newspaper, water collected in footprints in the fields. The windows streamed with all the different kinds of rain: sometimes heavy and lashing, sometimes sharp and sideways, sometimes grey mizzle which draped over like a net.

Pearl repaired the porch roof, put tape over the leaking windows, found an old sandbag and put it by the front steps. She tried going out but the rain drummed against her face, soaked the camera, sent the river slopping over the best paths. So she stayed in, listening to Ada pacing around the house, the floorboards creaking as she moved from room to room. Stopping at each window and looking out, fretting that there was nothing to do, she couldn't get to Judy's, she couldn't go up to the shop, her books and shoes were going mouldy because the house was so damp. Which was true. When Pearl took up the mouldy jackdaw and danced with it around the room, Ada did something new: she laughed then tried to hide it, her lips puckering like old fruit, shielding her mouth with her hand.

One particular evening, Pearl was struggling to resize a ring, which was always a pain in the arse, the metal either over- or under-heating. Ada was in the kitchen clattering pots and bowls. Pearl started to cut into the metal. A cupboard slammed. Then another. Pearl got up and stood at the door, listening, tracing her finger over the grain in the wood. No noise from the kitchen. When she went to look, Ada was sitting at the table with an empty bowl next to her.

'What are you making?' Pearl said. Hoped it was something with raisins, she couldn't get enough of them for some reason.

'There's no ingredients,' Ada said.

Pearl looked out at the belting rain. Could hardly see the car through the smeary window. But she knew that the rain was corroding what was already corroded anyway. 'The brakes are playing up,' she said.

Ada nodded. 'The shop's still open.'

'The brakes are playing up,' Pearl said again.

Ada's fingers tapped against the empty bowl. Chink, chink, chink.

Pearl watched the rain. Her fault, after all, that they lived so bloody far from anywhere. She went and got their coats and started the car. Splashed it through a deep puddle and turned onto the road. The tarmac was slick with rain. The windscreen gushed water. She drove slowly, knew she should have stopped and turned round but she kept going. Ada was sitting very still, holding her breath round every bend. Pearl changed gear, turned a corner and swerved to avoid a deep puddle, felt the brakes slacken and not catch. Slammed them and slammed them again. The hedge reared up, branches tore at the car and they were flung sideways. The engine went quiet, the car tilted into a ditch and both of them sat there, stunned. In the hedge next to them, baffled bluebells that had come up far too early.

For Christmas she bought Ada a set of cake tins and Ada bought her a leather notebook.

The next winter there were starlings, hundreds of them, in the bare trees. Ada started sleeping until midday; she confused litres with pints and grams with ounces; she came downstairs in the night and nibbled at a block of marzipan, leaving behind small teeth marks and fingerprints.

The winter after that, the river froze. Pearl thanked Christ it wasn't more rain, but after a few weeks, the steely quiet started to get to her. It seemed like, if you rapped on anything, it would ring out like metal. The water pipes froze and they had to buy bottles of water from the shop and Mick, that greedy bastard, put the price up each week. A pipe burst and left a brown stain on the ceiling that looked like someone giving them the finger.

Pearl wanted to show Ada the frozen river. The way it creaked, the bubbles and stones trapped in the ice.

'It's too cold out there,' Ada said. She had started drinking coffee, but only if she heaped in half a pot of sugar and about a pint of milk – wouldn't listen to Pearl's advice about the benefits of having it strong and black.

'It'll only take a minute,' Pearl said. She half expected Ada to say no, but Ada put her mug down and got up. Pearl pushed past and strode on ahead, suddenly worried – what if the river didn't look as good today, or the ice had started to melt?

But the river was still ridged with ice. Clear in some places, opaque in others, like someone had huffed on a mirror. A thread of silvery glints running deep in it, and blue and grey shadows.

Pearl cleared her throat. She wanted to say something about how strange the frozen river made her feel – uneasy but also astonished at the colours the ice could make. 'Here it is then,' she said. The cold air made her voice gruff.

'Yes,' Ada said. She looked down at the water.

Since when had Ada's cheekbones jutted out like that? And why had she started plucking her eyebrows so ridiculously thin and arched? Made her look as if she was constantly startled.

'It's thick,' Pearl said. And then, because she didn't know what else to do, because she wanted to show Ada how important the ice was, how beautiful, she stepped onto it.

The ice creaked. Pearl stood very still. After a moment, Ada stepped onto the river too. The ice groaned and shifted. A bubble contracted, then sprang back. They stood there for a long time, their hands in their pockets, staring down at their feet on the ice.

She bought Ada a recipe book that she had a copy of already. Ada bought her a camera bag that was too small.

And the next winter there was a spate of burglaries. First the pub had its window jacked open and the till raided. Then Luke's place – they took his whalebone with the patterns inked on. Then the new houses by the road – each time getting closer and closer.

Pearl fixed another bolt to the door, propped a chair in front of the handle, left the poker by her bed. She lay awake, listening. Jumped at every small noise. Went down to check the bolts and then check them again. A tight feeling in her chest which carried on all winter. She learned the particular nocturnal movements of Ada: how she would sit up watching TV until the early hours; how she would sneak out of the low study window, leaving it propped open with a book so she could get back in. How she would half-wake sometimes and murmur a name that Pearl didn't recognise; how she would make hushed, urgent phone calls, talking in stifled laughs and gasps, so that, however hard Pearl listened, it sounded like a different language entirely.

She bought Ada a purple scarf with beads on that Ada wore for one day. Ada bought her a bright green belt, which Pearl wore for two.

Storms the following winter. Trees tossed from side to side like an ocean; lightning, thunder, an oak cleaved in two and burnt inside. A branch smashed tiles on the roof. Pearl went up there and nailed the tiles back down, she bought wind-up lamps for when the power was out, she got ripped off in a deal for fuses which were all duds.

She found otter tracks and tried to tell Ada about them. But Ada only glanced at the photos, didn't want to know that there must be a den somewhere and that the spraint smelled like jasmine tea. So Pearl stopped asking what Ada was cooking. She went back to eating all her food out of tins: baby potatoes, peaches, spaghetti. She developed a peculiar fondness for those tinned sardines in tomato sauce.

But it couldn't go on forever. She found an old recipe that Ada had cut out. She put a handful of flour in a jar, added honey and warm water and left the jar in her study. After a few days there were bubbles. The acidic, pissy smell changed to something warm and yeasty. She took the jar into the kitchen and scooped some of the starter out and mixed it with flour, shaping it into a loaf. It rose overnight by the fire and Pearl kneaded it and shaped it again. She turned the oven on and slid the loaf in. She went back into her study and waited for Ada to come home. Got to work on a tricky bracelet, head down, hooks and pins out. Hours passed. She smelled something, thought maybe the wind had pushed smoke down the chimney and went to check the fire. It seemed OK. The smell got stronger. The fire alarm went off. The front door opened and Ada rushed into the kitchen with her boots still on.

Pearl slid the tray out. The loaf was black and smoke curled out of it. A deep, dark split in the crust.

'You made bread,' Ada said.

And Pearl felt such a fool that she said, 'No I didn't.' Took the thing out and threw it in the bin, where it smoked for hours.

For Christmas she gave Ada cash. Ada gave her some tinned sardines, but not the ones in tomato sauce.

Then there was that terrible winter that dragged on until April. The snow started falling and didn't stop. A thick blanket that covered everything. Sounds became muted, but not peaceful. Snow falling on snow, the world humped and submerged and unfamiliar.

Pearl bought a roll of cheap insulation, put tape over the draughty windows, tended the fire, using up more logs than she should have. Looking out for signs of spring. Winter dragged on and on. A single daffodil peeked out and, startled to see the white world, withered and turned brown.

The house was quiet and muffled. Pearl listened to Ada moving through it. She stood by the study door, running her finger along the grains in the wood. Suddenly thankful for the way the TV blared, covering up the small noises and echoes: the clink of cups and forks, the footsteps, the creaking springs in the sofa. Sometimes only a handful of words passing between them: please, thank you,

dinner's ready. As if they were struggling with a new and complicated language. Weeks passed and the snow didn't shift. She opened
the study window and scooped up a handful of snow from the
windowsill, went towards the kitchen ready to burst in and throw it
at Ada, make her shriek. But she stopped in the hallway, thought:
maybe next year, and let the snow drip through her fingers and onto
the carpet.

22

DECEMBER WAS RUSHING BY already. One morning Ada thought about snow as she opened the curtains, and then there it was: a dusting on the ground, as if a dandelion had blown apart in the wind. She shut the curtains, waited a moment, then opened them again. The snow was still there. She had been so busy at the pub, Val asking her to do more and more shifts – one minute trying to use up the rest of the deer, the next minute working out what the hell de-bearding a mussel was – that she hadn't noticed how short the days were getting, or how raw the air had become.

She went outside and touched the snow with her fingers. It was crumbly and fine, not like the heavy, cloying snow she remembered, which heaped up and stuck to itself like burs. But maybe that was to come. She looked up at the laden clouds. Almost clasped her hands together.

By mid-morning, the snow had disappeared.

The sound of hammering on the roof and then the ladder bouncing as Tristan went down to get more tiles. Replacing the ones he'd already prised off; nailing them on in neat rows. A work-belt slung across his hip. He'd made his way around the house looking for the source of the leak, running his hands up walls, levering floorboards. Decided that the only way was to completely seal the roof. So now he was up there every day, only stopping when it got too dark or the wind suddenly reared up.

When Ada was upstairs, she could hear him talking to himself about what he was doing: overlapping tiles, keeping the felt taut. His voice muffled because of the nails in his mouth. She kept finding reasons to go up and listen, or watch him on his breaks – he would go down to the river and rinse his hands in the water, or cut across the bridge and walk up one of the paths. Once he'd climbed halfway up a tree and sat on a curved branch. She would make herself turn and go back downstairs. Not what she needed to get involved with. Follow the recipe exactly and everything will turn out as expected.

But it made sense, didn't it? asking him to work on the house. Fix the leak, repair the walls. He was reliable, everyone kept telling her that, and he didn't have any other work on at the moment. It made sense, it definitely made sense. Get it done before winter set in properly.

She went into her mother's bedroom and looked at the wardrobe. Took a deep breath. Couldn't keep putting it off any longer. She opened the doors. The wardrobe was stuffed – coats and shirts and trousers creased into strange poses, like a line of people gesturing at different things. A row of felt shirts, drooping at the waist and unravelling. Baggy cords with damp brown knees and flecks of yellow grass. Wrinkled waterproofs, crushed shoes and knapsacks. A pair of waders slumped in the corner, a tide-line of silt around the thighs. The overwhelming smell was of mildew, but also soil and strong coffee. The oil used to clean jewellery.

Ada unhooked a shirt from its hanger. A tissue fell out of the sleeve. There was a rip across the collar. She folded the shirt carefully and put it in the box she'd brought up. Blew her nose on the tissue, which was running from all the dust. Then saw all the dust coated on the tissue. She picked up a pair of canvas shoes with mould around the eyelets and petrified laces. She put them in the box along with a bright green belt, a horrible thing with a fat buckle. The hangers swayed. Maybe that would do for now. But she made herself take out a stack of jumpers and lay them out on the bed. One of them was much bigger than the others; a man's jumper, navy with thick ridges. When she was growing up, she used to find things around the house: a bottle of spicy-smelling aftershave, a battered harmonica, a silver cufflink that had slipped under the carpet in the bathroom. Things that, one by one, disappeared, and she never saw again.

Ada folded the jumper neatly and left it on the bed. Then looked at the rest: all snarled together, the crusty wool stained and snagged. Could hardly untangle one from the other. She heaped the pile onto her lap and worked carefully at the wool, licking her fingers to gather loose yarn and threading it back onto itself, closing up the holes and finishing them with small knots.

The front door opened and she heard Tristan come in. The kettle clicked on. Ada tied one more knot, then went downstairs. Tristan was rinsing his coffee mug, his cheeks mauve with cold. 'Do you want one?' he asked. He'd left his boots by the door. Ada, her eyes acclimatised to noticing loose thread, saw a fraying lace, tattered heels on his socks.

She nodded and he reached up to the shelf and got another mug. 'I'll do it,' she said. She stood by the kettle; it seemed to take a long time to boil. Tristan radiating warmth and that bloody pine-and-soap smell, which stayed in the house for hours.

'I'm working around the chimney now,' he said. 'You know there's different stone there. All the rest is local stone but the chimney isn't.'

Upstairs, the wardrobe creaked open. 'Grockle stone,' Ada said. Then frowned and poured out hot water.

Tristan got the coffee and shook it in straight from the jar. 'Are you going to Luke's party at the weekend?' he asked.

She had forgotten about the party. Luke had mentioned it a while ago, a small gathering he'd said, for the festive season. She imagined awkward small talk in his living room, mostly people she didn't know. 'I don't think so,' she said. She would probably be working anyway. She took the jar from Tristan and spooned the rest of the coffee in. Regretting telling him he could come and go as he pleased – no idea he would be around this much.

Tristan stirred his coffee with his finger. Seemed to dislike spoons. 'You can tell how far the stone's come by the amount of quartz in it,' he said. 'A lot of people don't like working with the stuff around here, but to me, it's the best kind, splitting it open and finding a seam of quartz in there.'

There were bits of bark and tile snagged in his jumper. She wondered where he would go, if he had to move on. 'Are you going?' she asked. 'To the party?'

'I told Luke I would,' he said. He picked up his mug and crossed the kitchen. Bent down to tie his boots. 'He's worried no one's going to come.'

'Lots of people will,' Ada said. 'I'm sure lots of people will.'

Tristan shrugged. 'Maybe it will just be me and him. Talking about the good old days.' He whistled a bar of quavering music, then saluted her with his mug and closed the door.

The wardrobe doors clunked. The hangers rattled. Ada went back upstairs. The box had tipped over and spilled onto the floor. The clothes in the wardrobe were rumpled and very cold. Specks of snow on the edges of the sleeves. She crouched down and pulled out handfuls of shoes from the bottom shelf: trainers, walking boots, sandals with Velcro straps. A pair of leather boots, the heel cracked like paint.

'Don't get rid of those,' her mother said. She was standing by the window looking out.

Ada ran her hand along the cracks. Some of them had gone right through. 'I think they're broken,' she said.

'Everyone needs old shoes. You can get rid of any new shoes you want.'

Ada got back down on her knees and looked along the shelf. Saw hatched bootprints, tissues and dust. There was a slipper by itself in the back corner, worn right through at the toe and the heel. She reached in and brought it out, then glanced at her mother. 'There aren't any new shoes,' she said.

Her mother stared at the slipper as if she didn't recognise it. 'Do what you want then,' she said. 'Get rid of all of it.'

Ada put the slipper on the floor next to the box, then gathered up the tissues and threw them away. She looked through the hangers slowly, all the clothes blurring together, the smell of coffee and oil and grass getting stronger. She saw a shirt that used to be red and blue checks, the colours now faded and the seams unravelling like old cobwebs. An unwashed fustiness clinging to it. Imagined her mother wearing it, sitting by herself in the quiet kitchen. When before she had worn it to yank up weeds and sweep the chimney. She slipped the shirt off the hanger. 'I could keep this,' she said. The sleeves were edged with soot.

Her mother barely glanced at it. 'I never liked that one,' she said.

Then fleeces, all daubed with stains. Ada gathered them up and clutched them like a bouquet. They were much smaller than she remembered. 'I could wash these,' she said. What she wanted to do was wash them all, smooth them out, then hang them back up neatly.

'Get rid of them,' her mother said. 'Look at the state they're in.'

Ada held onto them. 'I could wash them,' she said.

But her mother was looking deeper into the wardrobe. There was a dress which had fallen off its hanger. She looked at it for a long moment and muttered something. It was a brown dress with an ugly band of shiny material at the hem and sleeves. A strange glittery belt around the waist and the neck cut into a hard V. Ada took it out. Swallowed. 'It's nice,' she said.

'You can keep it,' Pearl told her.

Ada fiddled with the belt – the material was very cold. Glitter stuck to her hands. The hangers clacked together softly. 'I don't think I need it.'

Her mother stared at the dress. 'Well I definitely don't need it.'

'I don't need it either,' Ada said. There was a price tag dangling down the back of it. The first price had been scribbled out and a new one had been written next to it. Less than half price. She swallowed again. 'You never wore it,' she said.

Her mother's face suddenly looked crumpled, her eyes pale and watery. She reached out and touched the hem, slowly working her fingers over it. 'Actually,' she said finally, 'brown would probably make you look ill.' Neglected to notice the brown jumper Ada was wearing right now.

Her mother turned away from the dress and started looking through the wardrobe again. Muttering, pushing things aside. Shirts and bits of snow fell onto the floor. She leaned deeper in, then stopped.

There was a green blazer and a skirt. The wool was thick and expensive and the blazer had brass buttons. One button was missing halfway up. Pearl moved her hand up towards it but didn't touch it. A baffled look on her face.

'When did you,' Ada said, then hesitated. 'When were these for?' The suit must have been there all the time, hidden behind the jumpers and tattered shirts. Ada looked at the thick wool. There was a faint trace of perfume on it. The shoulders stretched out of shape from so long on the hanger. Her mother stayed in front of the wardrobe and didn't answer.

The cardboard box was still almost empty. All the clothes and shoes from the wardrobe were piled up on the bed. Ada picked the green belt up off the floor and put it back in the box. Sure about one thing at least.

'Definitely keep that,' her mother said without turning round.

Ada pulled the hem of the skirt down over her knees, smoothed it, then pulled it again. It sprang back up and bunched around her thighs. The fabric too thin and clingy. She'd already had a shock off its crackling static. It hadn't looked so bad in the shop, but maybe that was because she hadn't been moving. And it was too much with her silky top and loop of beads, definitely too much; it was only a few people going round to Luke's after all. Impossible not to go, what with him worrying about nobody turning up, and even Val forcing her to take the night off – she wouldn't be serving food because she wanted to close the pub early and come along to Luke's herself.

Ada took the clothes off and let the cold air in the bedroom cool her down. Looked at herself in the mirror – her broad hips, the silvery shadows and dimples on her thighs, the ochre freckles below her belly button, her stomach soft and slack like good bread dough. Liked to think of it as having been pummelled by Pepper. The skin around her collarbone was almost translucent; turquoise veins, more freckles splashed like dripping paint. Some flecked across her breasts, more in the folded skin under her armpits. Growing into herself year by year, her body stronger, sturdier, more comfortable.

She kicked the skirt aside. A waste of money but she'd needed to go into town anyway; suddenly a lot of things that had accumulated: boxes to drop into charity shops, jeans and socks for Pepper, paint and filler for the house. And they'd get scurvy if they went much longer without proper fruit and vegetables. She bought pink wine and pastries to take to the party, tinsel to go over the front door. Looked everywhere for a Christmas present for Pepper, but saw nothing that would rival the chipped bird ornament she stroked every time she went into Mick's shop.

Ada had walked around the shops slowly, feeling dazed. Glad Pepper was at Judy's rather than tugging at her hand and trying to run off. It was only a small town but it had been a long time since she'd been in a crowd of people, bright displays in windows, the orange flush of street lamps. Everything glinted and caught her eye. But there were a lot of empty shops and boarded-up windows. Posters advertising clearance sales. Broken benches and bottles. Couldn't find the jewellery shop although she looked everywhere. The church had become a cafe, the library had moved into the corner of the information centre. But still the lovely holly tree she remembered from the car park, and the graffiti heart on the wall by the bank. She'd hurried past the estate agent's; she'd phoned them far too many times. All the houses on display in the window looked neat and idyllic, no sign of the dark, sprawling pictures they'd taken of Pearl's house.

She unpacked her old black dress – the one she wore for everything – and put it on. The material was soft and didn't cling. Could move without having to pluck it out of crevices.

The camp bed wheezed behind her. 'When did you last wear that?' her mother asked.

Ada dug into one of the bags and found her creased black shoes. 'I don't know,' she said.

'I know where you wore it,' her mother said. 'And I want you to tell me about it.'

Ada brushed her hair and twisted it into a knot, then undid it and let it hang down. Thought again about phoning Luke with an excuse – that the power had gone? He'd say come anyway. The car was broken? He'd drive over and pick them up.

'You can tell me,' her mother said. 'How many people came?'

There had been hardly any. Herself and Pepper. Luke. Two or three people shuffling at the back of the church. Ada had kept checking her watch, waiting for the stream of people. She crouched down and fiddled with her shoe. 'There were lots of people there,' she said.

A crushed leaf fell out of her mother's sleeve. She touched her fingers lightly together. The room was so quiet Ada could hear her watch ticking. 'I suppose I closed myself off,' Pearl said.

Ada took a step closer to the bed. 'There were people there,' she said.

Her mother suddenly reached out and gripped Ada's wrist. It felt like Ada had plunged her arm into the river. The watch ticked loudly. A draught caught the curtains and made them sway. After a moment, Pearl's grip loosened and fell back. Left Ada's arm blue and tingling. 'You're going to be late,' she said.

Ada lingered in the doorway. Halfway through the funeral, the church door had creaked open and she had turned quickly, but it had just been the wind.

'You're going to be late,' her mother said again.

Ada looked at the crushed leaf. As she went downstairs, she heard her mother muttering: 'I hope that godawful vicar didn't say anything pious about me. Because I told him once before that if he dared . . .'

Ada found Pepper by the kitchen table. Leaning on her elbow and crumbling bread between her fingers. She was wearing her shabbiest trainers and a sweatshirt with a dragon on it. Refused to brush her clumped hair. 'How long do we have to go for?' Pepper said.

'Not very long,' Ada told her. 'We just have to talk to a few people, be polite, and then say we're tired, OK?'

But it didn't end up like that at all.

A swathe of bright lights surrounded Luke's house. As they drove closer, Ada saw that there were at least thirty cars pulled up around the front. And more coming. Horns blared out. A cacophony of noise – voices, engines, snatches of clashing music. A big group of people crushed on the front steps. She held Pepper's hand and tried to get through. Someone called out; she stepped on someone's foot. Drinks were passed over their heads. Pepper stiffened, quivered slightly, then let out a high-pitched note from between her lips. Seemed to suddenly absorb the underlying energy, like a spring absorbing pressure. She broke away and vanished into the house.

Ada pushed her way into the kitchen. The hot fug of breath and bodies. No sign of Luke anywhere. She put her bottle of wine down, and the box of pastries, which were swallowed up on the vast table, amongst the huge bowls of crisps and cans of beer.

She opened a beer and drank some down. It was warm. The music in the kitchen was yowly jazz; in the hall, something with bass that thrummed. Voices roared and droned. Someone outside banged so hard on the window that it shook. A plate smashed on the floor. She glimpsed Luke through the kitchen door and waved, but he was swigging from a bottle and didn't see. He disappeared through the hallway.

Ada finished her beer and opened another. Ate some pickled onions out of a jar – then pushed them aside before she ate the lot. Two women next to her started dancing. They gave off a cloud of perfume and cigarettes; flinging their feet and elbows out. Another plate smashed. A dog bolted into the kitchen, skidded on the floor, turned and bolted out again.

The music got louder. A group of men surged in, went straight to the table and emptied one of the bowls of crisps. They spoke quietly to each other; their shoulders jostled; low laughter escaped like steam. One of them was Jake. He saw her and came over holding a mug of drink, said something that she couldn't hear over the noise. 'What was that?' she shouted. Cupped her ear.

Jake leaned closer. 'Who brought this stuff?' He held up his mug which was brimful with her pink wine.

'No idea,' Ada shouted. More people pushed in. She and Jake were pressed against the sink. The kitchen was boiling – her hair was damp against her forehead, her mouth dry. She opened another beer.

'Australia. Move out sometime,' Jake was bellowing. 'Forty thousand, fifty thousand a year.' She was close enough to see coppery bristles on his cheeks, and his long eyelashes, just the same as they always were. 'Me and a few of the boys,' he shouted. 'Enough work for everyone out there. Hot sun.'

Ada glimpsed Pepper slaloming among legs and chairs. A small boy following behind her. 'I've got to go,' she shouted. Gestured towards the hall. Jake nodded and made his way back to the table, stopping to adjust a blanket round the legs of an old man sitting in the corner.

The hallway was dark and the music throbbed. No sign of Pepper. She stepped on a kid with orange hair, who was gone again before Ada could see if he was alright. Someone grabbed her elbow. Mick. He guided her into a space, wanted to talk to her about working out some kind of special rate if he started supplying the pub. Maybe she could mention it to Val? Another man came up and dragged him away, saying, 'I've got the matches. Tell Luke I got the matches.' Then there was Luke himself, red and reeling. He bowed theatrically. 'Welcome,' he said. 'To my home.' Beery breath and his smart jacket with a rip in the shoulder. His eyes were watering. He staggered away towards the front door.

Someone pushed another drink into Ada's hand. A man draped in tinsel shouted that he could smell smoke. Ada leaned against the wall and closed her eyes. The wall felt sticky. Then, two cool hands touched her cheeks. 'Dance with me,' Judy said. She held Ada's hands and pulled her forward, whirled her around and bumped against her hip. Something loosening in Ada's chest.

She closed her eyes, felt the floor tilt, and opened them again. 'All these people,' she shouted.

Judy took off her scarf and shoved it in her pocket. It had parrots printed all over it. 'There's less than usual,' she shouted back. She spun Ada round in a woozy circle and Ada slipped, thudded into the wall. A picture shook and fell onto the floor. The glass cracked.

Judy picked the picture up. 'It was like that when we found it,' she said. She hung it back so that it was facing the wall.

Ada rolled her eyes. 'Good one,' she said. 'Luke'll never notice that.'

Judy straightened the picture. 'If he finds out, just tell him it was me. He owes me about sixty quid for duck eggs.'

Everyone suddenly surged towards the door. Judy swept one way, Ada another. 'Robbie's driving people back later,' Judy called. 'Come and find us.'

Outside, the freezing air felt good. A lot of people had gathered around a smoking heap of wood.

'That's pretty close to the house,' a voice said in her ear. Tristan. They stood and watched as Luke threw on more wood. Then Luke called something out and Robbie ran over with a can of petrol and boom, the whole lot went up and streamed into the air. Orange streaked with blue and green. Luke prodded it with a broom, didn't seem to notice how close the wind was pushing the flames towards the house. 'More fuel,' he shouted. He went inside and came back with a chair, which he threw on in a cascade of sparks.

Tristan's skin was glowing orange. Ada shivered and he leaned closer. She glanced at him, saw him looking at her, flicked her eyes away. Then back. He leaned down, his face tilting towards her.

'Your leg,' Ada said. 'Luke told me about your leg.'

Tristan frowned and straightened up. 'What about it?'

'The accident,' Ada told him. 'When you were travelling. You had to walk by yourself.' She breathed out slowly, held her hot palms to the cool air.

'Luke told you that?' He looked at the fire for a long time. 'I fell out of a tree,' he said at last. 'I was sixteen. It was a pretty small tree, so I tried to pretend it hadn't happened. I carried on for about a week. The break didn't set properly.' He shrugged; again that small twitch in his mouth that made it seem like he was about to laugh. 'If it had been a tall tree, it probably would have been different.'

'You could have just told everyone it was a tall tree,' Ada said.

Tristan rubbed his palm over his jaw. 'Yes,' he said eventually. 'I suppose I could have done that.' The bonfire sparked and cracked. Smoke poured upwards. 'Isn't that Pepper over there?' he said.

The little sod; she knew she wasn't meant to go near fire. Ada ran over the hummocky grass, but by the time she got there Pepper had gone. And when she turned, Tristan had gone too.

She went back into the hall. In the kitchen, Val was sipping tea among broken plates and spilled cutlery. Ada swayed and closed her eyes. Something thumped against the house. Two men hurtled through the door, trying to wrestle each other to the ground. Laughing but one of them with a bloody nose. Knocking into Ada. Then someone held her wrist and pulled her out of the way, pushing her up against the wall. Tristan's face so close, they knocked teeth together, his hand on her thigh, hers pressed onto his stomach.

Outside, the fire snarled and crackled and more petrol went on in a whoomph that seemed to shake the whole house.

23

PEPPER HELD THE BIRD ornament carefully. It was magnificent. She wrapped it back up in the tissue paper then went upstairs to her room and got a package out from under her bed. She held it behind her back for a long time, running her fingers over the edges of the newspaper. She had forgotten to get wrapping paper – had never bought a present for her mother before.

'You got me something,' her mother said. She unfolded each sheet very slowly.

Pepper licked her dry lips and watched. It seemed to take hours to open, and then there it was: one of the silver key rings from the cafe. An engraving of the river winding through the middle. It was a lot smaller than she remembered and not quite as bright.

Her mother said it was a lovely thing. She got her keys and threaded them onto the key ring. But she didn't say it was the most beautiful thing she had ever seen. And she didn't say that she would keep it forever. Not like Pepper had imagined when she had planned it with Robbie, slipping him the money she'd saved up so that he could go and buy it.

'You'll always have that now,' Pepper said. 'Won't you?'

Her mother touched the top of Pepper's head lightly. Then she put the keys down on the table and said, what about pizza? Which was their tradition – home-made pizza and ice cream all afternoon. And games: charades and Cluedo, which her mother tried to play tactically, going slowly from room to room, but Pepper slipped through secret passages and made wild accusations, winning every time.

The last day of the year. Her mother was working at the pub and Pepper was going too. She had never seen the new year arrive before and hadn't ever really noticed it. Usually, by the time she woke up in the morning, it had already begun. But now it felt like she was about to tip over a very steep edge, or that, any moment, the lights would go out and when they came back on everything would be different. She'd borrowed her mother's watch and she kept checking the time every few minutes. It was important to know exactly when it was going to happen.

The pub was so full that there was nowhere to sit down. Val had to move people around, push tables together and find an extra chair so that Pepper could squeeze into the corner. The windows had steamed up. A woman knocked into Pepper's chair. Pepper gulped her lemonade. Her throat was dry. She checked the watch again. Half past seven. There was a group of people standing so close that she kept having to lean out of the way of their arms. One of them said something about the holidays ending. Another one said something about children and school – the new term was almost here already. Pepper backed her chair away. She picked up a beer mat and started to shred it, layer by layer.

Someone carried a chair over and sat down right next to her. Pepper pulled another strip off the mat. 'I've never seen it as busy as this,' the man said. 'It's because of your mother's food. Everyone wants to try it.'

Pepper looked up and saw that it was Luke. He sipped his beer and froth bubbled on his top lip. 'Are you staying here till midnight?' she asked him.

'Thought I probably would,' Luke said.

Pepper moved her chair a bit closer. Spoons tapped, plates clattered together. But it seemed to her that everything was different to usual. The lamps were dim and buzzing and looked like they were about to go out. Three glasses had smashed already. There were a lot of people talking, but their voices would get louder and louder and then suddenly stop, and the room would go quiet. After a while, there would be murmurs and laughing and the voices would build up again, like gusts of wind that came and went.

She glimpsed her mother through the kitchen doors. In the car, she had told Pepper that people made resolutions at New Year, which were things they wanted to change about themselves. Every year she resolved to stop biting her nails and learn how to bake custard without burning it. What about stroking Shep? Pepper had asked, but apparently you couldn't make resolutions for other people. Pepper had thought about hers for a long time. She still hadn't decided. What should she change? And did it mean that, after midnight, she would be a different person to the one she had been before? She checked the watch again. It was quarter to eight.

Luke pointed to someone across the room. 'There's Neil Simons. I haven't seen him in here for years. Hardly ever see him out of his house.' Pepper looked and saw an old man sitting by himself, staring down into his drink. He was still wearing his coat, which had patches glued on. He twisted at his dust-coloured hair with his fingers. Luke kept his voice low. 'I probably shouldn't tell you. But he suffered a bad loss a few years ago.' He sipped his drink. 'Where do you keep your money?' he asked.

'In my envelope,' Pepper said. She didn't have much left.

'Well,' Luke said. 'Old Neil over there, his father kept his in his mattress. He stuffed it in and sewed it up. Thousands and thousands. Didn't tell anyone about it. So when he died, Neil put the mattress in a skip at the dump. He didn't find out about the money until a few weeks later, but the mattress had already gone.'

'Someone's got all that money,' Pepper said.

Luke shrugged. 'Maybe. Neil's given up on it now. But he could have done with it, poor bugger.' He leaned back. There was a bit of tattoo poking out above his collar. It looked like the tip of a wing and the end of a thin, forked tail. 'It's like the burial hoard that could be in my field. Some expert told me about it once. Meant to be amulets, brooches, coins. They said I should dig and see. I have a scrape around now and again but in the end you have to let it go.'

Pepper looked at the man in the coat. He was still staring into his drink. 'Why?' she said. 'Why do you?'

Luke nodded slowly. 'Maybe you're right,' he said. He sipped his drink and nodded again. Then he scraped his chair back and got up. 'I need to take a piss. I mean, a leak.' He pushed through the crowded bar.

More people came in. When the door opened an icy draught whipped round Pepper's legs. The watch ticked very loudly. She wiped a patch of steam off the window and looked out. Nothing but deep black. The reflection of her own face staring back in.

Luke came back holding another beer and a glass of fizzy orange for her. 'We've got food coming in a minute,' he said.

'What about them?' Pepper said. She pointed to the people standing at the bar. 'Tell me about them.'

Luke looked round. 'You see that woman in the green hat?' The woman was leaning forward and speaking to Val. Her scarf was trailing over the floor. She had very long orange hair that looked stiff, like brittle sweets. 'She's an expert on stars,' Luke said. 'She knows everything about them. Just woke up one day and decided to learn. Her telescope is this big.' He held out his hands to show. 'She can tell you all about the moon glowing bright red. And asteroids burning up right in front of her. And see the man standing next to her? He crashed his car and now he does stuff in his sleep. You know: walks around the house, walks down the road, cooks himself a meal. He can't remember any of it in the morning.'

'She just woke up and decided?' Pepper said. Still thinking about the red moon.

At the bar, a group of men started singing loudly. *She was a great-looking lass and her tits and her ass.*

Luke told her not to listen. But his foot jiggled along. 'They'll get Howard to do something next,' he said. And just as he said it, someone pushed Howard into the middle of the room and everything went quiet.

'What's he doing?' Pepper said. Howard stood very still. He cleared his throat. Then he started to sing. It wasn't like the men at the bar; it was deep and rich and slow. He kept his eyes closed. The song was about a woman who got lost and didn't come back and the person who loved her looked for her every day. Years passed and he kept looking. He got older and older and then, on the day he died, he finally found her. Howard finished and everyone whistled and clapped.

176

The song kept working its way around Pepper's head. It didn't seem fair, that he only found her on his last ever day. Her stomach felt very tight and cold. She looked at the watch. Half past eight.

Her mother came over and put a plate down in front of Pepper. Her cheeks were red and her hair was sticking to her face. 'Yours is coming Luke,' she said. Pepper watched her thread her way back towards the kitchen. The only person she stopped to talk to was Tristan.

The food smelled so good, onions and garlic sausages and potatoes covered in herbs and butter. She saw Luke looking at her plate and pulled it a bit closer.

'I wasn't going to steal it,' Luke said. Pepper hesitated, then offered him a potato. The smallest one she could find. She didn't think he would actually take it, but he put it in his mouth whole, which seemed like a waste. 'And see that man in the far corner?' he said. 'That there's Val's brother. They don't speak any more.'

Pepper chewed a big mouthful of food. 'Why don't they?'

Luke shrugged. 'No one knows,' he said.

The door opened again and another man came in, hunched in his coat. There was snow on his arms. It was Ray. Pepper slid down low in her seat. Her heart thudded. 'Ah,' Luke said. 'You know, it's a funny thing. He's started asking me questions about the house again. I thought he'd lost interest.'

Pepper put her hands over her ears. The watch ticked loud and deep inside her skull. She left her hands there for as long as she could, then took one off to check what Luke was saying.

'You'll like this,' he said. 'You see that man over there? I'll tell you a thing or two about him that will make your hair stand on end.'

Her mother came over with Luke's food and told Pepper she looked tired, was she OK?

Pepper hid a yawn. 'What things?' she said to Luke. 'Why will my hair stand on end?'

Luke put a hand to his face and stammered, looked at her mother out of the corner of his eye. Said he would tell Pepper another time.

Pepper turned over and kicked out a leg. Everything was very quiet. No singing, no sound of forks on plates. She opened one eye. She was in her own bed. Grey light came through a crack in the curtains. The watch was on the chair and she looked over at it. It was quarter to six. She lay very still and stared up at the ceiling. The stippled paint looked like a row of sharp mountains. She had fallen asleep and missed midnight. This was the new year.

Everything was very quiet. She got up and looked out of the window. It had snowed in the night. There was thick snow on the ground and the trees and everything was pale and grey and different. Things had changed shape, as if the snow was trying to hide them – the trees were heaped with lumpy snow and the ground was smooth and sloping and there were no stones, no tussocks of grass, no potholes in the yard. There was a wedge of snow on the car and another on the roof of the truck parked next to it.

She pulled on a jumper and socks and went downstairs. The kitchen was cold and dim. Snow had piled up on the windowsill. Shep was asleep on the floor, curled up on a sheet of newspaper. Pepper took a step towards him and he opened his eye, stretched and sat up. He whined. She stopped and watched him for a moment. Then she turned and went to the front door, put on her coat and went outside.

The snow creaked under her boots like polystyrene. A blackbird hurried in front of her, ruffling its feathers so it looked twice as big. Snow slumped off a branch and onto the ground. All the sounds were muffled and distant. Pepper turned and looked back at the house. No lights on. There were her footprints in the smooth snow. As if she was the only person left in the world. The prints looked small and unfamiliar. She stepped back and placed her boot in one of the prints, to make sure it was definitely hers. Her boot fitted. She took it out and made another careful print. Thought about the camera when she saw the contrast between the pale snow and the dark hatching of the boot – the mud and grass coming up through it.

The river was like cold metal; it was so dark grey it was almost blue. It wasn't glinting. There were thin patches of snow along the bank and bits of dusty snow on the roots. Small flecks of snow started falling and they landed on her face and melted.

The snow was deeper in the next field. By the hedge there were tiny splayed footprints, and a leaf skeleton that was so white and crispy it looked like something her mother had spun out of sugar. When she was spinning sugar, she would put her hands in a bowl of ice, then she would take them out and plunge them into a pan of boiling caramel. Every time, Pepper would hold her breath, waiting for the sizzling caramel to burn her hands. But it hadn't happened yet.

She kept close to the river, working her way along the bank. Muttered and hummed to herself as she walked, great-looking lass and her something and her ass. There was a flash down in the water. She fumbled for the camera, realised too late that she didn't have it. Her foot slipped on a flat stone and she fell, grabbed at the bank and clutched a handful of snow. She rolled down the mud and landed on sharp pebbles. A stick dug into her hip and her cheek was stinging. Pain jolted through her knee.

She lay there for a few moments. The river lapped at her hair. She clenched her fists and her eyes shut. Water worked its way through her coat. She bent her legs slowly and hauled herself up, keeping most of her weight on her arms. Brushed off mud and slush and stones. The bank was churned up where she had fallen. She tried to climb back up, got one leg onto a root before a hot pain sliced across her knee. Her hand slipped on wet mud. More snow started to fall, heavier snow that settled on her arms. Upriver, the way she'd come from, the water was choked with trees and boulders and there weren't any bits of beach. But downriver, there were enough bits of beach and roots and flat rocks to be able to walk on. Maybe. She hoped it would come out somewhere.

She splashed along the edge of the river and clambered over mossy boulders. Some of the shallow water had frozen and there were bands of ice around the bottoms of the rocks. Her knee kept giving out and she would jerk downwards, almost kneeling. Her socks were heavy with water, her toes numb and cramping. Nothing looked familiar at water level: a dead tree that had fallen; its roots heaving up a disc of earth; the surface of the river, which creased into seams and troughs. What was it the old woman kept talking about? Whether you could step into the same river twice. Look, Pepper had told her. You can, see? She had stepped into the water, then out, and then back in again. But today the river didn't seem like the same river at all. It looked flat and metallic and endless, and, now that she thought about it, where did the river actually stop?

'I wonder if I'll die,' she said. Maybe that could be her resolution: not to die. There was a lot she wanted to do: take a picture of a heron. Invent a new flavour of crisps. Find out if dinosaurs definitely had feathers. Go into space.

Her knee jarred with every step. No sound except the river clucking its watery tongue.

There was no one else around. And then, suddenly, there was a sheep on the bank above her. 'Brrroo gnnrrr,' it said. It stamped its hoof in the snow.

'I can't get up there,' Pepper said. Her teeth clattered together.

'Brrrurgh,' the sheep said. It stamped again. Its breath steamed out of its mouth and its teeth were brown and yellow. There was snow matted into its curly back.

'Do you know where we are?' she asked. The sheep stared down at her like she was stupid for even asking.

She turned and looked back the way she had come. No footprints. Smooth snow on the banks all above. It was very quiet. The river was fast and quiet. Brittle ice spread between the stones. It was like she had never even been there at all.

24

THINGS LOST, THINGS LOST . . .

. . . Things she had lost in the river: five shoes. Three lenses. A watch. A scarf. A small fortune. Her footing. Her favourite screwdriver. A tin of fruit. A tin of fish. Two gold fillings.

Things she had found in the river: purple stones, sheep bones. A leaf gone through to the veins. An oily rainbow. A piece of copper-plate. Blue eggs floating in a nest. Fertiliser. Five oars. An upturned canoe.

Things she loved about the river: its endlessness. Its silvers and rusts. Its babbling that sounded like an old friend.

Things she hated about the river: its rushing. Its endless rushing.

Things she loved about the river: the cold in your teeth like biting on ice cream. The way the water was smooth one minute and the next minute pleated like the top of a curtain.

Things she hated about the river: how it could never make up its mind.

Things she had found in the river: a drowned kingfisher. A tripod. Salmon shouldering against the current. A newly hatched dragonfly drying out its wings, bright as a carnival.

Things she couldn't stand about the river: its bloody-mindedness. How it churned everything up. How it reeled you in. How it reeled you in and didn't let go.

Things she could tolerate about the river: how it rose up in rain and shrank back down in good weather.

Things she had lost in the river: years and years and years.

Things she had found in it: warm pools. Peace. Miles of meshed and mossy roots.

25

THE SMELL OF EXHAUST through the draughty window. Ada lay on the bed and listened to Tristan's truck pulling away. The tyres crunched on snow. Hopefully it wouldn't be loud enough to wake Pepper up. She listened for movement in Pepper's room but couldn't hear anything. She licked her fingers and rubbed over her crusty eyes. Her throat was dry from shouting over the din at the pub. Still the smell of beer and onions in her hair. And Tristan's soap. It was New Year morning and she had broken her resolution already. Probably a new record. She bit her ragged thumbnail. Might as well go and burn some custard, get them all over with before breakfast.

She ran a bath as hot as it would go. The tank shuddered and the taps dribbled lukewarm water. She got in and lay back. The water was barely tepid, bits of old hair floated and got caught on her toes. There were red lines across the backs of her thighs from where the camp bed had dug in – nothing elegant about it.

She pushed her hair back with her wet hands. It was snowing; she could see it moving past the window, casting a murky light. It turned the bathroom a dim yellowish colour, like a pan of butter and water simmering. She leaned her head against the edge of the bath, then dunked right under, letting the thrum of the water push out all the thoughts that were circling and tangling together in her head.

The pipes were chuntering, or maybe it was Pepper speaking. She came back up, water streaming off her face. Her mother was sitting on the toilet seat. Her skin and hair were the same colour as the dim light and there was snow lodged under her nails. A rim of smooth ice around the bottom of her boots.

'And down there, in that shallow pool,' her mother said. Staring at the bathwater. 'There's a heron standing very still. It's seen something, its muscles are tensing up. There.' She jerked her neck forward. 'It caught the fish.'

Ada sat up in the water. 'I'm having a bath,' she said.

Her mother stopped talking. A shadow, which looked like spreading wings, moved across her chest. She looked up at the ceiling. 'The leak's going to come back through,' she said. She paused for a moment, then a moment longer. The bathwater started to chill at the edges. 'He hasn't been doing a very good job up there.'

'I just want to have a bath,' Ada said.

'He's very young,' her mother said. 'I suppose he's inexperienced.' A ripple moved under her skin: through her fingers and up the backs of her hands.

Ada reached forward and turned the hot tap back on. Cold water came out. 'The water's bloody freezing,' she said.

Pearl looked at her. 'You've got fat,' she said.

Ada crossed her arms over her chest. 'I haven't.'

'Around your waist.'

'Not much,' Ada said.

'No,' her mother conceded. 'I suppose it's what happens.' Her voice had gone quieter and she was studying Ada very closely. Taking in the lines and the creases. Lingering on Ada's face. Then she glanced down at her legs. 'It will take a while for those red marks to go, the way they've dug in like that.'

Ada closed her eyes and dunked under again. If she stayed under as long as she could, maybe her mother would have gone. If she could just stay under a bit longer . . . A bubble rose out of her mouth and broke on the surface. She came up gasping.

'The water is moving faster and getting deeper and there is a very loud drumming,' her mother was saying. 'There is a deep pool. The riverbed is very smooth. There is a very particular green stone with glints of orange which is actually an old chunk of copper, and a tiny fish darting. The water looks green and you can see right through it. A dipper just took off and is flying up the river, and the water is narrowing and the trees are leaning in.'

Her voice seemed to bubble and drum. Sometimes a silty crunch on her teeth, sometimes she seemed to be rolling stones around on her tongue.

Ada shivered. Thin feathers of ice had grown in the water around her feet. Suddenly reminded all over again how well her mother knew the place, how she'd belonged: the weather not difficult and unexpected, the river not strange, the valley not lonely or trapping. When Ada couldn't even remember what street she'd lived on five years ago, or what tree it was that had tapped against her window every night.

'And further down, the river widens into silty beaches. A dent in the middle where the little one landed. The stones all rucked up and disturbed but the water will work at them, soon they will be flipped back over.'

Ada sat up quickly in the water. 'What did you say?' she said. 'About the beach?'

186

'The little one had been there, you can see from the way the stones are.'

'Pepper?' Ada said. 'She's in bed.' A strange humming in her ears.

'You can see from the way the stones are all disturbed,' her mother said.

Ada lurched out of the bath, grabbed a towel and wrapped it around her body. She ran to Pepper's room and opened the door. There was a hump under the covers. She drew the blanket back slowly so that Pepper wouldn't wake up. There was nothing underneath. Ada was wet and shivering, dripping water everywhere. She ran downstairs and looked in every room. Then went back up to the bathroom. 'Christ, why didn't you tell me before?' she said.

'She's not there any more,' her mother said.

Ada went over to the window and looked out. It was still snowing, fat flakes that would cover any footprints.

'The water's slower in that bit,' her mother said. 'Eurgh, a sheep's got in somehow. There are enough bits of beach and root to carry on, and a bridge of flat stones. She will have gone that way. Yes, the bank is all churned up and there's a handprint in it. There are footprints going through a field.'

The phone rang, sudden and shrill. Ada ran to answer it. Her towel slipped off and she answered the phone naked, her hands too numb to grip the receiver – it fumbled, almost fell. It was Judy. She said they'd just found Pepper wandering across one of their fields, cold and wet and hungry.

'I'll be there in ten minutes,' Ada said.

The car skidded on the snow but she drove quickly and didn't meet anything coming the other way. Her hair was soaking. Her skin was freezing and her damp clothes stuck to it. Another new year that had gone tits up already – not sorted, not settled, and rushing to find her daughter, who she hadn't even known she'd lost.

She pulled up outside the house and went in. There was Pepper, wrapped in a blanket, telling Judy and Robbie that this was the third time she'd almost died – the first being the time she drank the very old apple juice in the fridge and threw up so many times she couldn't remember her own name. She was about to tell the second but stopped when she saw Ada, and her face flushed at being caught out boasting.

Ada went over to her, still shivering, water dripping off her hair onto the floor. 'What were you doing?' she said. 'You should have told me where you were going.' There was a cut across Pepper's cheek, and she reached out to touch it.

Pepper scowled at her. 'None of you were awake,' she said.

Ada stopped, felt her own face flush. No one spoke for a few moments. Judy passed her a towel.

Pepper tipped back in her chair. After a while, she said: 'And the second time was when I touched a wire on a plug and it—'

'Why don't we make breakfast?' Judy said loudly. She glanced at Robbie.

'Toast,' he said. 'We could have it with eggs and tomatoes – does that sound OK?' He started carving bread into thick slices. He was wearing a sweatshirt with something written in Spanish and a picture of a palm tree. Socks that seemed to have shrunk in the wash – the heels halfway down the soles of his feet.

Ada sat down at the table. She blotted at her hair with the towel. The kitchen was warm and she stopped shivering, now just felt very tired. She leaned her head on her arm. Judy put a mug of coffee down next to her, then draped a cardigan over her shoulders. Ada closed her eyes. Listened to Judy and Robbie's quiet noises as they made breakfast; talking about whether the snow was setting in, could Judy check if the toast was burning, something about the cows, back to the snow again. A comforting rhythm to their voices, the way their sentences blurred into each other's. When Ada opened her eyes, the snow was falling thickly past the window.

'Let me have a look at your cheek,' she said to Pepper. It looked sore but not deep. She asked Judy for some cream to put on it. But Pepper squirmed and said it stung. 'It needs to be clean,' Ada told her.

'It doesn't have to if it doesn't want to,' Pepper said. She put her hand up to her cheek and wouldn't move it. Ate her toast in huge bites, spraying crumbs everywhere.

'It's setting in,' Robbie said, looking out of the window. He held his plate up so there was a shorter distance between food and mouth.

'It'll be fine,' Judy said.

Robbie paced while he ate. 'I thought it was meant to have stopped by now.'

'If you choke I'm not doing that manoeuvre on you again,' Judy told him.

He sat down, but sideways, so that he could get up more quickly. Judy put her hand on his jittering leg.

'Finished,' Pepper announced. Her fork clattered down. She resisted catching Ada's eye and hummed shrilly.

Robbie pushed his plate to one side. 'What about that trick I showed you?' he asked. 'Have you practised it?' He reached towards her ear and pulled out a coin.

Pepper snatched at it. 'I'll do it,' she said. She waved her left hand elaborately while hiding the coin up her right sleeve. Then shoved her hand into Robbie's ear and tugged. The coin thudded onto the floor. 'Arseballs.' She got down on her knees and scrabbled around under the table.

Ada closed her eyes again. When she opened them the sky had turned very dark and more snow was falling, wet flakes that piled up on the window ledges. Judy looked out of the window. 'We should go and check the animals,' she said.

'I'll do it,' Robbie said. Pepper followed him out into the hallway.

When they had gone, the kitchen was very quiet. Judy was still standing at the window. 'The roads are going to be covered soon,' she said. 'Your car is already.'

Ada propped her head up on her hand, trying to stay awake. The kitchen so warm and the smell of toast and butter. Steam blurred the windows. The TV in the background. 'I'll wait a bit longer,' she said.

Judy put the kettle on for the third time. Filled the sink, took her ring off and put it by the taps, then started going through the pile of plates.

'I should be helping,' Ada said.

Judy turned to look at her. 'Don't worry about it,' she said. 'You should probably catch up on sleep, young lady.' Putting on her Uncle Granville voice: prim and high. Which was also the voice she used to slip into in school presentations when she got nervous.

Ada got up and went over to the sink and trailed her fingers in the water. 'Remember that plan we made? You were going to be a chemist, and I was going to do that thing where I went round to people's houses and read to them.'

Judy put a handful of cutlery into the water. 'You went round to Mrs Henderson's house and sat in her kitchen the whole afternoon, reading. She didn't know how to get rid of you.'

'I was brightening her day.'

'You made her miss her hospital appointment.'

Outside, Robbie and Pepper loaded the truck and got in. Doors thumped. The trailer rattled. Judy was watching Robbie out of the window. He looked up and saw her, both their mouths moved, almost too slight to notice, but some kind of shared signal.

'It's peaceful here,' Ada said.

'Yes,' Judy said. 'Sometimes.'

'I can see why Robbie never wanted to leave.'

Judy stopped washing and left her hands in the water. 'He worries so much. The uncertainty. Costs going up. We're only just breaking even. All the new regulations. He thinks we should stop. Sell the place and move into town. Find stable jobs. It's me that won't let us.'

The snow fell down in front of the window, blurring the farm buildings and the fields.

Ada moved her hand through the thinning bubbles. She was close enough to see the measles scars on Judy's forehead. After a while she said, 'The snow's probably quite deep on the roads now.'

'It will be,' Judy said.

'Maybe I should stay a bit longer.'

'You could stay over, if you want.'

There were bubbles in Judy's hair, tinted rainbow colours. 'Maybe that would be better,' Ada said. She watched the snow come down. Her hands tingled as they warmed up in the water. The kettle steamed. 'But it did brighten her day,' she said. 'When I got to the end of a sad story, she kept wiping her eyes.'

'That's because she had cataracts,' Judy said. She splashed water over Ada's hands.

Ada splashed back. 'Exactly,' she said. 'That's exactly why I thought I should go and read to her.'

191

Outside, the snow came down thickly and silently and heaped up against the bright windows.

Ada slept on the fold-out sofa, which sagged in the middle like it had been punched. It smelled ancient and musty; a cloud of dust puffed out when Judy unfolded it and they clapped their hands to clear it. The pattern was orange and brown daisies and coffee stains.

She turned over, exhausted, but couldn't sleep. Pepper had gone to bed hours ago. She'd insisted on sleeping upstairs in the spare room, and had pretended to be asleep when Ada went in to check on her.

There was a noise and someone shuffled into the room – Pepper, clutching her duvet. She stood in the doorway. 'Robbie made a funny noise,' she said. 'Like he was scared.'

She lay down next to Ada. Cold and rigid.

'He does that sometimes,' Ada said. 'When he's asleep. It's just a bad dream.'

Pepper stayed still for a long time. Something clicked in the kitchen, a gate creaked outside. Then she turned and burrowed into Ada's side. Her eyelashes tickling Ada's neck. It was very dark. The clock ticked softly. Ada thought Pepper had gone to sleep, but then she said: 'Judy doesn't want to have any children.'

'How do you know that?' She moved her leg out from where Pepper was crushing it.

'I asked her.'

Ada smoothed back Pepper's hair. 'Not everyone wants to,' she said.

Pepper nudged her bony legs in closer. 'I probably won't have any myself,' she said. Then she turned over, fell asleep and slept like a drunk, heavily and full of noise. She groaned and the breath in her nose rattled. Ada held her tight.

It seemed like only minutes after she'd gone to sleep, before there was any glimmer of light, when she heard Judy and Robbie get up. Moving around upstairs. Laughing quietly together. They opened the door and went outside and something metallic clanged and echoed in the sharp air as they said good morning, good morning, to the animals.

The snow had turned slushy enough to drive back. Ada felt a tickle in the back of her throat and through the day it got worse and worse. By the evening her throat was like a blocked gutter, swollen and sore, and every time she swallowed something in there got irritated and made her cough. Her eyes were red and streaming. Skin prickly and her scalp felt like it was full of cold sand.

She made Pepper a bowl of rice and beans, then went upstairs and lay down, shaking and clammy. Her legs ached and she kicked them around, couldn't seem to keep them still.

'Why do you look like that?' Pepper asked. Hovering at the edge of the bed, picking at the sheets.

'Have you brushed your teeth?' Ada said. Pepper nodded. 'Are you in your pyjamas?' Pepper nodded again. 'You should go to bed in a minute,' Ada told her. 'And could you move those balloons out of the way?' Her head swilled. Balloons were the last thing she needed. She closed her eyes. Pepper said there weren't any balloons. Ada slept. When she woke up it was very dark. She coughed, then couldn't stop coughing. Thought she saw her mother standing in the doorway. That same look on her face she always had when Ada was ill. Ada had always thought it was anger, but now she recognised the worry in it. How lonely she must have felt out here, watching, listening all night to the way Ada was breathing.

The camp bed groaned and the springs dug into her. She

twisted and moved her legs. After a while, she got up and moved into her mother's bedroom, into the bed, the sheets cold and musty but soft. She closed her eyes. A weight creaked down at the side of the bed. A cool hand, wet and grainy as snow, pressed down on her boiling forehead.

26

SHE WASN'T A SICKLY child, but when Ada did get ill it was sudden and forceful. And it was so much worse when she was younger – when she was three, or four, or five, and she was shivering and refusing to drink and her feet had gone so clammy that she left small, damp footprints across the kitchen floor.

This is how it went: first there would be a tinge of red in the corner of her left eye. Then she would start rubbing her throat, certain that there was something stuck in there. After that, a rattly cough, shivering that wouldn't stop, and then she would go upstairs and lie down in the dark, saying, no lights, no lights, they hurt my eyes.

Pearl would stand by the bed and listen to the way Ada was breathing. Was it shallower? More laboured? But it was just a cold for God's sake, maybe the flu at worst. It happened to everyone. She would make hot-water bottles and find the cough mixture in the bathroom. Dip her finger in and taste some of the purple syrup herself. Straighten the rucked-up sheets. Feel Ada's head, which would be boiling one minute and chilled the next. 'It's just a cold,' she would tell her.

Hoping that Ada would suddenly sneeze and blow her nose like anyone else, rather than lying there with a bruised and grey-looking face, her legs pedalling restlessly against the bed.

She always stayed in Ada's room the first few nights. Dragging in that wretched camp bed she had bought especially, lying stiffly, not sleeping. Trying to decide what was best to do. Drive out and get someone, or wait it out? When Ada was three, Pearl had packed her into the car and driven to the doctor's in town. It had been late afternoon and dark. The journey had made Ada sick and, when they got there, the doctor said it was a cold, just a normal cold, and it would have been better to keep her warm in bed. A patronising sod of a man, if Pearl remembered correctly. As if he knew what it was like to be stuck out here alone, listening to Ada shrieking about her throat and legs. Seemed only right when Ada threw up on his desk, bits of slushy liquid splashing over his expensive pens.

But if only she could go back now and tell herself, lying there in the dark, that the fever would break, that it always broke in the end. Spare herself those long hours, the hollow, aching feeling in her chest, wondering why there was no one that she could call on for help. No parents from the school that she could ring up – how had it got to that stage? A few stilted conversations that she had let dry up, a few invitations that she had declined. She'd stopped joining them at the gate after a toddler a woman was holding had pointed at her and shouted: old! Why is she so old? But sometimes, half asleep, her imagination conjured up a knock on the door and she would stumble out of bed to answer it, opening up to the rain and the wind.

By the second day, Ada would be delirious. Pearl would go upstairs to check on her and find her sitting rigidly upright, pointing at the wall. 'Look at those bright lights,' she would say. Pointing at a dim, grey wall. 'Look at the way they're moving.' Or she would whirl her arms in front of her shouting, bats, bats! Pearl would hold Ada's arms down, trying to stop her plucking invisible bats out of her hair. When she was five, she fell out of bed trying to reach a rope bridge she'd seen swinging across the room. When she was six, she'd spread her arms wide and bowed to the chair in the corner, saying, welcome to my country, her sweaty hair sticking to her forehead. And Pearl had snorted with laughter, then felt so awful that she'd spent an hour rubbing Ada's back, right between the shoulder blades, to help her get to sleep.

It always seemed to happen at the worst possible time. Just when the dragonflies were hatching on the river; those few precious days. Or when there was a rare hoarfrost in the woods. Or when she had finally been given enough work to tide them over and she needed to be at her desk all day and all evening, her back aching, her fingers getting calloused, the sickly smell of oil and polish on them, looking forward to the time when she didn't have to do it any more, when there was enough money for her to turn the work away.

Countless times it happened. And the worst time – that week in March when Ada was eight and the daffodils and garlic were just starting to push up. Luke had come over. They didn't know each other very well, just enough to say hello over the years, maybe stop if they passed each other on the road. She had fixed one of his watches – he'd come over to pick it up and ended up staying the whole morning. Offered to look over the car once or twice when it was playing up. But that day, when she answered the door, he seemed different: dressed even smarter than usual, the glint of cufflinks, his hands shaking. She'd thought someone had died. Remembered staring at his broken nose, from where a door on a boat had crashed open in the wind. But he'd come to ask her over for dinner. He'd said it so quietly she had to ask him to speak up. Next weekend, Saturday, he said loudly. Was she allergic to anything in particular? And she had said, limes, she was allergic to limes, but only the skin, not the juice, if he wanted to use the juice then that was OK with her.

She got ready carefully. Put on a brown dress that she had bought in a sale. Wrapped around some beads. Had some trouble rolling on thin tights and when they were finally on they felt strange after her loose jeans. And her smart shoes were hard and unfamiliar, her make-up had dried to crusts in the pots. She brushed her hair for a long time and pinned it up, enjoying all the complicated twists and flicks. Then she went downstairs to find Ada, explain to her again that she would only be gone for two hours, that she would lock the door, that Luke's phone number was on the table. But Ada was upstairs in bed, coughing, shivering, rubbing her throat, saying she had seen a horse galloping through the house.

Pearl had taken off her beads and peeled off the dress, a ridiculous thing anyway, made her look like she was trying too hard. And the price tag had been dangling down her back the whole time. She stood by the phone for ten minutes before dialling Luke's number. Her hands shaking. She told Luke she wouldn't be able to make it after all, then waited for him to say, come next week instead, but he didn't, and she couldn't bring herself to suggest it either. Neither of them had mentioned it again.

Pearl put the phone down, put her head in her hands and wept, making sure she kept it short and quiet. When she went back upstairs, she glimpsed Ada running into her room from the landing, jumping to avoid the sharp floorboard, not shivering, not coughing, then diving under the covers. But when Pearl came in, she hacked and held her head and groaned the deepest, most heart-rending groan, it seemed almost impossible that she could have made it up.

*

198

Now, Pearl stood next to Ada and watched her sleeping. Not a pretty picture: her nose red and swollen, her top lip chapped, grey cheeks. But sleeping quietly in Pearl's old bed. Pearl remembered the long nights alone in that bed, how cold the sheets would get overnight, the sound of the rain against the windows, the wind rattling. Sometimes, when Ada was small, she would come in and climb under the covers and ask things like: why is the sky so high up? Why do we have to sleep? What are all the different ways people die?

'I don't know,' Pearl would say. 'I don't know.'

Outside, the snow was getting deeper and still falling. There was ice in the corners of the windows and the corners of Pearl's eyes. Snow building up under her tongue. She rolled it round and round. Felt each piece of snow as it landed and melted on the river, which was cold and stunned, running slower than usual, stiffening like a joint.

She made her way through the house, leaving piles of snow and ice behind her as she went. She was stiff and slow but her footsteps were steadier, more solid; she could see where she was going now that her eyes weren't murky and streaming. No buckling bones, no persistent feeling of being dragged at. No stumbling, nothing jostling. No sound of the river roaring, but rather, the faint ping of growing ice. Her toes crunched.

Down the stairs, through the hall and down into the study, where she had always retreated to. Someone had tidied away the photos she had spilled. She stayed by the bottom step and didn't go in any further. The room was much smaller than she remembered. And the curtains that sickly orange colour; had she chosen them? She couldn't remember. If all the time she'd spent here was calculated, how much would it have been? This one little room, out of anywhere in the whole world.

Something caught her eye on the shelf. The camera the little one had been using. She went over to it. Her old camera, and there were the others on the shelves. The one with the dodgy lens, the one she had dropped and dented. She ran her hands over them. Ice crept onto the lenses and powdery snow clung to the straps.

But how had it happened, this fascination with cameras? When had she become someone whose first thought on a stormy day was to go out and take a picture? Pearl thought back over it. There was no sudden decision, no sudden urge, as far as she could tell. She had just found a camera. Yes, that was it – Ada had been ill and finally fallen asleep one afternoon. Pearl couldn't leave the house, but she couldn't settle; couldn't concentrate on work, couldn't concentrate on any book. So she'd come into this room and looked through her old boxes of stuff. All the things she'd never bothered to sort out: folders and files and crappy ornaments. A set of old cutlery. And a camera that she'd hardly ever used before. No idea why she even had it.

She'd taken it out of the box and looked at it, unclipped the cap and fiddled around with the dials, just about worked out how to adjust the focus. She went over to the window, opened it as wide as it would go and leaned out. Then aimed at a twig covered in lichen, pressed the button and the camera made a lovely whirring sound. She aimed again, focusing on something blue up in a tree which she thought might be a kingfisher but actually turned out to be a bag snagged on a branch. Just those two shots, and then she'd closed the window and put the camera away. But the next day there was a rainbow and she thought she might as well take a picture of that. And the next day a fish jaw had washed up on the shingles and it looked like a mouse-trap. And the day after that, there was a dipper on the rocks and she didn't have the camera so she'd run all the way back up to the house to get it.

Pearl picked the camera up, fumbled it, then cradled it in her stiff hands. It fitted so particularly in her palms: the shallow grooves down each side, the cool plastic, the weight of it. Although not weighty enough. There was no film inside. She found one in a drawer and carefully fitted it in. Now she could sense the chemical tang in the film, feel the light bouncing off every surface. She lifted the camera up and looked through it. The lens smudged with ice. She rubbed it off and looked again. Saw snow falling wherever she aimed.

She lowered the camera and blinked. Outside the window, the little one was crouched down in the snow. Her face all creased up and frowning as she studied something on the ground. For a second, Pearl thought it was Ada. The same expression, the same intense concentration. Bits of hair flying out in the wind, red cheeks. Pearl stepped closer to the window. She looked tiny out there, crouched in the snow. A small, dark dot. How lonely. How lonely it must have been for Ada out here, left behind in the house while Pearl went out looking for her dragonflies and her hoarfrosts.

The snowflakes were falling faster now, whirling in curved patterns, like flocks of knot showing their pale bellies. As Pearl stood by the window, memories started coming in flurries. Broken glass; someone beckoning her out into the river; a dent in the side of the car. Memories drifting and piling up quietly, like letters on the doormat of an empty house.

She raised the camera again, her arms numb and stiff, her joints grating over ice. She aimed the camera and moved her finger over the button, tried to push it down, summoning up the force of the water, how it snapped sticks and forced reeds to bow their heads. Her finger was on the button and she aimed at the little one and she pressed it.

27

'COME ON,' HER MOTHER called from the car. 'We're late already.'

Pepper bent down to look at the snow. It had been trampled and there were muddled tracks and marks. It was hard to tell if there were paw prints there or not. There were bits of feather and bird prints, maybe a speck of grey fur snagged on a bramble.

Her mother called again. Pepper walked slowly over to the car. Snow clung to her trousers. Everything was hushed. She stopped and pretended to get a stone out of her shoe. It was very cold, probably too cold for a cat to be outside by itself. Maybe his fur would freeze. Snow pattered down from trees and branches. It was like a lumpy blanket over the ground.

The car engine hacked and stuttered and then started up. Pepper had one more look around the garden. Then she got in the car and slouched down in the front seat. The tyres crunched on snow and juddered over the potholes in the lane. The snow on the road was thinner and bits of grit flicked up at the windows.

'You won't have to go for long,' her mother said.

Pepper slouched down further in the seat. Now and again a glimpse of the river through the trees, grey and wide and cold. She picked at a loose thread on her belt. She was wearing her old green jumper and the horrible black shoes with buckles on, which rattled like her broken lunchbox whenever she moved.

Her mother kept glancing over at her and then back at the road. She drove slowly over the snow. Her nose was still red underneath but she didn't have to lie in bed any more. Pepper had spent two days eating cereal and washing her bowl up carefully. She'd made herself a cup of coffee the way her mother had it, and sat for an hour trying to drink it.

Her mother picked at the side of her thumbnail. 'It will be OK,' she said. But it wasn't her that had to go.

They turned into a narrow road and there was a brown house and then a postbox. After a while, her mother pulled in next to the pavement and stopped the car. 'Why are we stopping here?' Pepper said. A sudden hope that her mother had changed her mind.

'That's the school,' her mother said.

It didn't look like a school. There were four green cabins with flowers and huge insects painted on them. A small concrete playground with a wooden train. She stayed in the car. She could hear other children screaming and running around.

'I'll come in with you,' her mother said.

Pepper picked at her lips. She shook her head. Kept herself very stiff and upright when her mother kissed the top of her head.

She got out of the car and held onto her bag. Didn't look back as she made her way over to the playground. She stood at the edge and waited. There were red and blue circles painted on the ground. She waited in a blue circle. After hours and hours someone blew a whistle and everyone went inside. There were only two classrooms, one for older people and one for younger people. You had to sit on a table with people the same age as you. Petey was in her class and a boy she had seen at Luke's party. She recognised almost everyone.

The teacher had very short grey hair and three rings on each hand. One of them had a purple stone on it. She showed Pepper how to hold the pencil so that it didn't keep slipping. She had a funny way of saying the letter R. There was a green dinosaur on her desk which nodded slowly. When a girl with a fat plait in her hair threw a paperclip at Pepper, and Pepper got up and tangled it into her plait, the teacher didn't shout. She talked to both of them and then she took Pepper out into the corridor and showed her a line of framed photos. Each one was of a different class. And there was her mother, standing in the front row of one of the pictures. She was very small and her hair was tangled and she wasn't smiling. She was looking away from the camera and up at the ceiling, where the sun had turned a window bright white.

At lunch, she ate her sandwiches with Petey, then went outside. 'Let's sit in the train,' she said.

Petey shook his head. 'The older class don't let us sit in it.'

Pepper looked over at the train. 'So?' she said. Someone kicked a football into one of the carriages. She chewed her lip and was relieved when Petey shook his head again.

'I'll show you something,' he said. He went to the corner of the playground and prised up one of the concrete slabs. Underneath there were hundreds of pale worms. 'No one else knows about this,' he said. He watched the worms for a minute, then took a book out of his bag and told her about all the kings and queens that had been beheaded. He liked to read about things that had happened a long time ago.

'Why can you read books so well?' Pepper asked him.

Petey shrugged.

'But you can't draw very well, can you?' she said.

'No,' Petey said. When he drew, the pencil wobbled and none of his lines joined up. When he tried to draw people, their eyes floated outside of their faces. He had been born with yellow, wrinkly skin and had to be put under a lamp to change it back to pink.

In the afternoon there was a game in one of the snowy fields. The first team to grab their flag and run all the way back to their own side won. The girl with the plait tried to trip Pepper up, but she dodged out of the way and stamped on her toes. And Pepper's team won, and she rescued Petey, who had been captured straight away and was stuck in prison.

Then, suddenly, she was back out in front of the school again, and her mother was waiting. She looked cold. She'd been waiting by the gate rather than in the car.

'Was it OK?' she asked. She unlocked the car and they got in. 'Was it OK?'

Pepper shrugged. 'I dunno,' she said.

The car was so cold that Pepper could see her breath floating out, but her mother didn't turn the engine on. 'What's that in your bag?' she said.

Pepper showed the picture she'd done. 'The teacher said we had to draw our Christmas lunch.'

'You drew our pizza,' her mother said.

'The teacher said she wished she could have had pizza. I told her we almost didn't because the oven stopped working until you kicked it. She said, sometimes that works for her too.'

Her mother sat with her hands on the wheel. 'So it was alright?' she said.

Pepper glanced at her, then slouched down in her seat. 'I stuck a paperclip in a girl's hair and stamped on her feet,' she said. Just so that her mother knew she couldn't trick her into things and expect them to turn out OK.

They had to bring something in to show what they enjoyed doing at home – but it couldn't be TV or computer games, or animals, alive or dead. Pepper hovered outside the study for a long time before she went in. She'd left the cameras on the shelves but they had been moved around – one of them was on the desk and another one was lying on the floor. She picked them up and wiped them with her T-shirt. They were very cold. She looked at the camera she'd been using before. There was a film in it; it felt heavier and she could see a code written behind the see-through plastic. She looked around the room. The curtains swayed slightly in the draught. She turned and went to get her coat.

The snow was a lot of different colours when you actually looked at it. At first it just looked white, but there was grey in there and yellow and blue and sometimes purple shadows. She aimed the camera and pressed the button. When she clicked the lever across, the number on the dial changed. She made her way slowly down towards the river. She aimed at a blackbird that looked even darker against the snow; held the camera steady, then adjusted the focus.

'Down here by yourself again,' the old woman said behind her.

'Hmmmm,' Pepper said. She concentrated very hard on the blackbird. It shuffled and moved to one side. She readjusted her settings.

The woman cleared her throat. 'You're by yourself a lot, aren't you?'

'That blackbird will hear you,' Pepper whispered. She aimed the camera again. The river drummed behind her. Snow pattered down onto the blackbird's feathers and it ruffled itself up. Its bright yellow beak had a snowflake on the end – if only she could get it now . . . her finger hovered, about to click.

'Is it lonely, being out here?'

More snow pattered around the blackbird. 'Sometimes,' Pepper said. She focused in again.

'Is it?' the woman stepped closer. 'Because maybe if I'd done things differently.'

The blackbird was right in the centre. One more second. Got it. Now the blackbird was hopping to one side, leaving behind clear tracks. She moved forward.

The woman followed behind. 'I just think, maybe if I'd done things differently.'

Pepper blinked. She kept the camera steady, watching the blackbird.

'But I tried my best. I'm sure I tried my best, didn't I?'

The blackbird turned and stared at them, then flew away, spraying up a fine mist of snow. Pepper lowered the camera. The woman was covered with snow and her hands looked cold and grey. Her boots were coated in thick ice. She was always by herself too. 'I don't feel lonely when I take pictures,' Pepper told her. She put the camera carefully back in its bag.

'No,' the woman said. She looked towards the house. 'It's good for that, at least.'

A week went by, and then another. Pepper went to school every day. She would hang her bag and coat on a peg with a picture of a flower on it. It was meant to be a primrose but it looked like a fried egg. The important thing was to stay very quiet when someone else was talking. And you had to think carefully and try to ask a question. Pepper had a lot of questions. There were jars of pond water and jars of clay and a big computer on a table in the corner. Some days there was an assembly where everyone went and sat in a big room and someone talked about boring things like Hope and Sharing and Health. Petey always listened very carefully. Some days she spelled a word exactly right, other days the letters went upside down. There was a huge book of birds with the names written in very big letters. The girl with the plait came in wearing purple shorts and boots up to her knees and she got sent home. The best place to go at lunchtime was the pond at the bottom of the playground. If someone was sick on the cement it got covered up with sawdust. The boy with orange hair collected scabs off people's knees and elbows. The girl with black hair had a thing in her ear so that she could hear what people were saying. It was OK to copy someone's work if you gave them your biscuits, but not your apple. If she tried to distract Petey in class he would close his eyes. One afternoon, they had to draw the house they lived in. Pepper bent over her paper and scratched with a thick pencil. Tried to capture the sprawling bits of the house, the bending trees, a glimpse of the river. Smoke winding up. She worked over break time. Dark, deep pencil lines and lots of crossings-out but she finally finished it. 'Well,' the teacher said. She went to get another teacher to look. The picture was pinned up in the corridor for everyone else to see.

Everyone said that the snow would go away but it didn't. It hung around on the ground and the trees and it didn't melt. Like it was waiting for something. By the road, there was a drilled yellow pee hole where a dog had been. But still no sign of Captain. If he had frozen to death somewhere it would be her fault. She went out every morning to check the food scraps and look for signs, but there was nothing.

Her mother kept buying bags of food from the shop. Just in case, she said, looking out at the snow. She bought bags of bread and about a hundred tins. Huge bottles of water. She put the bread in the freezer and whenever the power went off, the bread would soften and crumble.

It was Saturday morning. The mid-January sky like dusty slate. Pepper was under the kitchen table, looking for a piece of toast she'd just dropped. The phone rang and her mother answered it. Her voice sounded surprised, then went very quiet, then she didn't speak for a long time. 'OK,' she said finally. She came back into the kitchen, sat at the table and went back to beating the mixture in the bowl. But a lot slower than before.

Pepper stayed under the table. 'Who was it?' she asked. 'Are we going to the pub tonight?' She studied her mother's legs and feet.

'Not tonight,' her mother said.

Pepper found the piece of toast but didn't eat it. She pushed crumbs around the floor, waiting for as long as she could. 'Who was it then?' she said.

Her mother stopped mixing. 'It was Ray,' she said.

Pepper's stomach jolted. She stabbed the crumbs into the floor. 'He said he didn't want it.'

Her mother's foot twitched. 'He wants to come and look at it again,' she said.

Pepper stayed very still. 'He said he didn't want it.'

The spoon moved slowly in the bowl. 'I thought that too,' her mother said.

A heavy, pumping feeling worked its way through Pepper's arms. Her hands felt very hot. It was her fault, it was her fault.

Her mother pushed the chair back and crouched down so that she could see under the table. 'He just wants to talk about it.'

'Talk,' Pepper said. 'Ha.' She pointed wildly at nothing.

Her mother was quiet for a long time. She shifted and her knees cracked softly. 'Maybe you won't have to go to school for much longer anyway.'

Pepper picked at her lips. Either way it was a trap.

'We can try somewhere else,' her mother said. Her voice was strange and quiet. 'We'll find somewhere else, OK?' She breathed out slowly.

The sharp crumbs bit into Pepper's fingers. 'But is he definitely going to come?' she said.

Her mother suddenly reached out and held Pepper around the wrists. They stayed like that for a moment, then she tugged her out from under the table. They both lost their balance, her mother fell sideways, Pepper sprawled face down across her mother's chest and hip. The tiles were dusty. Her nose dripped onto her mother's neck. They lay there on the cold floor. The clock ticked loudly. 'What are we doing?' Pepper asked after a while.

Her mother sighed. 'I don't know,' she said.

Pepper wiped her nose on her sleeve. 'I suppose you are trying your best,' she said. Her heart beat hard and fast and she could feel through her chest, like an echo, her mother's heart doing the same.

28

ADA GOT OUT HER crumpled bit of paper and looked at it again. She'd written down a plan for the evening service but had suddenly decided to put meringue on the menu. There were a lot of egg whites that she didn't want to waste, but they took a long time at a stupidly low temperature which meant nothing else could go in the oven at the same time. Skewed her whole timetable. She looked at it again. What was it that Ray had said on the phone? Something about coming over to look at the house again. But when? What had he actually said? She stared down at her schedule. If she got the onions on at four and the meringues were already in the oven then maybe . . . there was a loud clattering up on the roof. Loose tiles in the wind. Tristan said he needed to come and nail them down but Ada kept making excuses: that the weather was too bad, that she didn't want him to catch her flu. Trying to untangle herself. She hadn't seen him since New Year.

She sat down at the table and crossed out the thing about onions. If she moved them back, then maybe there would be enough time for everything else. The lights flickered. The fridge stopped, then struggled and started up again. She got up and checked the fire. There were enough logs in there but she put another one in anyway; at least there would be heat when the power finally went. Back into the kitchen. The potatoes needed to roast at some point. It was like those horrible maths questions at school. If she put the meringues in at four, and the sausages in at five, how long would she have to roast the potatoes? There was another loud thump on the roof. And if the potatoes were stubborn bastards that happened to take over two hours to roast, what then? The sound of a tile slipping. Or if the meringues went in earlier and were completely done and out the way by four . . . then she would have to be at the pub right now and already have them in the oven.

She needed to prep some of the food now. Val had asked her to pick potatoes up from Mick, so she could parboil those – that would be something. She started washing and peeling. Someone knocked on the door and she went to answer it. It was Tristan. He looked at the knife clutched in her hand.

'I don't know how I screwed up all the timings,' she told him. She went back into the kitchen and carried on chopping. 'But I should have started this about three hours ago.'

'Listen,' Tristan said. 'I just thought I'd come over and . . . ' He looked down at her schedule. 'Well, you've got two o'clock written twice here, for a start,' he said.

'Where?'

'Just below where you wrote, why the hell doesn't Val have a decent oven by now? in capital letters.' The lights flickered again. His hands looked cold. He took his coat off and put it over the chair. 'I could help you peel,' he said. 'If you want.'

I could help you peel. It sounded like something someone had whispered to her once in a sleazy bar, a long time ago. She passed him a knife. They stood hip to hip at the sink. Loops of peelings by the plug. Ada's in hacked chips, Tristan's in long, curved strips, almost peeling a whole potato in one go. She and Judy had once peeled apples whole and thrown the skin on the ground – it was supposed to show the first letter of the name of the person you would marry. Judy had thrown hers carefully and made a skewed R. Ada's had twisted and broken apart and didn't look like any letter at all.

It was snowing again. Just the sound of the knives working, the tap sending out slow drips. A small frown on Tristan's face as he concentrated. Graceful with the knife, giving it the same careful attention he would to carving something out of wood.

She watched his hands. The wide knuckles, the pale skin under his thumb. A bit of potato stuck to his sleeve. Remembered the way he had held her shoulder blades as if they were delicate ornaments. 'You have nice fingernails,' she told him.

'Do I?' He looked at her ragged nails. 'You have bloody fingernails,' he said. 'Is that normal?'

Pepper came into the kitchen. 'I'm meant to be at Judy's,' she said.

'Shit,' Ada said. 'I was supposed to take you.' She looked at the potatoes. Wondered for a second if she could simmer them on the car's heater.

Tristan put down his knife. 'I'll take her,' he said. 'I'm going that way anyway.'

Ada pushed her hair out of her eyes. 'OK,' she said. 'Thanks.' Reluctant, now that he was here, to see him go.

She helped Pepper wrap her old purple scarf around her neck; it looped down twice over her chest. Something she had started wearing to school. No fake illnesses to get out of it yet, no phone calls from teachers, although Ada still jumped whenever the phone rang.

213

On their way out, she heard Pepper ask Tristan if Shep minded sleeping on newspaper.

She put the potatoes on the hob, then started packing up ready to go. But the snow was falling a lot heavier now and settling over the ice around the front steps. Suddenly seized by the urgency of it. The clouds were dark grey and swollen. What if they couldn't get back through tonight? Or snow started to drift up against the door?

She went outside and found the shovel. Carried it over to the front steps and began scraping. The front door creaked open and her mother was standing in the doorway watching. Ada carried on shovelling. The cold bit into her fingers and she couldn't seem to shift the snow properly – she was just making a different pile in the middle of the path instead.

'There's no point doing that,' her mother said.

Ada scraped at the snow, which was icy and grey and smeared with mud. 'I've got to try and move some of it,' she said.

Her mother looked down at the steps. 'The snow was getting in through the kitchen window,' she said.

'What?' Ada said. She looked up quickly, but the windows were all shut. She worked the shovel over a slab of ice; it slipped and grated against her heel. She bit her bottom lip, had to stop herself throwing the shovel down and kicking it.

'Through the kitchen window,' her mother said. 'I'd left it open when I was out shovelling in the lane.' She bent down and picked up a chunk of ice.

Ada looked out at the lane. The snow was settling on it. 'Should I clear the lane instead?' she said.

'I was shovelling all morning. And all the time the snow was getting into the kitchen.' Her mother studied the ice carefully. 'It soaked into one of the sockets and blew it.'

Ada raked hair out of her eyes. 'The windows are all shut,' she said.

'And another time, I was shovelling snow away from the steps when I should have been shovelling around the car,' her mother went on. 'I couldn't get out for four days.'

Ada looked over at the car. The wheels were surrounded by an inch of snow. She stopped scraping the steps, started walking over to the damn car.

'There's no knowing which is best,' her mother said to the ice.

At the pub, Ada whipped the egg whites into peaks. Made her think again of the snow. Couldn't seem to get away from it. A difficult and slow drive over, a thin layer just starting to settle on the roads.

Val steered her over to the fridge. 'I got landed with all this garlic-cheese stuff,' she said. 'So maybe in the next week or two you can make something good out of it. Look up some recipes or invent something. It's stronger than you'd think. Pungent almost. Got to get it used up before it stinks the fridge up. And I need to talk to you properly about longer hours. Got to get the summer menu planned, make a big deal out of it. Bring in some of the tourists; they go straight past up here. And Valentine's Day, only three weeks away now. Have you had any thoughts on what we might do? I was thinking filled pasta in the shape of hearts, something red stuffed in there. Something simple. Perhaps a dessert with champagne in it, charge more than usual – champagne jelly, although I wasn't sure if jelly made it sound cheap. Do you think you could do that?'

'I've got to get these in the oven,' Ada said. Couldn't deal with all Val's pressure at the moment. She needed the money to sort the house, but couldn't sort it if she was always working. Either way she

215

was stuck. Unless Ray finally came over to talk, like he'd said he was going to.

Howard was back. He came in from the bar and looked in the fridge. The stocked shelves seemed to fill him with despair. 'I can't plan for summer at the end of January,' he said. 'I can't even look at that cheese stuff without my heart twingeing.'

She asked how his heart was, as if asking after a relative. Then wished she hadn't when he launched into a long and complex explanation. Vascular tubes all wrong, weak muscle condition. He pumped his hands like he was playing an accordion, oomp pah, he said. Then showed it slowing and wheezing. 'Anyway,' he said. 'I'm not touching anything to do with that cheese. Do you read your horoscope? Mine says: "Now is not the time." I think it could be applied to this.'

He'd made a batch of his special hotpot – potluck, he called it – but she managed to convince him to leave out the raisins, remembering the weird tough consistency and the way they stuck in people's teeth. Pepper picking them out one by one saying, rabbit poo, rabbit poo. She put the meringues in the oven, then got out the onions for her stew. Realised how similar it would be to hotpot and quickly switched her idea again. Something with pasta, some kind of rich sauce. She started chopping the onion, found the bunches of kale she'd asked Val to get in – it always tasted sweeter after frost and ice.

'I could help you do that,' Howard said. 'Chop it up and wash it.' He put the kale in the sink. 'I could do a few easy jobs. I don't mind doing prep.'

'OK,' Ada said. She hated prep the most, or maybe the washing-up. She crouched down and peered into the oven, checking the meringues. Howard added a handful of raisins to his pot with a sly look when he thought she wasn't watching. Then he got to work slicing, working the knife like a lever so that the kale came out in very thin, even pieces. 'Learned that technique in catering school,' he said. 'Took a month. Like a card trick – it's all in the sleight of hand, see?' He showed again. 'We used to have competitions. Learned to slice pig cheeks so thin they were translucent.' He smacked his lips against his hand.

'Listen you two,' Val said, coming back in and carrying on where she'd left off. 'What about a themed menu in the summer, eh? I was thinking, June, you build it around strawberries – strawberry salad to start with, strawberry mousse to finish, what main courses could have strawberries in do you think? Does strawberry lasagne sound weird to you? And then maybe a saffron thing for July, conjure up the sun. Everything bright yellow. You'd have something like smoked haddock, the stuff that's dyed yellow, maybe mushrooms in a sauce, colour it with turmeric. Paella, lemon posset for dessert. Although what is posset anyway? I thought it was baby sick, but I just read a recipe in a magazine the other day.'

'It's a cold dessert,' Ada told her. 'Chilled and set, like syllabub.' But also the slushy, milky sick a baby brought up. Had never been able to eat the dessert herself.

'Syllabub?' Val said. She turned the word over in her mouth. 'Syllabub?'

'I can't think about this now,' Howard said. He rubbed over his old burns with his thumb.

'We need to talk about it,' Val said. 'I've got a feeling about this.'

'I won't be here in the summer,' Ada said. Strawberry lasagne would be a bloodbath. But liked the sound of a strawberry salad, could play around with colours, maybe the sharp contrast of vinegar drizzled over.

'I've got a feeling about this,' Val said again.

Ada stirred her sauce. 'Arseballs,' she said. It had got lumps in when Val distracted her.

'That always happens to me,' Howard said. He passed her the sieve. 'There's nothing else for it.'

Val went out and a moment later called back in again saying, someone wants a slice of the pie you made the other day, is there any left? And two hotpots, put them in bowls not on plates. Put some of that kale with it.

Ada looked over at the hotpot. 'Howard?' she said. 'Could you go and ask Val which pie she meant?' Howard sighed, dried his hands on his apron and went out. Ada quickly picked out all the raisins and threw them in the bin, before dishing up two servings.

Just as she was leaving, Clapper came over to her from the bar, holding something. It was a green box wrapped in layers of elastic bands.

'It's for the little one,' he said. 'From Petey. Strict instructions that no one else can open it.' He tapped his nose.

She took the box and put it in her bag carefully. There were coded symbols on one side. Couldn't believe that Pepper had made a friend, and that they had a secret language already.

It had stopped snowing but there was a smooth layer on the ground and the trees. Everything silvery. She stood for a moment, breathing in cold, grainy air. It felt good. The sudden hush and chill of being outside, the air raw and hard. A sense of being scoured. Under the pub's lamp, the world glinted. Black branches against white, like lines of ink. The valley suddenly changed, draped in snow like furniture draped in sheets. But the same smokiness to the air, the same dry tang in the back of her throat. The air crackled. She stood and breathed it in.

The road had been gritted. She drove slowly. Another car's lights emerged in the distance like dim moons. She turned into the road towards Judy's, the headlights swept over the hedge, and she slammed on the brakes. The car stalled and was silent. Tristan stepped out of the hedge, where he had jumped back to get out of the way. He came over to her window and put his hand on it. He was wearing a black coat, scrappy at the edges like an old biscuit, and a navy knitted hat. A simple recipe for death: narrow lanes and dark clothes.

'You shouldn't wear dark clothes at night,' she told him. 'Hasn't anyone ever told you that?'

'I was just going for a drink,' he said, gesturing towards the pub. But he walked round the car and got in and she started it up and drove.

Snow had been pushed to the sides of the road in heaps, like crumbling walls. More snow collected in potholes. She glanced at Tristan, saw the freckles on his cheeks, thought of the tea-coloured freckles on his back. Stopped herself. Looked again. Tapped her fingers against the wheel.

'I should have finished nailing the tiles on,' Tristan said.

Ada turned down a narrower lane, which looked like a white carpet unrolling. Then another. She had no idea where she was going. 'You know I'm leaving soon,' she said. 'Don't you?'

'Of course I know that,' he said. 'I'm working on your house.'

There were lines in his face she'd never noticed before, faint etchings around his eyes and mouth. Ada nodded. 'Good,' she said. 'That's good.' She kept tapping her fingers.

Tristan wiped the steamed-up window with his sleeve and looked out.

'Because I don't know when it will happen exactly,' she said.

219

'I know,' Tristan said.

'It's just too much work,' she went on. 'And too isolated, too hard to get around. That's what I always said.'

'I know,' Tristan said.

'And Pepper. You know I've got Pepper. I just wanted to get the whole thing done as quickly as possible and get out.'

'I know,' Tristan said.

There was a lay-by in the road and she pulled in and stopped the car. Her hands still gripping the wheel. 'You know? You know?' Something unravelled and snapped in front of her like a flag. Tristan just going along for the ride.

Tristan turned round sharply. 'Yes,' he said. 'I know, Ada. And you knew as well. But there's nothing I can do about it whether I want to or not. Do you know that?'

'Do I know that?' she said. 'Of course I know that. I know the hell out of that.' She always got lost in arguments; what did she know? She knew nothing. She got out of the car. Her breath billowed out. Her cheeks stinging. Snow crunched. She climbed up the bank towards a low fence, a field beyond covered in snow. The field was smooth. No marks, no tracks. Her boots sank, leaving deep prints. She walked a wide circle. Heard Tristan get out of the car and climb up the bank. Felt him watching her. She looked up. God, that stupid hat made him look young. He'd found a curved stick and he held it in front of his mouth. First curved downwards, then gradually making the ends point up. Behind it, his own mouth in a lopsided grin. And this was her problem, this was definitely her problem: when it came down to it, she would do anything for a really good grin, all chapped and bemused and leaning teeth.

Tristan walked into the field, put his hands in his pockets and started pressing his own deep footprints into the snow.

From above, the field was stamped with wide arcs, like links in a chain, each one getting smaller and closer as they slowly circled each other in the snow.

29

THE BUCKLES ON PEPPER'S shoes rattled. She sat on the stairs and pressed her feet against the rails. Waiting for her mother to get off the phone. 'Could you say that again?' her mother kept saying. She shook the phone and looked at it. 'All I can hear is crackling.' She shook the phone again, listened, then put it down.

'What is it?' Pepper said.

'I think the school's been closed,' her mother said. She picked the phone up once more and listened. 'It's not working,' she said. She went over to the window and looked out. It had been snowing heavily all night. In the distance, the moor was submerged. The clouds were so low and bulky it looked like they were going to land on the ground. There were drifts of snow all around the house and the wind was getting stronger, flinging snow against the windows.

Pepper pressed her feet hard against the stairs. They were meant to be doing pictures with chalk. And she wanted to show Petey her knee – she had a bruise that was changing from purple to yellow. 'How long for?' she asked. Trying to keep her voice casual.

'All this week,' her mother said. 'The snow's forecast to get worse.' She stared out of the window.

'But maybe the week after,' Pepper said. She ran her finger over the shiny wood. There was a black knot in the step she liked to sit on, which looked like a spider in a web. She touched the fat middle. The day stretched out ahead of her. She followed the spider's web with her finger, round and round and then round again.

The snow made the house seem dim and green. Her buckles rattled. She got up and went down the hall, looking again at the pictures along the wall – she had looked at them so many times she knew them off by heart. The kingfisher on the branch over the river; the paper turning yellow in the right-hand corner. The picture of the wren in the bank – the shadow of the person taking the photo spilled out on the grass in front. The one where the water was so flat that there was a whole tree reflected upside down in it. And there were fingerprints on the wall around the pictures. Different-sized ones that Pepper liked to put her own fingers against. In the other houses they'd lived in, the walls had usually been scrubbed so hard that there was no sign that anyone had ever lived there before.

There was a lot of noise coming from the kitchen. Her mother was looking in all the cupboards and filling a bag with packets and tins and pieces of bread. Pepper watched from the doorway. 'What are you doing?' she asked.

'I've got to go and check on Luke,' her mother said.

'Why?' Pepper asked.

Her mother gestured outside. 'He's in the house by himself.' She put another tin in the bag. She went to the door and put on her coat and scarf and gloves and a hat. Then she took her coat off and put on the long brown one that was hanging by the door. 'Stay inside, OK?'

she said. 'And don't touch the fire. I won't be long.' She pushed the door. It only opened a few inches, so she shoved it hard with her shoulder. It scraped past a heap of snow, then closed softly.

Pepper stayed in the hall listening for the car, but it didn't start. She went upstairs and just glimpsed her mother trudging up the road through deep snow. She watched until she couldn't see her any more. Now Luke was in his house by himself, and she was in her house by herself.

The house was very quiet. She went and stood by the fire. It was very low. There were a lot of logs stacked up at the side. She put the oven glove on and opened the stove door carefully. Then she placed two medium-sized logs on the embers. Let enough air whoosh in so that they caught and then closed it again. There. A burning smell. The glove was smouldering. She stared at it. Smoke curled out. She pressed it against the slates for a long time with her eyes closed. When she opened them it had stopped smoking.

An hour passed, and then another. She wasn't scared of the house's noises any more: the creaks, the groans, the soft chunterings. It was like the house was talking to itself. When it was windy, the upstairs windows shook, and when the water was low in the tank the radiators banged. Once, when the wind was very strong, it shook bits of old horsehair out of the beams because part of the house used to be a stable. There was a beam in the kitchen with a stain that looked like a bat, and a crack in the wall by the phone that was so deep that, if she picked at it, she could slide most of her hand in. Her coats and boots were lined up by the door. She knew the best place to watch the road, the best places to hide, the best place to stand if she wanted to listen in to conversations. She avoided, without even noticing, the rusty nail sticking out of the third step, and the sharp tile by the door in the kitchen.

She went into the study, picked up the camera and a bird book and took them under the kitchen table. Got back up and found a tin of cherries in the cupboard. She opened them and crawled back under the table, ate them one by one, dripping dark syrup over the floor. She hummed to herself. Turned the pages slowly. There was a picture of a heron in the book. She studied it for a long time. Snow fell outside the window. She turned the page slowly. A grey shape moved past the window. The glass rattled. She stopped humming. She held the page very still. The window rattled again. She closed the book and crawled out, then looked outside. Saw nothing but deep snow. She opened the window. Snow whirled and landed in the sink. There was a paw print in the snow on the windowsill. She closed the window and went to the hall, then pushed the front door open as hard as she could. The world was deep and white. She stepped out into it. Almost fell down the buried steps. 'Captain,' she called. She blinked snow out of her eyes. She took another step out. Could hardly see through the snow, but there was the cat, turning to look at her. There was snow all over his ears and his face. His tail looked like a white brush.

She stayed by the door. Captain turned back and looked out at the snow, towards the trees and the river. There was a scratch on the back of his leg and a tuft of fur missing from his tail. His ears pricked up and alert, his back quivering. His fur blending in with the snow, moving his paws carefully. His ears twitched. He lifted his nose, sniffing things on the air that she would never even know about. She stood and watched him and she didn't call.

But the cat didn't move away. He turned again and looked at the house. He took a step closer. Snow matted onto his fur. Then he jumped lightly onto the tree stump, then along the row of plant pots and onto the front steps. He disappeared into the house.

Pepper left the door open. She went back into the kitchen and sat under the table. Captain moved around the edges of the cupboards, the melting snow slicking his fur. His paws trailed snow over the floor. Pepper opened her book and turned the page. Watching Captain out of the corner of her eye. He snaked around the kitchen, jumped up on the side and drank some water from the sink. Then jumped back down and rubbed against the oven.

'You don't have to stay in here,' she told him. 'I left the door open.'

He stopped rubbing and looked at her. Then he went out of the kitchen.

Pepper turned the pages of the book without looking at them. Her eyes felt hot and she blinked them over and over. After a while, she got up and went out into the hall. The snow had piled up around the door and it was very cold. She pulled the door closed and leaned against it. Her mother had been gone a long time. She picked up the phone and listened: there was no dialling tone. She checked the fire: it was OK. She checked the windows were shut: they were. The window in the study rattled. She glanced in. Captain was sitting on the chair in the corner. Padding his paws down on the cushion, as if he was plumping it up. There were tearing noises as his claws dug in.

She went in but didn't look at him. She reached up to the shelves and spent a long time choosing a book. She took down a big colour-ful one. 'D i p p e r,' she spelled out carefully. 'Dipper.' Glanced over at Captain. He was sitting up and looking at her. 'It's just letters,' she told him. 'Nothing to be afraid of.'

He put his head to one side. She put the book down and stood in front of him, then stretched out her hand a little. Captain flinched and made a funny noise in the back of his throat. She took her hand away. At school, she didn't like it when she had to hold hands with people in a line. They always had dry or clammy skin or sharp bits of nail. She always kept her hands behind her back.

'I don't mind,' she told him. She sat on the floor next to the window and opened the book. Snow slid down the glass. The jackdaw's loose feathers ruffled in the draught. She felt something by her leg. Captain had jumped down from the chair and was standing next to her, looking at a trailing thread on her jumper. She snapped it off and pulled it along the floor. 'What is it?' she said. 'Get it Captain.' He stiffened up and arched his back. His tail very rigid. Then he pounced on the thread. Pepper pulled it away. His claws almost grazing her hand. She pulled it along the floor again, standing up this time. 'Come and get it,' she said. Captain swiped and his claws caught her on the thumb. She jerked her arm backwards, hard and fast, and heard, rather than felt, her elbow smack into the window. There was silence. Then a hot jolting pain swept down her arm and the wind howled in and there was glass on the carpet around her feet. She turned and looked. The window had cracked right through. Snow whirled in. Dark grey sky. Then, suddenly, there was a face at the window – the old woman, standing outside and staring at the glass.

Pepper blinked, looked again and saw only snow, swirling and intense, like the time she had split open an old pillow and feathers had poured out; drifting down and settling over her bed and her pencils and her shoes.

30

THAT WINDOW HAD BROKEN before. Yes, that was it: it had broken and he'd picked up a piece of glass and cut his thumb. Pearl remembered the bead of blood, the look of surprise on his face when it had rolled down over his wrist. She could remember the way his eyebrows had furrowed, the slight puckering on his bottom lip, but not his actual face, not the particulars of it. Frank. She said his name out loud, in the snow. What exactly was his skin like? What exactly were his eyes like? Nothing came back as vividly as the broken glass, the smear of blood, more brown than red, like glimpsing a deer rushing through trees.

That was when it all changed, although the day had started like any other. One of those mizzly winters, no snow, but the rawness of it exceptional. The house full of damp and smelling like a ditch and the fire puttering and not generating enough heat. Pearl scoured back over it, looking for signs. They had woken up early, as usual. Eyes bleary and the sheets chilled overnight. Those precious few moments before the day began, when they would lie side by side, hips touching, looking up at the ceiling; the stain from the burst pipe – which Frank said looked like an owl and Pearl said looked like an umbrella – and the stippled paint, bits cracking off in the night and garlanding the bed like confetti.

Their breath floated up in front of them. 'Frank?' Pearl said. 'Did you have any dreams?' It was what she always asked in the morning. Usually, Frank would say something about cities underwater, or bailing out a sinking boat with a tambourine. Always a sense of urgency, some kind of impending disaster. Although he also had a recurring dream about sitting peacefully on top of a stalled Ferris wheel, looking out over millions of tiny bright lights.

Frank stared up at the ceiling. A muscle in his eyelid fluttering – he was never completely still for one moment.

'I dreamt about an island,' Pearl told him. 'It was getting smaller but there was a tree right in the middle. I started climbing. There was a phone up there and it was ringing and ringing.'

Frank shifted, kept his eyes fixed on the ceiling. 'Well,' he said finally, 'why didn't you answer it?'

And then the first noises from Ada, like an alarm clock, the clucks and the mewls and then the roaring, tiny fists red and clenched at the outrage of waking up. Frank stumbled out of bed and went to her, rocked her and soothed her and Pearl remembered now: how tall he was – how small Ada looked with Frank's long arms wrapped around her. The slight stoop he had, as if he was constantly under a ceiling that was too low. And his thin hair: long and wispy around his ears, full of static, and the same dry colour as oats.

Frank's side of the sheets turned cold. Pearl got up and sat on the edge of the bed. Starting the day exhausted, one day blurring into the next. Confusing when was night and when was morning. Four months of heating milk, swiping through dishes, collapsing in chairs – not asleep but not awake either. Baffled, stunned even, by the mess, the noise, the constant cycle of washing and meals and washing. Forgot who she was almost. Ten seconds in the shower: just enough time to scrub on soap and rinse. Forgot what her own body looked like. The milkman came to the door and she gave him letters to post.

But Frank sang to Ada while he dressed her, he cooked while Ada was sitting in the sink. He would put her in the hood of his coat and take her outside. Paint strange swirling pictures to put on her wall. Warm the milk up patiently to just the right temperature. And it was only from time to time that he fed her spoonfuls of beer when he thought Pearl wasn't looking, or left her under the desk in his study because he'd forgotten she was there, or got a bemused look on his face and said, how do you do, as if she was a stranger.

Pearl came downstairs, smelled the usual morning smells: toast burning, sour milk, baby shampoo, coffee. Got Ada fed while Frank sorted out the fire – couldn't help noticing that he took a long time about it, and when she went to look, he'd piled in enough logs to burn all day and probably overnight as well. When she went back into the kitchen, the washing machine had spewed black liquor all over the floor. She called to Frank but he was thumping around in his study. She put Ada in her basket, then looked at the instruction manual – tried to figure out the mechanisms and the diagrams but it was impossible. She hit the pipe with a spanner, mopped up the liquid and switched the machine off at the plug – the best she could do.

There was murmuring and banging coming from the study. Frank's work not going well again. He came into the kitchen and held up a ring. 'Look at this,' he said. 'I can't get the stock to go in.' Pearl took the ring from him and looked at it. He'd cut the metal unevenly and hadn't heated it enough to make it malleable. He wasn't patient, always struggling with the work, always restless, God knows why he'd got into it in the first place – he wasn't good with anything fiddly or small. He liked daubing paint, chopping hunks of wood, smashing old fence for kindling. He went over to the radiator and gripped his cold hands on the top. Any minute now he would come over and hold them against her cheeks. She waited, then waited some more.

'I'll have a look at it,' she told him finally. She carried Ada into the study and put the basket down on the floor. Put the ring in the holder and studied the stock.

Frank followed her in. He went over to the window and paced. 'The river's so loud,' he said. 'You can't get away from it.'

'What did you expect?' Pearl said.

He stared up at the sky, where a vapour trail bloomed like spilled paint. His thumb moved along the window, smoothing the paint over and over, slowly rubbing the paint down to bare wood. He glanced down at Ada and back up at the vapour trail.

Ada slept on. Morning turned into afternoon. For lunch, Frank cut thick slices of bread and cheese. They ate in the kitchen, their chairs pulled up in front of the radiator. Wet clothes on the airer next to them. And had they spoken? Pearl racked her brains but couldn't recall if they had spoken. All she remembered was the rich taste of the butter, the way that Frank ate his bread slowly, relishing every bite. How he'd speared chunks of cheese and apple with the sharp knife and put them straight in his mouth. Maybe he'd mentioned the jackdaws in the chimney, maybe she'd talked about the car's creaking brakes. Both of them slipping into criticisms of the place when they had nothing else to say, working each other up, until Pearl felt like she was sinking under all the repairs that needed doing, the money they'd already spent, how much more wood they had to buy now that they had Ada. But maybe none of that had come up. Maybe they'd just sat there quietly, huddled against the radiator.

Drizzle bloomed in the air and drops of water hung off everything. It was so raw and cold that the house seemed to shrink into itself and tighten. At the bottom of the grass, the river was running fast and low. You could see stones through it, showing through like a spine.

She went back in and had another look at the ring while Frank fed Ada.

'We've run out of milk,' Frank said, coming in. 'Normal milk I mean. I'm going to go and get some from the shop.' He put Ada down next to Pearl. A sudden energy to the way he moved: he tucked Ada's blanket elaborately, kept raking his hand through his hair, he came up and stood very close to Pearl and touched the tips of his fingers against her cheekbone. His fingers were very cold. His breath fast and shallow. He turned to look at her again from the door, then went out and got in the car. The engine started up then stopped. Started, coughed, then stopped again. Nothing for ten long minutes. Then Frank came back in. He hadn't put a coat on. 'I need to get milk,' he said. His voice was tight. He tapped against the door with his fist.

'You finish this,' Pearl said. 'I've softened the metal and opened it up wider. There's not much left to do.' She touched Ada's soft arm. She was sleeping again. 'I'll go and get the milk.'

'How will you?' Frank asked.

Pearl looked out of the window. 'I'll have to walk,' she told him. She pulled on her boots and the long brown coat that Frank had bought her. Far too expensive. And not her style at all. Too practical, too waterproof, but it was warm, something in the seams that kept the wind out. 'I'm going now,' she called.

Frank didn't answer.

'I'm going now.' Determined he would know how annoying it was, having to walk all the way to the shop. She stood on the top step of the study. 'If I twist my ankle again and it gets dark you'll have to come out and look for me.'

And that's when it happened. Frank stood up, took a pair of pliers from his toolbox and hurled them at the window. The glass cracked outwards, then seemed to hold for a moment before shattering and falling onto the carpet. The room was very quiet. They both stood there and waited for Ada to howl, but she didn't wake up.

Drizzle rushed into the room. The sound of the river was even louder now, drumming away at the bottom of the field. Frank went over to the window and picked up a piece of the glass.

'I'm going now,' Pearl said.

It took her nearly three hours to walk to the shop and back. At first, her legs ached and her knees cracked. Her chest was tight and heavy. The raw air made it difficult to breathe. But, after a while, she started getting used to it. And felt better – the cold air felt good in her lungs, her legs got into a steady stride, her thoughts steadying. Her heart stopped racing and beat firmly and in time with each step.

When she opened the front door, the house was quiet. Ada was still asleep in the kitchen and Frank had tucked another blanket around her.

She called out to Frank but he didn't answer. She knew immediately that he wasn't there but she went round the house checking anyway. Up the stairs, into every room. She put the milk away in the fridge and saw that there were two bottles in there already. She went back outside and walked around the yard. The car was still there. There were no bags missing, no other clothes except his good pair of boots. His wallet had gone but the bank book was still there, the dwindling figure of their savings stamped at the front. The ring was on the desk, fixed now and polished up to a gold shine. And he had put a piece of board over the broken window. Not a rushed job either – he had cut and fitted it neatly so that it would hold. It seemed like a kind thing to do. And by the way he had done it, she knew that he wasn't coming back.

Although she waited. When Ada woke up she sat with her by the fire and waited. All night, holding Ada in her arms as she grizzled and drifted in and out of sleep. Listening for Frank's footsteps coming up the steps by the door, listening for his cough, his voice. But he didn't come back.

She made up stories. He might have had an accident – maybe he'd been hit by a car, had lost his memory and never remembered the house, or her. He didn't have his coat – he should have taken his coat. Or maybe he was being held somewhere. Or maybe he was . . . Then she would stop and shake her head. She warmed her hands up on the radiator and held them against her face.

Forty-five. With a baby. On her own. Again, she went back over that morning, that day. 'Why didn't you answer it?' he'd said about the phone in her dream. He'd rubbed his thumb on the paint on the window. Should she have known when he banked the fire up so high? Why hadn't she checked to see if they actually needed milk? She remembered the bright fire and the bottles of milk so clearly, but still couldn't remember the particulars of his face.

The morning came in grey and damp. A glimmer of brightness in the distance. Still Pearl sat by the fire. Nowhere else to go, but she whispered to Ada that they wouldn't be staying here, not for long anyway. They wouldn't end up staying here for long.

31

THE SNOW WENT UP to her ankles, then her shins. Ada waded out of the lane and onto the road. No fresh grit – the snow packed down and slippy in the middle, a few tyre tracks veering in wide arcs. Gravel and leaves trapped in there like fossils.

She moved over to the edge of the road, where the snow was more powdery and easier to walk on. Her feet sunk in with each step. Snow fell on her hair and stuck to her coat. Everything was thick and white and silent. She hefted the bag over her shoulder. Tins dug into her back. Luke lived a long way from the shop and there was no way he'd be able to get out in his car. She had moved restlessly through the house, couldn't stop imagining her mother out here alone; cold, struggling with the heating, with the power, no way of getting out. No one around to help. She'd grabbed things randomly – a tin of spaghetti, a packet of custard, three bars of chocolate – pulled on her boots and gone.

The road curved through the valley, following the river. It climbed higher on the way to Luke's. It was difficult going uphill and she slid and grabbed at the hedge, which snagged on her gloves. And it was impossible to see any of the potholes until her foot was already in them, her ankle almost twisting. Once she stumbled and her arms disappeared into deep snow.

She brushed the snow off her coat. Breathed in icy grains through her nose and mouth. The sloping fields ridged with snow, besieged hay bales, laden trees. A tipping scarecrow, eye-to-eye with the snow, coat flapping in the wind. She walked faster, thinking again about those last few winters. What if there'd been power cuts? What if there'd been no heating or hot water? What she should have done years ago. She clutched the bag and turned round a sharp bend in the road. There was Luke's place in front of her, the snow covering up most of the blackened remains of the bonfire – there were still streaks of soot on the walls where it had licked at the house.

She was covered in snow when she knocked on the door. Out of breath, wet hair in her eyes. There was no answer. She looked through the window. There was a light on in the kitchen but no sign of Luke. She tapped on the glass. 'Luke?' she called. Saw the reflection of her own anxious face staring back out at her. She banged on the front door, then rattled the handle, but it was locked. She ran round to the back of the house and looked in. The TV was on, the news flickering across the screen. A blanket slumped on the floor by the chair. She should have come before, she should have come before. She shouted Luke's name and thumped on the glass.

There was the sound of a key in the front door and it opened and Luke was there, standing on the front step. 'What the hell's the matter girl?' he said. He was pulling on his coat and boots. 'What's happened?' He was wearing pyjama bottoms and a red jumper under the coat.

'I was knocking for ages,' Ada said. Her breath rasped in her throat. 'What were you doing?'

'I was upstairs,' he said. 'Jesus, what is it?'

Ada wiped her nose and her eyes with her sleeve. Her legs were shaking. 'I was knocking for ages,' she said. 'I thought something had happened to you.'

Luke stopped tying his boots. He looked at Ada carefully. Then he untied the laces, took off his coat and beckoned her inside.

She went in, took her boots off and hung up her sopping coat. Luke gave her a towel and a blanket to put over her wet legs. He pulled out a chair for her at the kitchen table. There was an oil heater sending out waves of heat, a bright lamp, the radio playing quietly in the background. She rummaged in the bag. 'I brought you things,' she said. 'I thought you might need them.' She put the tins out on the table, a crushed packet of crackers.

'You didn't have to do that,' Luke said.

Ada unpacked the last tin, then saw the fresh loaf and the pot of jam, smelled the baking smells and saw the oven door was ajar, cooling.

Luke put the kettle on and got out plates. Opened the crackers, cut slices of bread.

Ada looked at the motley spread of crap she'd brought. 'God, you don't need this,' she said. She started to pack the bag up again, blinking her eyes. They felt sore from the snow. But Luke stopped her, put the things she'd brought away carefully: the custard, a handful of dusty tea bags. Said he'd have the soup later. His favourite flavour. Then he poured out tea and sat down. 'I'm surprised you made it through,' he said. 'I saw the road wasn't gritted.' He put a handful of crackers on his plate and spread them with butter.

Ada pulled the blanket tighter over her damp legs. She took a slice of bread and spooned on a thick layer of jam. Ate it in four bites. Luke cut her another. She rotated her stiff ankle. 'I nearly didn't,' she said.

Luke leaned forward, resting his elbows on the table. 'You just walked over three miles in some of the worst snow we've had in the valley,' he said.

'Three miles?' It hadn't seemed that far.

'Just to come and see if I was OK,' Luke went on. 'I heard that Robbie and Judy can't even get their truck out. And the pub's closed. And Larry Reams? Jake's friend? He slipped over and broke his leg and his arm, got a cast all the way up.' He bit at his cracker.

'I almost did that,' Ada said. 'There are potholes everywhere.'

Luke leaned back in his chair. 'Like your mother,' he said.

Ada shook her head and rubbed her ankle again. 'She would have been here hours ago.'

'Not at the beginning,' Luke said, then looked surprised when Ada leaned forward and asked him what he meant. He touched his hair. 'I suppose I haven't ever told anyone this story.' He reached forward and lifted up his mug, sipped the tea, then held it in both hands. 'It's nothing much though,' he said. 'Not even a story really.'

'I'd like to hear,' Ada told him. Thought of when he had told the story about Tristan's leg, and the one about the bees that someone had smoked out of their chimney, only to see them swarm down the chimney next door. Practically rubbed his hands together with relish and leapt straight in.

But now he started, faltered, then started again. 'It was the first time I saw your mother,' he said. Gulped more tea. 'She must have only moved into the house a few weeks before. It was winter. A terrible time to move in but there you go. Snow was half a foot. Less than now. But it went on for almost a month. I was driving along the road, on my way into town I think it was. This was a long time ago of course,' he said. 'More than thirty years. I hadn't been in the area that long myself. Had enough of the sea at that point but that's

238

another story.' He stopped and glanced over at the wall, then carried on. 'I was driving slowly through the snow and I came round that bend on the bottom road – you know the one, where the tree leans over and it looks like someone pointing.'

Ada nodded. She knew the exact place.

'I came round there, and there was your mother.' He stopped for a moment and took another swig of tea. His voice was hoarser than usual, as if a wheel that normally turned smoothly had a rusty axle. 'There she was. Standing in the road. You probably don't believe me, but she was walking along in these thin blue shoes, just straps across them and hardly any sole. No hat, no gloves. Thin trousers. A smart coat, not very thick, the snow going right through it. Not like that brown one you wore over here.'

Ada had a sudden memory of something her mother used to do, which had always seemed so out of place. She would polish her walk-ing boots. She kept a stack of different-coloured tins of polish in the cupboard under the sink, and every Sunday evening she would get out her boots, choose a tin, and scoop out little divots of expensive polish – the kind people normally used for work shoes or special occasions. She would wipe off the mud and clinging moss, then work the polish in carefully, buffing up the cracked leather until it shone. Ada could almost smell the polish here now, in Luke's kitchen.

'She was hobbling,' Luke said. 'I pulled in and asked if she was alright. It turned out that she was trying to get to the shop. She was going completely the wrong way, but I didn't tell her. I thought it was best not to tell her.' He smiled and lines spread all over his face. 'She didn't know about the potholes. Couldn't see them in the snow. She'd twisted her ankle in one of them and could hardly walk on it. I told her I'd give her a lift back to the house. She got in and sat down very carefully. I remember her hands were clasped like this.

And some kind of perfume that stayed in my truck for a week.' Luke shook his head and let out a long breath. 'All she talked about was how they wouldn't be here very long, how it was a stop-gap; doing up the house with her husband, Frank, I mean . . . well, your dad.' He rubbed over his face and went quiet for a moment. Ada smiled and shrugged, waited for him to carry on. 'He'd seen the house, thought it would be a good place to live for a few years. Cheap, you know, and right by the river. It only took ten minutes to drive her back. But her hair dried, in the heat. It curled up at the back, I always remember that.' He looked down at his hands. 'Like I said, it's not much of a story.'

Ada was quiet for a long time. Looking round at his small kitchen: a set of china plates painted with cherries, binoculars on the windowsill. A pot of cream paint and a brush – maybe for touching up after the party. There was a framed photograph of a goldcrest on the wall – a picture her mother had taken. She'd always said it was one of her favourites. He must have put it away somewhere safe for the party.

She glanced at Luke, who was still looking down at his hands. What was it her mother had said about the snow? She'd left a window open and it had come into the kitchen and blown a socket. And it hadn't even crossed her mind to shovel round the car. 'She had a suit,' Ada said suddenly. 'Hidden in the back of her wardrobe. And sometimes she slept with a lamp on, because she didn't like the way it was pitch black.'

Luke nodded. 'She didn't like the sound of the owls at first, either,' he said. 'And what about her temper? When she would curse the roads and the tiny shop and the power cutting out. And the rain. She used to hate getting wet in the rain. But she couldn't use an umbrella because it was always too windy.'

'The rain?' Ada laughed. 'That's nothing compared with the fire. I once heard her shout at that thing for over an hour. I went out and came back and she was still going.'

'She put it out once,' Luke said. 'Threw a bucket of water over it. Then later she had to dry it out and relight it all over again.'

'And what about when she kicked the car and bruised her toe?' Ada said. 'She broke a bit off the number plate.' Her turn to look down at her hands. The corner was still chipped off the number plate; she'd forgotten until now how it'd happened. She finished her bread. One more spoonful of jam as a chaser. The clocked chimed. 'I didn't know you made your own bread,' she said.

'It's Pearl's starter,' he said. 'I make one loaf a week, rise it up over-night. None of the digestion problems you get with commercial yeast.' He got up and brought back the jar of starter, which was full of bubbles. 'You'll probably find a jar of it in the fridge at your place,' he said.

Ada touched the edge of the blanket. 'I threw it away.'

'Here,' Luke said. He opened his and scooped a spoonful of the mixture into a clean jar. 'Leave it open somewhere warm to get it going.' He said she should take some of the bread too, he had plenty. Maybe a bottle of milk, and why not the rest of the jam as well? He had a spare jar himself anyway. He packed the things carefully in a bag and it was only when she was halfway back down the icy road that she realised he'd given her much more than she had taken to him in the first place.

She hiked back through the snow. Didn't find it such hard going this time. Her feet in cold, clinging socks, but once she got walking they started to warm up again. It was easier downhill, and she leaned her weight back so that she didn't slip.

It was getting dark already, the sky turning olive-coloured. Snow poured down silently. If it carried on like this they wouldn't be able to get out for days. Ada walked along the road. Noticed the blue shadows on the snow, the hollow tree by the fence, leaves encased in muddy ice, as if they were trapped in amber. There was the tree that looked like someone pointing. She stopped under it for a moment. There was the caved-in fence where people took the corner too fast. There was the scarecrow. There was the gate made out of an old bed frame. Small way-marks, like a different set of road signs.

At the top of the valley she stopped and looked down. The trees white and feathery in the snow, the shape of the river through them. She knew where the house was exactly, even though she couldn't see it. Just a faint twist of smoke from the chimney.

She came down the lane towards the house, which was just as low and slumped and askew. But the windows glowing yellow. She took off her sodden boots and rolled up her wet trousers, called to Pepper and heard her answer in an odd voice. There was no one in the kitchen. She called up the stairs. Heard the familiar noises of her mother moving around in the study. But when she looked in, it was Pepper. She was standing next to the window and there was a freezing draught coming in. A cracked hole in one corner and broken glass on the floor.

'I was going to fix it,' Pepper said.

Ada went over to feel Pepper's elbow, which was lumpy and scratched. The lights flickered. The pipes groaned and shuddered as usual and she could smell chimney smoke getting pushed back into the house by the wind. 'It's OK,' she told Pepper. Snow blew in through the broken window and landed on the carpet.

32

SNOW PILED UP AGAINST the door, and the wind, coming from the north, froze it into yellow hunks. The ice wore away at the paint, which crackled and split. Some flaked off, some clung on with the lichen, which was crispy and stubborn, spreading over the door by a fraction of a millimetre.

The windows shivered in their panes. Snow spattered. The frosty draught worked its way through putty, eroding it crumb by crumb.

The steel roof twanged in the cold like an instrument.

And in the chimney, smoke struggled out into the snow. Brewing into icy smog. Stunned by the cold, it hung droopily, strung across the trees in hammocks.

The walls breathed in snow. The cement weakened – loosening bricks, loosening plaster. The house buckled by a fraction of a millimetre.

Sloppy snow fell into the fire and made it sizzle.

Pipes clanked and froze. The taps were turned and turned but no water came out. The taps screeched. Ice in the pipes expanded and a crack appeared – the beginnings of a split in the metal.

Footsteps creaked like pipes. When a face stared out of the window, it looked like a blur of snow behind the old glass.

The footsteps were like stones turning in the river, the hushed voices like branches rubbing together. At night, the house moved restlessly, like the river moving underneath the ice and the falling snow.

Lights flickered. The sun didn't rise above the valley. Everything was muted and dim, like a lid had been put over.

A hand pressed against the window.

The snow prised off tiles and the last of the leaves. Heaping itself against the roof and the walls, heaping itself against trees, which retreated into themselves, biding their time, living off stored reserves of sugar.

Ice grew on the coldest parts of the house: on the windows and the edges of the gutter. It grew thicker on the slowest parts of the river: the pebbly shallows and the sluggish pools. The ice changed water into glass, changed glass into brittle feathers.

And across the valley, snow pressed itself into nooks and runnels. Ice finding its way into fissures, wearing at them, chipping away like an excavator. Snow-battered, wind-battered, battered by cold. But barely a fleck in the valley's long memory. Like a shiver that gives goosebumps one moment and is gone the next.

The river cut through clay and granite, digging itself deeper by a fraction of a millimetre.

The clogged pipes groaned and settled. The footsteps slowed and settled. Curtains stayed drawn. A lamp flickered on and off. Smoke struggled out of the chimney. The house leaned against the snow. Paint crackled and clung, holding on for at least one more winter.

33

PEARL FELT EACH SNOWFLAKE as it swept in and settled on the house. But she couldn't settle; no, she could never settle. It was just a stop-gap – that's what they kept saying. One year, two years, maybe three at most. After all, the house was cheap, they could do it up, sell it on for a profit, then go wherever they wanted. Frank could start up his jewellery business, finally make use of the tools and books his father had left him. Work from home – no one telling him when his day should begin and when it should end. He had meetings with the jewellers in town, put out adverts, pinned a poster up at the shop. Pleased when the work started to trickle in.

But Pearl had nothing to do. It was an unfamiliar feeling. No work, no one she knew in the area, nowhere to go to pass the time. She tried to paint the window frames but she didn't know you had to strip the old paint off first, sand the whole lot down, prime it and then paint. She just slopped new paint on over the old stuff, made the whole thing look bumpy; the old paint showing through grey underneath like the beginnings of a bruise. She tried to get into cooking – always said that if she had the time she ought to try and get to grips with it. But it was too much fuss. She scorched onions and singed butter. Couldn't whip up eggs into peaks; they ended up looking more like the floppy scum that floated on the river. Much easier to eat things out of tins, that's what they were there for, nothing wrong with a good tin of spaghetti followed by a tin of mandarins for dessert.

And she looked for work. Endlessly. Of course she knew it would be hard – a rural area, the nearest town an hour's drive away. She was prepared to drive, but hadn't quite realised the extent of the roads' narrowness and bloody danger. But she got out the phone book and rang around. Eventually got asked in for an interview at a small office in town. She'd only been out in the car a few times before – it was cheap and she didn't trust the brakes. It was a horrible mustard colour and even worse than the green one she bought after. But she couldn't just sit inside all day doing nothing. So she got in the car and drove out, took a corner too fast, met a car coming the other way, swerved, and found herself nose down in a ditch. Got out shaking. A gouge down the passenger door from a sharp branch in the hedge.

The man driving the other car got out slowly and came over. He was wearing a denim jacket and a red hat with a picture of a football on it. He put his hand on the bonnet and patted it. 'I've had a crash with this car before.'

'It's second-hand,' Pearl said. 'We only just bought it.'

The man tapped the bonnet again. 'Quite a few years ago now. Almost the same place.' Still he patted the bonnet. 'I wonder when the third time will be.'

Pearl stepped round the car and looked at the ditch. 'I need to get into town,' she said.

'Dunno how you'll get someone to tow you out,' the man said.

'I need to get into town,' Pearl said again.

'You won't get anyone out today,' the man said. He patted the car once more. Then he walked back to his car and got in. He sat there for a full minute without moving. Then he got back out, went round to his boot and found some rope. 'I suppose I should help,' he said. He tied the rope to both cars and dragged hers out, his wheels spinning on the wet road, flicking mud all over her clothes. It was late by the time they had finished and no time to get into town. She drove back to the house slowly, phoned the office and was told that they had already found someone else that afternoon.

She read all the books in the house. Things that the previous owners had left behind: musty yellow crime books, a book about someone who went to live on top of a mountain and didn't see anyone else for forty years, a boring old book about birds, some crusty tome full of advice about hairstyles and keeping the house clean. She read the jewellery books too. Spent afternoons turning through the thin pages. Diagrams and pictures and figures. Most of the words she didn't understand: filigree, mantel, switch lock. Like it was written in another language. She would read and watch Frank getting on with his work – polishing links and chains, soldering. Once pointed out that she thought he had put the mechanism in the wrong way round. She managed to get a stopped clock ticking again. The satisfying whirr of the cogs as they turned smoothly at the back.

She got the local paper delivered and circled the job adverts. Read the thing from cover to cover: the letters people wrote in about roads and meetings, complaints about errors that had been printed. Recipes, photos of babies, wood and cars for sale. Became almost addicted to the weekly article about the reverend's eighteenth-century diaries – what he was doing this time two hundred years before. Visiting the elderly; burying parishioners that had died of typhoid; interviewing for a new schoolmistress when the other one ran away and didn't come back.

There were adverts for cleaners, vets, carers, warehouse packers, dental assistants. For caravan park attendants and seasonal pluckers. She applied for everything. Lost count of the number of letters sent back. *I'm sorry but you do not fit our requirements. I'm sorry but the post has already been filled. I'm sorry but you do not show sufficient experience.* She crumpled them up and threw them away, hiding them under the other rubbish so that Frank wouldn't see them and feel sorry for her.

'Maybe we should go out,' Pearl said. 'Go up to the pub, or the cafe, or something. Try and get to know people.' She paced around the house. Looked out at the fields and the trees, the glimpse of river. What had she expected, exactly? Where she had imagined stillness and quiet there was restlessness: rushing water, swaying trees. Where she had imagined meadow there was mud. 'Have a drink, get talking to people,' she said.

Frank came over and stroked her hair, twisting it around between his fingers. His nails were bitten down to the skin. He twisted her hair slowly. What he did when he wasn't listening, but it felt nice, his fingers working through, kneading her scalp. So that she could almost feel it now, the memory of it ingrained somewhere deep, like the way the river kneaded the bedrock.

In the end she went up to the cafe by herself. The door had those long wooden beads over it and she pushed through them, got tangled, then found a table in the corner. Sat down. Got back up. Sat at a table in the middle, by the door. She was the only customer there. A young man came out and she ordered lunch and a cup of tea. He came back with the tea and put it down carefully, as if he had been practising. Pearl sipped and waited. The door opened and a man came in, but he was just delivering something in boxes. He got the boxes signed over and left.

Pearl's lunch came and she pulled the crusts off the bread.

A woman came in, smiled at Pearl, went to the counter and ordered something. Pearl waited for her to turn round and come over to find a table, but she stayed at the counter, talking to the waiter about his father – was he OK now? Could he still drive? What about the concert on Saturday (what concert? Pearl didn't know anything about a concert) – would he still be able to make that?

Pearl pulled at the bread. Her tea went cold in the cup.

The waiter hovered. In the end came over. 'Shall I take that for you?' he said.

When she got back to the house, Frank met her at the door holding a stuffed jackdaw. 'I found this in a skip,' he said.

'Where?' she asked.

He waved his arm. 'Look at it. Look at the condition of the beak.'

It was an ugly, weird thing. A bulbous beak and squinting eyes. The feathers still soft and glinting blue.

'Where did you get it?'

'I'm going to put it by the door,' he said. 'Like a lookout.'

His hair was sticking out from the wind, his eyes roving as he clutched the bird. She smoothed his hair down. She touched his racing chest. She loved him very much.

There was an advert in the paper for work at the local shop. Four mornings a week, to put the bread and pies in the oven, to serve on the till, stock shelves, answer the phone for milk orders. She wrote and rewrote her application, crossing things out, then writing it up again until it was good enough for bloody Harrods. Signed her name carefully at the bottom, handed it in and waited. Nothing for three days, then the phone rang and she was asked in for an interview. The owners, a husband and wife in their sixties, were standing behind the counter when she went in. She could see herself now: palms sweating, shaking. For a part-time job. Putting bread in the oven and taking it out again when it was done.

The owners, what were their names? Sheila and someone or other. They had owned the shop for years but needed extra help now. Sheila having to go into town for her appointments and therefore not always able to serve behind the till. Pearl nodded. 'You can't be in two places at once,' she said. She put her hand in her pocket and held her button. They looked at her and didn't smile. One of those couples that had grown to look almost identical: ruddy, collapsing cheeks, smiles that turned their mouths downwards, eyes that roamed. And their voices affronted, as if they had some important task to do that was constantly being interrupted.

They ran over what she would have to do: the early hours, could she handle early hours? The oven would get boiling, did she understand the risks? Could she deal with difficult customers? Could she work out the right change if the till broke?

Pearl said she could do all that.

'It's difficult work,' Sheila said. 'The oven gets boiling.' She drummed her hands on the counter. Her nails were painted blue. Her eyes flicked over Pearl's face, down to her too-smart shoes and back up.

Pearl took a breath. 'I could do a good job here,' she said. 'I need something close by, I'm reliable. Get to know people here better.'

They nodded, their faces like slammed doors. 'Have you worked an oven like this before?' the husband asked. He showed her into the back room, where the big oven sat in the middle like a shrine. He showed her how to turn it on, how to adjust the timer.

'I haven't used one like this before,' she said. 'But it seems easy to pick up.'

'It's harder than it looks,' he said.

The wife was opening and closing the till. 'And this needs an experienced eye,' she said. 'The buttons are temperamental.'

Again, Pearl said she could pick it up. She had worked with tills before, more complicated ones.

'More complicated?' they said dully.

They didn't phone. Days passed, and then a week. Frank went up to the shop to buy bread and came back raging. Told her that the job had gone to a woman who lived next to the school. She had botched up Frank's change. He threw the bread down and clenched his fist, said he would never shop there again as long as he lived. Pearl calmed him down, telling him that it was OK, and that they had to shop there unless they wanted to drive an hour every time they wanted milk. Soothing him, as if it was him that had been passed up for the job.

In her first month at the shop the woman burned her hand on the oven; in her fourth, she stole thirty pounds from the till and the charity box and then left. They didn't re-advertise the job.

Pearl stopped circling adverts. She didn't go back to the cafe. Sent Frank up to the shop whenever they needed anything. She stayed in and read the local paper. Two hundred years ago, the reverend was collecting for a fete and visiting parishioners during a spate of measles. He'd had to ride into town to buy material to repair the church roof.

She tried to talk to Frank about their plans. It was a nice place, of course she could see it was a nice place, but how long were they planning on staying? Especially if she couldn't find work. Maybe six more months, Frank said. A year at most. He should probably try and make something from this jewellery work, pay for some of the more expensive repairs on the house. And in the meantime, something was bound to come up for her. Pearl nodded. Noticed that the chain Frank was mending had been attached the wrong way round, but she didn't say anything.

One afternoon there was a knock at the door. Frank was out on one of his walks through the woods and across the moor – each walk seemed to be taking longer and longer. Pearl went to answer it. There was a woman standing there. 'Yes?' Pearl said. Hoping that she wasn't selling something or collecting for some project or other. It was almost impossible to say no. So far she'd given money to repair a church window and to buy a set of swings, even though there wasn't a park as far as she could tell. And she'd bought an iron and too many dusters to count.

'Pearl – is that right?' the woman said. She looked about forty, the same age as Pearl. A helmet of tight dark curls framing her face, holding her hands out in front of her as if she was protecting herself from something. She carried on. 'I heard about you, from Sheila at the shop.' Some kind of smile twitched in the corner of her mouth. 'Apparently she was very concerned you didn't know how to work an oven.'

Pearl felt herself stiffen and flush. 'I know how to work an oven,' she said.

The woman's smile faltered for a second. 'Anyway,' she said quickly, 'I've got a bit of work. At my business. It's not much, two days a week. Answering the phone. Paperwork. You'd probably find it boring but I thought I'd offer in case.'

Pearl stayed in the doorway. Could still recall the feel of the door-mat's bristles against her bare feet. Why hadn't she said anything? She willed herself now, looking back, to say something. Take up the offer, ask about the business. Anything. But she didn't. She stayed in the doorway, still flushed and stiff, moving her toes over the bristles. Eventually said, like a fool, 'Of course I know how to work an oven.'

The woman nodded and smiled, then walked back to her car and, just at that moment, a blackbird started singing on the roof – it was the first time Pearl had properly listened to how clear and lovely its song was, how it sent out a cacophony of notes and knitted them back together.

34

SOMETHING WAS DRUMMING. IT woke Ada up and she lay there, listening. At first, she couldn't place the sound – something beating against the windows and the roof. It didn't sound like snow, but snow was all she could think of. Four days in the house with snow piled up all around. It filled her thoughts: snow heaped against the door, snow pressing against the windows, snow sliding down the panes. The dim, snowy light. At first, she and Pepper had watched it out of the windows, talked about it endlessly. How deep it was getting, whether the flakes were bigger. Then, slowly, they stopped talking about it. They let the snow build up and they didn't try to sweep it away. They stayed in their pyjamas; they ate out of sauce-pans and stopped washing up. They stoked the fire and slept next to it all afternoon.

When Pepper went to bed, Ada would stay up and walk around the house. Listening to the quiet noises: tools jangling against the desk in the study, her mother's hushed voice in the kitchen, boots creaking slowly up the stairs. The sounds comforting and familiar, hour seeping into hour, until Ada couldn't imagine anything but this: the hushed house, the snow. The other world – the one of trees and grass and roads and work – had disappeared.

The drumming grew louder. She got out of bed and opened the curtains. There was rain running in torrents down the dark window. She put on a jumper and went downstairs. It was very early. The rain thumped against the house. She clicked on the light. Nothing. The fridge was silent. She tried the light again, but the kitchen stayed dark. She was standing in something very cold and wet, which soaked into her socks. Could hardly see anything. She crouched down and touched the floor, felt slushy snow and hunks of ice. She followed it over to the corner of the kitchen.

'There you are,' her mother said. She was sitting in the armchair, hands gripping the sides. Her voice sounded further away and melting snow was dripping off her and pooling on the floor.

Ada knelt down next to her. 'The rain woke me up,' she said.

'Milder air sweeping in and colliding with laden clouds,' her mother said. 'I think there's going to be a lot of rain.' She seemed to sway slightly on the chair.

'It'll stop soon,' Ada said. A cold feeling starting to work up from her feet. She tucked her legs under her and shivered. An hour passed, then another. The kitchen started to get lighter. The light grey and smeary through the rain. Which beat and hammered without cease. As it got lighter, she could see that the chair her mother was sitting in was drenched. Icy water was pouring off Pearl's clothes, her hair was flat and tangled, the edges of her trousers and sleeves suddenly threadbare and crumbling.

And outside, the rain took bites out of the snow. The smooth white world was grey and moth-eaten, melting into slushy puddles like icy soup. The rain uncovering what the snow had hidden:

there was the holly bush, revealed suddenly like a skeleton. There was the moor, blearily shrugging off its thick blanket. A torrent of rain poured in a sheet off the roof and over the front steps. The snow on the windows dissolved and ran down like soapy water. Clumps of grey and yellow slouched at the foot of the walls and the sides of the road. A messy thaw. Underneath, everything bedraggled and shivering.

Something knocked against the house. Snow falling down off the roof. Her mother seemed to slump forward and then she got up and staggered across the kitchen. Melting snow sloshing over the tops of her boots. Ada got up quickly and followed her. Her mother made her way slowly down the hall towards her study. As she was going down the steps, another heap of snow slid off the roof and she fell against the door, caught herself just as Ada rushed forward, and disappeared down into the room.

Then Pepper was calling from upstairs. 'What's that noise?' she said. 'What's happening?' She sounded half asleep and frightened. Ada went up. 'I can hear something loud,' Pepper said.

'It's raining,' Ada told her. She pulled back the curtains so Pepper could see.

Pepper got up and pressed her face against the window. 'The river is very loud,' she said.

Downstairs, amongst the sounds of the rain, Ada could hear thumps and bangs coming from the study. She told Pepper to get dressed and brush her teeth. But to be careful, none of the lights were working. Then she ran downstairs and looked in the study. The cardboard she'd taped over the broken window was hanging off and soaked with rain. There was no one in the room. But there were boxes piled on the desk that hadn't been there before. Ada lifted the flaps. The cardboard was wet. There were cameras and books and photos packed neatly inside.

She looked around the room. No clutter on the floor or under the desk. The desk was empty. The small bookcase by the door was empty. The lowest shelves on the walls were empty.

There was a noise behind her and Pepper came in. 'You've packed the cameras away,' she said. She looked warily in the box. Ran her fingers lightly over a camera and rubbed at a dirty mark on the lens. 'Why did you pack them?'

Ada looked once more around the half-empty room. 'They're yours now,' she said.

Pepper looked at her out of the corner of her eye. 'Mine?' she said.

Ada nodded.

'To keep?' Pepper closed the box up as if looking at them was too much to bear. Then she crossed the room and came back with a pen. She frowned and started writing. A tense jitter in the muscle on her top lip. She gripped her writing hand with her left hand to support it. Moved the pen very slowly. The letters came out big and wobbly, but clear.

'You wrote your name,' Ada said.

The rain was so loud it was like someone knocking on the door and then Ada realised it was someone knocking. She rushed over, hoping it would be Tristan – there'd been no way of contacting him since the snow and a week seemed like a long time. Suddenly it seemed like a really long time. She touched the backs of her hands against her cheeks. No idea what she would say to him, but she flung the door open, imagining his wet hair and the way he would lean against the door frame.

Slushy snow pooled on the front step. It was Ray, hunched under the splitting porch, his coat drenched and the hood pulled low over his eyes. 'Your phone's down,' he said.

Muddy snow spattered off the roof. 'Everything's completely gone,' Ada told him. Had to speak loudly over the torrent.

'I thought I'd just come over,' Ray shouted.

'OK,' Ada said. Realised she was blocking the door. But still she stalled. 'I can't believe how quickly this came on,' she said. Gesturing to the rain.

'Yes,' Ray shouted. He hunched down in his coat as more water spilled onto him from the porch. 'I haven't been able to get out till now.'

Rain soaked through Ada's socks. 'I guess you want to come in then,' she said finally.

'That would be good,' Ray said. Ducked another fat splash.

They went into the kitchen. Ada took his coat and put it in the sink, where blue water streamed out of it and down the plughole. His pale jumper was covered in blue dye. His trousers were stuck to his legs and wet snow clung to his shoes. He raked at his hair. 'Listen,' he said. 'I told you I'd been thinking about the house, didn't I?'

Ada picked up his coat and wrung it out, so that more water and dye oozed. 'You shouldn't put this back on when it's like this,' she said.

Ray looked at it. 'The first time that gets properly wet and this happens. I paid quite a bit of money for it as well.' He plucked at his jumper. 'Look at this,' he said. 'What am I meant to do with this?'

'You'll have to soak it,' Ada told him. 'Rub a bar of soap on it, soap gets out anything. Just a plain bar of soap.'

'Just plain soap?' Ray said. 'I can do that.' He wandered around the kitchen, pulled out a chair, sat down then got back up again. 'It's cold in here,' he said.

Ada lit the gas with a match and put a pan of water on to boil. 'Everything's gone out,' she said again. The gas and the rain roared.

259

'It's some place,' Ray said. 'Power going out all the time, the river getting high like that.' He went over to the window and looked out. 'No electricity a lot of the time, no phone, the heating powered by the fire. It's no way to live, is it? Driving everywhere, the roads terrible as they are and nobody within a mile. Cost of petrol. This cold valley. I don't blame you at all for wanting to get out. Been thinking of moving into town myself. I know the benefits: can walk everywhere, pick up food when you like. You fancy a pear and you can just go and get a pear.' He stopped and looked at her.

'A pear?' Ada said. She watched the water in the pan as it started to boil, silver bubbles erupting at the bottom and rising. Reminded her of the intricate beads her mother had once fixed onto a bracelet.

'Yeah, a pear,' he said. 'Or an orange, whatever you like. But as I was saying before, I'm interested in the place. You've got a good location – I think people will like that. Had to have a think about it for a while, but I've come to my conclusions. I think I can take it off your hands.' He rubbed his throat with his thumb.

Ada watched the bubbles rolling on the water.

'So I'm willing to make you an offer.' He named a figure that was significantly less than she'd asked for at the beginning. Said it like he was doing her a favour. 'It needs a lot of work,' he said. 'But I can do that. You wouldn't have to worry about it any more. I guess it's got potential in a lot of ways.' He was speaking a lot faster now. He slurped at the coffee she gave him and added three spoons of sugar.

Ada looked out at the pouring rain. The snow going crumbly and grey as old pastry. Things underneath battered but emerging.

Ray said: 'Alright, alright, I'll give you what you asked for.' He stood behind a chair and tipped it backwards and forwards. 'You're right. I was being cheap before but you're right.' He wiped at his forehead. 'I shouldn't have even said that.'

Ada shook her head.

Ray named a figure that was over the original price. 'Hell, woman,' he said. 'You haven't even got electricity. Look at this place.' He tapped on the counter, on the sink.

'I changed my mind,' she told him.

Ray put down his half-finished coffee and touched his coat in the sink. 'You changed your mind,' he said. His sleeves dribbled dye down his hands. He put the coat on and it clung to his arms and wrinkled. 'I suppose no one can stop you doing that.'

'Soap,' Ada told him. 'Remember? To get the dye out. Rub it with plain soap.'

He stopped in the doorway and looked out towards the road. Water was pouring down. 'Snow-melt,' he said. 'From up there.' Pointing at the moor. 'And all this rain.' He shook his head. 'Listen. There's going to be a lot of water coming down here soon. It was running down the road when I was driving. Watch out OK? I think you've got it coming.' He said it kindly. He pulled at his shrunken coat, put the hood up, then turned and ran to his car, splashing up snow and water.

Ada stood for a moment in the doorway. A lot of water coming. She ran out to the barn, found two sandbags and slung them against the front steps. Glimpsed the river running very high and fast. It was dark brown and choppy. As she watched, water spilled over the top of the bank and sank into the rain-soaked grass.

The rain chewed snow down to wet crust. The roof streamed like washing. Trees dripped. The moor shucked off snow and was soon back down to bare husk.

And the water had to go somewhere. It ran down the moor in rivulets that joined up and became a torrent. Over saturated bogs, through knotted grass, into fields and lanes. It gushed down the roads, overflowed ditches and drains. Bubbled out of grilles. The snow melted off trees in the wood, and the melt-water poured with the rain into the river. The river swelled and thundered through the valley. It doubled its width until it had flowed over the banks towards the house. It soaked through the grass and met the water pouring down from the road above it.

'Why's there water coming into the house?' Pepper said. She lifted her foot up and looked at it. Then crouched down on the kitchen floor and poked at a seeping puddle. Ada looked. Water was rising up through the floor and spreading, darkening the tiles as she watched. 'I put out sandbags,' she said. 'I put out sandbags.' She went over to the window and looked out. No grass. The house on a shallow lake. Trees standing in the middle like waders sifting through an estuary.

She ran out and down the hallway. Saw water pushing in under the front door, more rising through the skirting and floorboards. The lino in the kitchen was lifting and peeling, a tile floating off already. The water pushed up and spread and in minutes was a centimetre deep. Brown, gritty water, bits of crap from the fields and the road brought with it.

'Captain,' Pepper shouted. 'Captain, where are you?' She splashed into the hall, calling. 'Captain will drown,' she said.

'He's probably upstairs already,' Ada told her. 'Go and look.'

Pepper ran upstairs and then back down again shouting that he wasn't there. Ada went through the house looking. How had it happened so quickly? She stood on the top step of the study and looked down. The room was filled with a foot of dirty water. It lapped against the bottom step. Captain was on the armchair in the corner, asleep but twitching, his hackles rising as if his dream-self knew what was coming. The water just touching the bottom of the seat. 'He's down here,' she called.

Pepper rushed in and stopped next to Ada. 'The cameras,' she yelled.

'They're OK on the desk for now,' Ada said. 'Get the cat upstairs.'

Pepper ran and got a blanket, waded through the water and shoved it over Captain, hauled him upstairs as he struggled and hissed inside. 'I'm trying to save you,' Pepper shouted at him.

Ada stepped into the cold water and lugged a box off the desk, carried it through the hall and put it halfway up the stairs. Went back to get another. The rest of the books were safe on the top shelves. She touched them as she went past, a page tearing in the damp and sticking to her hand.

She heard Pepper come back down and suddenly wail, 'Where is it? Where's it gone?' She came down into the study and plunged her hands in the water. 'My button,' she said. She sifted through the water and then went out of the room, still looking.

'Stay upstairs with the cat,' Ada called. 'Don't let him come down.' Then she ran down the hallway, stopped, shouted 'Gas', and went through the kitchen to turn everything off. She went to the front door, opened it, and started to brush the water out. There was a huge puddle on the front step that kept washing in. Rain drove into her face. She turned and saw her mother leaning against the wall, shaking her head as if trying to clear her thoughts. Water pouring down her hair and her back.

'Sandbags,' Ada said. 'Are there any more?'

Her mother shook her head. 'Just let it come,' she said. 'There's no stopping it.' Her voice drummed like the rain and water streamed down her face and dripped off her hands. Ada stopped brushing and leaned the broom slowly against the door.

Her mother staggered and held onto the wall.

'I don't know what to do,' Ada said. A cold feeling pumping in her chest. The water gushed like a tap. Pushing in and out of the house like something breathing.

Her mother's eyes were swimming with murky water. She let go of the wall and stood for a moment, swaying, then she stumbled down the hall and towards her study. Stood in the deep water at the bottom of the steps.

Ada followed her. Her mother's skin seemed to ripple and stretch, grit lodged under her fingernails. She was trailing her fingers through the water. 'The window broke,' she said. 'And the snowball dripped through my fingers.' She swayed, then stepped back to get her balance. 'Fob watches,' she said. 'The lovely way the oil smelled. I never thought it would become my favourite smell. Or matches. And the bread when it was baking. But the bread burned and I threw it in the bin.'

Ada watched her closely. There was so much water dripping, it was hard to keep her in focus. 'I ate it,' she said. 'I took it out and I ate it. It was perfect in the middle.' She'd cut the burned crust off and the middle was soft and full of air.

'You ate it,' her mother said. Her knees gave way and she stumbled, almost fell right into the water. Her arms plunged in. 'It's dragging at me again,' she said.

Ada moved forward but her own legs buckled and went numb. She crumpled onto the top step. 'Try and hold on here,' she said.

'It's a strong one,' her mother said. 'There's no question about that.' She closed her eyes, then opened them. 'It's crashing into things. Boulders, trees, taking everything with it. A branch is getting hauled right under.' She slipped again. Water rushed over her skin, turning it murky and thin. Ada could almost see the window through it.

'Tell me what birds you see,' Ada said. Her legs were so cold.

'You don't want to hear about that.'

'I do,' Ada said. 'I do.'

'Well,' her mother said. 'There's a pied wagtail on the highest rock, keeping its distance from the water. And a heron in the flooded field. By God it looks happy, extended fishing grounds. What is one person's disaster is another's opportunity.' She closed her eyes again. 'And a kingfisher just speeding downriver, trying to find a branch to land on. Like a bright bolt. Yes, and a wren watching it all from a tree, and a crow just over there.' Her foot drifted backwards with the water. 'The crow's waiting, just waiting to see what happens. Biding his time, the canny devil.' Her voice flooded with water now, the water pouring off her clothes and lapping against the walls. The current pulling at her. The water surging and rain pouring. Mixing everything up, loosening grips, churning leaves and dragging back silt and grit and stones, dragging everything back down to the river.

Ada stayed sitting on the step for a long time, watching the water. Listening to it like a voice that faded and surged and faded again.

35

EVERYTHING WAS POURING AGAIN, everything was on the move. The snow restless as it melted – breaking up and spreading and letting go of itself.

Pearl felt very thin and stretched. Once again the sound of the river was deep and unremitting; she could taste ditches and fields and wet carpets. She looked down at herself and saw only water – brown and gritty and strangely still. But there was a great dragging pressure – an unrelenting pull, as if a plug had been unstoppered somewhere.

She was taut and cold and aching. She lapped against walls. She split the desk's wooden legs. She toppled a lamp. A wire fizzed. A coat slumped like a drowned body. A notebook fell off a shelf and its sodden spine tore. The pages floated – all her observations, all her lists; hours and days and years. A record of her attentiveness. Now dissolving in the water, the ink thinning like skin.

The river roared. She was hauled downwards and out – through plaster and brick and cobwebs, through mouse tunnels and the gap under the door. Suddenly merging with rain and huge puddles.

Gravel from the road, a shoe like a bloated fish. Sweeping past swampy grass, past clumps of sludgy snow and drooling ice; the water rushing back down to the river, more water spilling over the bank and pushing up towards the house. Pearl caught in the middle of it – the river pushing and pulling like the pumping of silty blood.

Everything teemed. The bank crumbled and Pearl went with it – back into the churning river, which was bloated and brawny, ripping up roots and hurling branches as it went. Bowling a tractor tyre along like a toy. Juggling a ripped fence. She saw the house as she went, standing among shallow water like something marooned. Propped up and grey and bedraggled. An infuriating place. But it was hers. Yes. It was hers. Where she had ended up. Not what she had expected, but perhaps not the worst thing, to have had her life here. For it to have become home without her noticing. Her rapids, her slushy snow, her watery, boggy greens and greys. Her pain-in-the-arse remoteness, not seeing anyone for weeks. Her power cuts, her seeping and ancient moor. Her birds, her narrow and bastard roads. Her flooding river: brown and silver and fat as a trout.

Down the bank and into the pounding current. There were no slow, quiet parts of the river now. No eddying, no stagnant pools with nests of caught sticks and feathers. The water riled everything up. Leaves split and tore. Branches snapped and were flung down-river. Pearl swept out into the middle where the water was fastest, hurtled down and round the bend and . . . wait. The house was about to go out of sight. She clung onto a boulder instinctively. Somehow managed to grip onto the stone's rough edges, work her way into the moss and cracks and haul herself up. She stared at the house. She wasn't ready. Suddenly, she wasn't ready.

She clung on. The river rushed past her and through her and its roaring was so loud, so steady, that she stopped hearing it. In amongst the ceaseless pressure everything became silent and calm. The browns turned into greens and yellows, the water glinted, and she remembered the first time she had stepped into the river. The first cold shock of it.

It was early spring and they had just moved into the house that winter. The first daffodils coming up like lamps, and the ramsons' white flowers coating everything as if the snow had never left. Their pungent smell after it rained. The wind whipping. Silky buds on the alder trees like mice. Frank opening all the doors and windows to air the house and saying that he was going to teach her to swim. It was never too late to learn, apparently. He knew a nice easy stretch where the river wasn't too deep, the current slackening and good to swim against.

Her hair had lifted up in the wind. The river was wide and glittering and they walked down the long grass, along the bank and down onto a shingly beach. Pearl took her shoes off and hobbled on the sharp stones, her soles not yet toughened up. No cracked, hard skin back then. She watched Frank take off his belt and his trousers and his shirt. He waded in. The colour of his body against the water: the creams and coppers and dusty purples. His spine like the lovely bumps in a chrysalis.

Pearl took her clothes off down to her underwear, felt Frank watching her, and folded them carefully. It was very cold. She waded in, the freezing water pushing against her toes, then her ankles, then her thighs. She waded over to Frank and ran her finger down his back. She had only known him for a year.

'Sit in the water first,' he told her. 'So that you get used to it.'

They sat in the river, their skin gleaming and pale and looking not part of themselves at all, but part of the rippled and moving water. She could feel the current tugging at her and the wind pulling at the water's surface and at the surface of her skin, making creases and

268

goosebumps. Everything glittered green and copper, like a rusty coin being cleaned.

Frank knelt up and showed her how to lean forward and move her arms. 'Try dipping your head under,' he said.

She did, and got a shock of cold, blurry darkness, came up coughing.

'Keep your mouth closed,' he said.

Pearl spat out a mouthful of water. 'I did,' she said. Her first taste of the river, dank and fresh at the same time. She tried again. She dipped her head under and water streamed down her hair and back. It felt better this time; she kept her mouth closed and opened her eyes, saw brown silt and stones mixing. Frank's feet among grey pebbles. She reached down and touched his toes and Frank ran his hand down the inside of her arm, then guided her into deeper water so that she was in above her waist. Her skin tingled. He let go of her and swam a few strokes out into the middle and beckoned her. She leaned forward and pushed with her arms. Her knees scraped along the stones, something in her wouldn't let her knees go and she stayed there, attached to the stones like a weed. Tried again. She pushed off and her knees lifted and she was moving into the river, actually moving through the water, buoyed and lighter than she had felt before, stronger than the current, moving towards Frank's arms. (And there was no need to go into the fact that a few strokes later she floundered and her arse floated up. What mattered were those first few strokes, cold and bright and wonderful.)

Now, Pearl clung to the stone. Alongside saturated moss, which was old and strong and probably didn't even notice. Still she held on. The river dragged and she streamed out like a flag. Rain drummed. Pearl closed her eyes. Felt the water spreading and she a part of it, flooding through the valley.

269

Water poured down through the woods from the moor, picking up mud and clay and pine needles. The river slopped over the bank and onto the paths, scouring earth and leaves. Mixing with the rain and overflowing pipes. Gurgling up through drains and spilling out onto the roads. Reeking, mulchy water, full of dirt and rust. It carried sticks and sweet wrappers, tin cans, plastic bags, unidentifiable crud from a dumping place, a cup, a blanket, a handful of batteries.

And on the road outside their house, Clapper and Petey picked the rubbish out of the drains to help the water go down. Clapper picking carefully and Petey holding the bag as wide as it would go.

The water flowed out of the top fields, some of it bubbly with chemicals and soap, and streamed down the road that wound through the valley. Past front doors, past gates and down the hill, where cars had to stop and put their handbrakes on tight.

Over potholes and gravel, past verges and fences. Down towards the shop, where it pooled by the front door. Mick swept at it with a broom to keep it from getting in. He was wearing his wife's old waders – too tight and wouldn't go over his knees. He swept and swept, beating the water back. Praying that the water would stay away. His wife had been the canny one; he had stopped paying the insurance to save money.

The water poured down the narrow lanes and past the pub. Val heard the torrent and knelt on her bed to look out of the window. Saw the water whisking past, then turned over and went back to sleep, unalarmed. Making up for all those lost hours.

Down the valley and into Judy and Robbie's farm, where it lost speed and spread over the lower fields, turning them to glistening marsh. Judy and Robbie up all night dragging in sheep and moving cows. The water not deep enough to do much damage; but more work, and more worry, and no sleep for them.

And at Luke's place, the water ran through the garden and turned the bonfire remains into a charred stew. It started to pool in a long, deep hole in the garden, but Luke was nowhere to be seen.

A telegraph pole sparked and cut out. Everyone in the west of the valley lost their electricity. The Trewins made a grill out of a metal bucket and some coal and cooked rounds of sausages.

A group of bungalows was surrounded by hoarded sandbags.

The cafe was above it all and missed everything.

And what was happening at the house? The water was still pushing up through the foundations, filling the house with a shallow layer. Who was that? The little one, coming down the stairs, getting the broom and starting to sweep water out of the door, saying, go away, go away. And where was Ada? There she was, still sitting on the study steps, looking around like she didn't know where she was exactly.

'Come on girl,' Pearl muttered. 'There's only one thing you can do.' Still Ada sat there. And then, finally, she got up and went over to the desk and picked up a plastic box. She opened the window, bent down and started bailing. Throwing out box after box of water. 'That's right,' Pearl said. Although it probably wouldn't even touch it; but what else was there to do? She watched them sweep and bail. It was out of her hands.

The river swelled. A huge pressure, like cloth that was as taut as it could go at the seams. Pearl saw something glinting in the water. She reached down and grabbed it as it swept past. Her button. She clutched it tightly; although she couldn't remember why it was so important . . . it was before all this, back before all this even happened. There was a lot more to go over, a lot more to sift through until she was back at the very start. Everything glinted silver and rushed fast and deep. An overwhelming circling feeling – the water seeping into mud then draining back, always separating and joining,

271

always the backbreaking, bending feeling of the river trying to meet itself at the beginning.

A heavy branch crashed into the rock and Pearl slipped and scraped against the edge. The water slowly prising her off. She dug in harder and then stopped. Felt the current tug at her. The river calling out. She couldn't cling on forever. It would be ridiculous. How long had she been here already? It felt like a long time. It felt like enough time. The water glinted and galloped. It peaked and folded, transforming second by second. Maybe better to see where it would take her.

So she let go.

36

'JUST CHECK ONE MORE time,' Pepper said. She stood by the car and picked at the rust. The water had worn the gravel away from the tyres so that they were sitting in deep holes. And the rain had got in and pooled on the seats.

Her mother leaned in and turned the key again. Nothing happened. 'We've tried it twelve times now,' she said. She adjusted the straps on Pepper's rucksack, then on her own. 'Ready?'

Pepper moved her feet around in her damp boots. If she squeezed her toes really hard, cold water bubbled up. 'Do we have to?' she said. It was a long way up to the shop.

'I thought you said you'd die without milk,' her mother said. 'Come on, it won't take too long.' She started walking up the lane and Pepper followed behind her.

The road was slick and wet. Water gushed down gullies on either side, and piles of sticks and leaves were caught in the drain covers. The trees dripped, the sheep dripped, the fields were bogs instead of grass. Everything was soaking, especially the house. The water had got into all the rooms downstairs and left them mucky and reeking. Everything smelled like that bus-station toilet she'd been into once; the one with the skull painted on the wall and the woman lying on the floor singing. The water hadn't cleaned the house at all; instead, it had smeared mud and sludge on the carpets and black gunk on the bottoms of the walls. The floorboards were warped and dirty and the paint was bulging and brown. Chunks of plaster were cracking off. The kitchen door wouldn't close properly any more. And strange things had washed in and been left behind when the water went away: bits of fence and plastic, a bright yellow glove next to the study window, a rusty horseshoe by the car.

She caught up with her mother. 'But how long exactly will it take to clean?' she asked.

'We talked about this,' her mother said.

The grass on the verge had been flattened by the streaming water. 'But a long time,' Pepper said. Waited for her mother to say she didn't know, or that it probably wouldn't take very long.

'Yes,' her mother said. 'It will take a long time.'

Pepper thought about the photos on the walls: one of them had fallen down and got ruined. Others were so damp that the corners had started to rip. And the carpet in the study was going to be rolled up and thrown away, and maybe the desk would have to go too – its legs were splitting halfway up. It wouldn't be the same any more. But they were going to put wax on the floor instead of the carpet and it would smell nice, like pine trees, and there would be new paint on the wall in the kitchen and she was allowed to choose the colour, except she wasn't supposed to choose black, or dark red, she was supposed to take her time and choose properly. 'And we will still be here,' she said.

Her mother touched a crumpled leaf in the hedge. 'Yes,' she said.

They walked for a long time. The roads and the drains slurped water. The shop's sign dripped and the door was soaking, but when they went in, Mick was triumphant: he had kept it all out of the shop. He bowed low as they came in, pointed out a picture of a dog wearing a sombrero in a newspaper, opened a can of lychees and ate them straight out of the tin one by one. 'Little brains,' he said to Pepper, who watched the juice run down his chin.

They got firelighters and matches, milk, tins, cereal, cat food and bread. Pepper worried about how heavy it would be walking back, but her mother only packed the light things in her rucksack.

'You took a hit down there I bet,' Mick said. He rang in the last tin. 'Still,' he said, 'I'm sure a certain young fellow won't mind giving you some assistance from what I've heard.' He ate another brain then licked over his front teeth.

There was a moment of silence and Pepper held her rucksack very tightly. Then her mother rolled her eyes. 'That's pretty old news by now,' she said. She packed the last tin in the bag. 'Next you'll be telling me you haven't heard the latest about Val's brother.'

Mick blinked. He fiddled with the cuffs of his jumper. 'I guess you'll need more wood now anyway,' he said. 'Bet yours got soaked when it poured on you down there. Special deal, seeing as you're so needful of it.'

'We'll think about it,' Pepper told him.

Mick glanced at her, his hand hovered over the jar of pink lollies on the counter, but then he took it away again. Maybe another time.

They were halfway back to the house, a packet digging sharply into Pepper's back, when there was the sound of a truck behind them. Her mother held Pepper's hand and told her to press as close as she could into the hedge, but the truck stopped next to them. It was Judy and Robbie. Robbie stuck his head out of the window. 'It's Luke,' he said. 'We're going over there now.'

They got into the back. There was a draught coming in from a gap under the door. The seats smelled of straw and chewing gum. A cold feeling started gnawing at Pepper.

'What's happened?' her mother said.

Judy drove quickly down the narrow roads. 'We don't know exactly,' she said. 'Tristan phoned us. He couldn't get through to you. Said he was passing Luke's and called in but couldn't find him. Then heard a noise from in the garden. Down in some huge hole. Been out digging or looking for something, I don't know. He went out for another go in the rain and the sides collapsed. He couldn't get back out.'

Pepper sucked in her breath. Her stomach clenched like she was about to be sick. Her mother turned to look at her. 'He'll be OK,' she said.

But Pepper closed her eyes tight and felt the car sway. Muddy water flicked onto the windows and ran down the doors.

They pulled up at Luke's house. Pepper stayed behind in the doorway. She heard everyone talking at once and then there was Luke's voice. It sounded just the same as it always did, maybe a bit quieter. She went through the hall and looked into the kitchen. He was sitting in a chair covered in blankets and hot-water bottles. Streaks of mud down his face and neck. Shep came over and sniffed her feet and she stroked him and didn't look up.

'I think he's got a bruised ankle, something wrong with his rib and a chipped tooth,' Tristan said. 'He won't let me take him to hospital.'

'Hospitals,' Luke said. 'More likely to die in one than out. I read that somewhere but I forget where.'

276

Pepper concentrated on Shep; his curly fur, his rough tongue lolling out.

Tristan sat down at the table then got back up again. He went over to the corner and started slicing up bread with a big knife. Judy switched the heater on to the highest setting. She and Robbie said they'd go upstairs for towels and spare clothes. Her mother went over and stood close to Tristan. Tristan carried on sawing the bread. She reached up and put her fingers under his hat and moved it so she could say something in his ear. He stopped sawing.

'Come here,' Luke said.

Pepper looked up and saw he was talking to her. She patted Shep once more, then went over to Luke. She picked her lips. Kicked his shoelace around the floor with her foot.

He leaned over and spoke quietly. 'There wasn't much there,' he said. He smiled and there was even mud on his teeth. But there was an old coin on the table next to him, battered and mouldy and bent.

'You found something,' Pepper said.

'There was something,' he said.

Pepper nodded. She prodded at his shoelace. 'It's one of the best coins I've seen,' she said finally.

Luke pulled at one of the blankets. Then he bared his teeth. 'I bet my chip is bigger than yours,' he said.

As he got more tired, he began to describe how it had been when the mud started slipping on him, and what it was like trapped there in the dark, not knowing if he would get out. His leg crushed, his mind wandering. Thought he was back in the bed where he was born and if he just unwrapped the blanket, if he just shouted a bit louder, then he would be able to get up and get on with things. Which he did.

*

277

Pepper went to find Captain and make sure he was OK with having Shep in the house. It was late afternoon and dark. Captain hissed and backed away. Probably best to keep them separate. The fire was roaring and every single window was open even though it was cold, to try and get rid of the damp. All the sodden things had been piled up outside: one pile for saving, one pile for throwing away.

When she got back into the kitchen, Tristan was chopping onions and his eyes were watering. He'd brought over a camping stove to cook on because their oven didn't work. Her mother's hand was on his back. The sizzling oil and the sizzling onions covered up the sour, fetid smell in the kitchen.

Later, her mother smoothed the covers around her in bed. She smoothed and then she pushed at the lumpy bits in the mattress. 'Do you like Tristan?' she said eventually.

Pepper traced the stars on the duvet. 'Do you?' she asked.

'Yes,' her mother told her. 'I do.'

Pepper thought about it. 'I like Shep and Tristan the same.' She propped herself up to look at her mother better. 'He looks younger than you,' she said. Thought about when her mother's knees cracked, and the tiny grey hairs behind her ear.

'Do you think so?'

Pepper nodded. 'He doesn't have lines like this,' she said. She put her finger on the creases around her mother's eyes.

'Maybe he hasn't laughed as much as me,' her mother said.

Pepper patted her mother's hand. The dry knuckles and the scalds and the bitten skin. She patted and patted.

In the morning they got out buckets and mops and soapy water. The bubbles had rainbows in them. The disinfectant burned up Pepper's nose. 'This better not happen again,' she said.

'It might,' her mother told her. She wiped the wall by the front door.

Pepper crouched down and scrubbed at the floor. Remembered something that Petey had told her. 'Judy and Robbie's animals,' she said. 'Why do they have them there?'

'What do you mean?'

'The cows and stuff.' She dunked her sponge in the hot water. 'I stroked them.'

Her mother stopped wiping. 'You know why,' she said. 'It's a farm. They milk some of them and they sell others for food.'

Pepper nodded and slowly lifted the sponge out. Wrung it out so that bubbles and grit dripped back in. Vowed then and there that she would never eat meat again. Another surprise for her mother.

She scrubbed for a few minutes, then she put the sponge down and went into the study. The windows were wide open and the wind was blowing in. The bare floor was dark and gritty. They kept finding pins and clips and bits of jewellery in between the boards. There were coins and a gold ring, like treasure. All the boxes were stacked on the shelves out of the way. Pepper went over to the box with her name on it. Patted the dusty jackdaw as she went past. She could hear the river, high and drumming. She found her camera, leaned out of the window and took a picture of the wide puddle outside. Then went back out into the hall and took one of her mother scrubbing the bit of floor Pepper was meant to be doing, her hair tied with a scarf. A flash of Captain's tail. Shep drinking the horrible water pooled by the front door.

She put on her boots and coat. 'Come and see the river,' she said to her mother.

'I better finish this,' her mother said. Shep came over and sniffed her hand and she moved it away.

Tristan came out of the kitchen and pounded Shep's back. 'Don't take it personally buddy,' he said. He ran his hands down the hinges on the door.

Her mother reached out and touched Shep's ear with the back of her hand. 'There,' she said.

'Come on,' Pepper said. 'I want to show you.' She shoved her mother's coat at her and told her to put it on.

The ground was like a bog. Sucking at their boots. Mud and water clagging on their heels. Her mother stopped and looked back at the house and said something about the tiles.

'Come on,' Pepper said. The grass was yellow and crushed. There was a tideline of wet leaves pushed halfway up the field. She looked around for the old woman but couldn't see her anywhere. 'Petey says it's going to snow some more,' she said.

Her mother stopped again and bent down to adjust her laces. 'I hope not,' she said.

The grass got wetter and wetter and then there was the river, heaving past their feet. Wide and deep and brown, with thick swells moving through it. A magnificent booming sound, like a metal drum rolling around in a gale. Most of the rocks were covered, just a few grey tops jutting out, and the bank had crumbled, whole chunks fallen away like the river had grabbed handfuls of it.

'Look at all that stuff,' Pepper shouted. There was a tree stuck under the bridge. And a road sign, and a tractor tyre, and what looked like a front door – the handle still hanging on it. Torrents and creases; the water overlapping itself, crumpling under its own weight. And the floodwater had scoured the ground, exposing all the trees' roots underneath. 'Look at it,' she said.

'I am,' her mother said.

Pepper looked at the trees in front of her and then at the next field over. There were still shallow pools of water spreading over the grass. And there was something standing in the middle, something grey and hunched. She closed her eyes, then looked again. It was still there, standing very upright and not moving. Pepper didn't move. The heron was big and grey, almost purple in places. It had a bright white neck and a black bit of punky hair at the top. It looked like it was wrapped in a tatty cloak. And its yellow eye was staring down at the water. She reached for the camera but the heron looked over and shuffled its feathers. Then it hunched forward and glared right at her. A bolt of joy passed through her.

'Frank,' she said. 'Frank, Frank.'

'What did you say?' her mother asked.

'It's what the heron says,' Pepper told her.

'Yes,' her mother said quietly. 'I think I knew that.'

The heron swivelled its head and then it shifted, flexed its shoulders and took off downriver, crying out as it went. Wings wide, legs dangling, almost skimming the top of the water.

'It won't have gone far,' her mother said. She walked through the grass the same way that the heron had gone. 'They don't usually fly far when they get disturbed. There's a wider bit further down here they sometimes go.' She started walking along the bank.

'How do you know?' Pepper said. But further down, exactly where her mother said, there was the heron. Hunched over at the edge of the bank, staring down at the fast-moving water. 'What's it doing?' she whispered.

'Hunting,' her mother said. 'Looking for fish.'

They crouched down in the wet grass and watched. Pepper took the camera out of the case. She adjusted the focus very carefully. The heron stepped through the water, moving further along the bank. She started to roll up her trousers. 'I need to get closer,' she said.

281

There was a wide shingly beach below the bank and her mother held Pepper's arm and lowered her down.

The wet stones glinted dark grey and orange, like rusty pipes. They crunched as she stepped forward. Water swirled among the pebbles. The first icy shock as it crept into her boots. She squatted down and lifted the camera.

The heron was looking at her again. She held the camera steady. Thin mist clung to the edges of the bank. She heard her mother jump softly down onto the beach. She glanced back and saw her standing on varnished stones, watching.

She turned back to the heron. It was standing so still; she had enough time to get it exactly right if she just waited, if she just waited a bit more. She adjusted the focus again and looked. The heron moved to one side. She followed it with the camera, waiting, waiting. The heron stopped moving and hunched forward. It stood so still. She had it in focus but she waited a moment longer, it was important to get the clearest shot, to capture exactly how it was, right now, with the wet stones and the crushed grass and the mist. She made one more small adjustment, held the camera steady, noticed the orange beak and an orange leaf floating past, and then she clicked the shutter, and just at that moment the heron took off again. Maybe she had caught it, or maybe she had clicked too late and there would be a wing, a foot, glimpsed in the corner of the frame as the heron glided out of sight, streaming out beyond the picture like a kite. But she could try again and again and again and . . .

37

HERE SHE WAS AGAIN, back by the river. Freezing water rushing under her feet. Stones flipping like drop-scones; purple and green and mackerel-coloured. Fragments of smashed terracotta, stirred-up silt, peaks and creases and wrinkles. The bank worn down to pale roots, tangled inside like the workings of a body.

More beautiful than she remembered. Ada watched Pepper crouch down, almost kneel, in the water and aim the camera at the heron. Her mouth twitching with concentration. Keeping herself very still, but not rigid, not fraught; a calmness in the way she held the camera and waited. The water pushed past, restless and glinting. Soaking through the seams of Ada's boots, making her toes prickle. She had forgotten, or maybe never noticed, the sound the river made when it lapped at the shallow edges, how the drizzly mist clung to the surface like static on fabric. And all the shifting colours. She'd thought of it as dull and monotonous, the same old river from one moment to the next. But it changed second by second: now a clump of feathers tumbling down, now a plank of wood, now the water riled up around a snapped sapling.

Ada watched the heron – solitary, hunched, staring fixedly at Pepper. It was standing very still, just its eyes flicking between Pepper and the water. Pepper's finger hovered over the button.

'Take it,' Ada whispered. The heron was shuffling its feet, an agitated twitch in its feathers. Pepper raised the camera, pointed it, and clicked. At the same moment, the heron took off, clattering up out of the water, soaring away with its legs dangling. Its croaking calls merging with the sounds of the river: with the water glugging around the rocks, the deeper thrumming like boots thumping across a floor, or doors opening and closing. And the rhythmic click of stone against stone, like a clock ticking. And the saffron glints like jewellery scattered across a desk. The low rumbling sounds, as if someone in the distance was coughing and clearing their throat.

Pepper turned and started to wade back over to Ada, her trousers soaking, holding the camera carefully so that it didn't get wet. She kept talking about getting a TV, so they could watch cartoons, and the news, and those cowboy films where everyone walks off into a sunset. Ada glanced back at the house, just glimpsed the dripping roof, the battered chimney. Thought of Tristan waiting for them in the kitchen. The mouldy floors and warped doors, the grass in front churned with mud. No sunset there, but a February fog, woolly and glorious.

She looked downriver at the old bridge. The water was moving in wide, choppy waves, making its way past all the branches and bits of fence that had banked up. Further down, on the other side of the bridge, there was a deep pool. When the river was calm, the water there slowed down and turned very clear. Tiny fish darted through it and insects skimmed over the surface. It was the place her mother used to go to swim. She would slip out early in the mornings, before Ada woke up, and come back with soaking hair and goosebumps all over her arms. And one morning, Ada had got up and followed her.

It had been early spring, the first hints of pale shoots, a solitary bumble-bee working its way around the trees. The sky grey and still. She could see herself now, hiding behind that tree, leaning against the rough bark and chewing the ends of her hair. There she was: the same age as Pepper, just a bit taller, digging into the bark with her fingers and watching her mother wade into the water – her pale legs and arms, skin soft and slightly slack, turquoise veins, a black swimming costume. Ribbed lines around her ankles from where her socks had dug in. Her mother's hair was longer back then, a rich auburn tinge to it, and it curled in the damp around the nape of her neck. The wind lifted it softly. She waded into the water step by step, and the water was so clear, Ada could see her feet moulding themselves around the stones. Step by step, her eyes fixed on the water. Freckles flung over her shoulders like salt. The river lapping around her knees, then her thighs, and she crouched down in the water and let out a quiet gasp at the cold.

Ada had stopped picking at the tree. She leaned forward, watching. Her mother spread her arms out and then she pushed herself forward through the water. She hardly made a sound. Leaves and seeds floated slowly. A small ripple circled out, growing wider, the circles doubling then tripling, then washing up against the bank below Ada's feet. Her mother's skin looked green and yellow, her arms pale and wavering. Like a strange underwater flower blooming.

And then she'd ducked under. One moment she was there and the next moment there was just a wide circle of ripples moving slowly outwards.

Ada stayed very still and watched the water. What thoughts had passed through her mind, exactly? There she was, behind the tree, chewing her hair instead of her nails, wearing her favourite glittery jelly shoes. Her skin smooth and cold: no scars, no dents, no scalds. But what had she been thinking? She couldn't remember. All she remembered was the sound of the wind through the trees, how she had turned over a loose stone with her foot, waiting, watching the ripples spreading out and out . . .

38

AND OUT SHE WENT. Spreading and dissolving in the water, stretching into peaks and humps, creased, folded, scouring stones and bending sticks.

Out she went. Rushing and drumming, the house receding in her mind. Which filled instead with currents and eddies and melted snow. With silt and icy stones. She split and dispersed, shedding thoughts of watches and pins, of lenses and boots and chimneys; roiling over rocks then scattering in refractions of bright light.

Down through the woods, past roots and mushy leaves. Snatching at the trees' cast-offs – their branches and twigs and wintry paraphernalia. Past boulders swathed in moss like winter coats, past networks of tunnels deep in the bank, past pools and brand-new, snowy waterfalls. Then there was something croaking above her and a heron flew over, wings spread and feet dangling, and for a moment they drifted side by side and then the heron was away, calling out frank, frank, and Pearl listened and thought: what a lovely sound, and she made it echo off the corner of a stone.

Past oak and beech and hazel that thinned, becoming gorse, bilberry, dry-stone walls. Down a set of jangling rapids and out onto the lower slopes of the moor, the riverbed stripped to bare granite. A few seams of quartz and mica. Browny-yellow seepage of bog and iron; the sudden taste of sheep dip and peat. And what was that tang? Ammonia? A walker just taken a piss in a stream.

And out she went. Washing off the edge of the moor and through something dark and prickly: a pine plantation. No light straining through, a resiny smell, needles stitching together into floating sheets. Split cones and sap, shadows darting, and then there was the wide grey sky and the trees opened out onto fields. The river surged and flooded over the bank and beached among the mud and grass. Horses raised their hooves and flicked their tails and shucked flies off their backs.

Part wallowing in shallow floodwater, part rushing past farms and barns and warehouses, past storage containers and supermarkets. Through the edge of town and siphoned into the middle, hemmed in by brick walls. Slower, glassier and more viscous, a nice change really, the soupy stillness. And a new kind of flotsam: an oily rainbow, crisp packets, algae, socks, plastic bags like collapsed moons. A bright cufflink that floated in circles. Tins sunk under the surface, which she scrubbed clean and then left behind. A sort of pent-up pressure, everything moving forward very slowly, stagnating, impatient shoving from the back. Then faster, and a great roaring sound ahead and just at that moment, a yellow bowl bobbing in the water and Pearl circled it, just managed to send over a gentle ripple, and then the bowl had gone and she was pouring downwards, an overwhelming plunging sensation because Christ, it was a weir, the unforgiving cement and then the steep drop on the other side.

288

Halfway to the sea and the first bite of saltiness. The wind turning the surface choppy and cold, and everything widening. No more ferns at the edges but, instead, seaweed, and the banks softening to marsh. Mud and water mixing into squelchy clay. Mile after mile of mudflats and claggy sand. Purple stones, dead green crabs on their backs with their legs in the air. The ribs of a boat. A bleached buoy. A thousand insects scavenging. Birds scattered all around, little brown ones on the mud, something with a curved bill probing. Their names . . . she let them sink into the mud, where feet and beaks sifted through, searching for whatever was lurking underneath. The sand and the mud sucking. Clumps of barnacles and inky mussels, flat white shells as big as saucers. The sea smashing its crockery. Pearl sunk into sticky mud, made runnels in the sand. She rolled her own name around on her tongue, where it mixed with salty water, turning opaque and gleaming. And then she dropped it.

Out she went. The river colliding with the sea. Fresh and salt water knuckling against each other, pushing the river into pleats. The river forced backwards and down by the tide, bending under the surface like a muscle under skin. And for a moment, the river was suspended, stuck between push and pull, and she remembered the first time she had seen it. She had expected a small thing: a ditch, a brook, muddy and oozing. But there it was: a silver slice, teeming and roaring. A messy cacophony of a river, all grunt and galumph and glinty rapids; wood and chemicals and blood and bits of stone. The sound of it all around, the smell of it all around, entangling everything.

A button dipped and floated on the waves. Where had it come from? She saw it through a haze of salt and blurry light. Maybe she would follow it, cling to the ingrained pattern and go out further and further. Maybe she would work herself into the clay and transform into something unrecognisable. Or maybe she would sweep into a rockpool and be sifted through by fat anemones. Or maybe the clouds would break, and the sun would lift her from the surface and carry her inland, back over the farms and the fields and the woods. And when it rained she would be back at the beginning, where the river was just a trickle in the middle of the moor. Conjuring itself drop by drop.

Acknowledgements

THANK YOU TO MY agent Elizabeth Sheinkman and my editor Helen Garnons-Williams for their encouragement, advice and enthusiasm. Thank you to everyone at Bloomsbury. Thank you to Jon McGregor for all the support he has given my writing; Ellie Roberts for the excellent and thorough notes on how to butcher a deer; Emma Bird for her memories of back boilers; Guy Bower for reading an early version; and Mum for patiently reading all my drafts. Thank you to Ben for everything.

A NOTE ON THE TYPE

The text of this book is set in Adobe Garamond. It is one of several versions of Garamond based on the designs of Claude Garamond. It is thought that Garamond based his font on Bembo, cut in 1495 by Francesco Griffo in collaboration with the Italian printer Aldus Manutius. Garamond types were first used in books printed in Paris around 1532. Many of the present-day versions of this type are based on the *Typi Academiae* of Jean Jannon cut in Sedan in 1615.